CW00383051

The Old And
The Young

To Betty and William
from their sister

The Old And
The Young

Margiad Evans

with illustrations by the author

introduction and notes by
Ceridwen Lloyd-Morgan

seren

seren
is the book imprint of
Poetry Wales Press Ltd
Wyndham Street, Bridgend, Wales

© The Estate of Margiad Evans, 1948
Introduction and notes © Ceridwen Lloyd-Morgan, 1998

First published in 1948
This edition published in 1998

ISBN 1-85411-221-X

A CIP record for this title is available from
the British Library

All rights reserved. No part of this publication may be reproduced,
stored in a retrieval system, or transmitted at any time or by any means
electronic, mechanical, photocopying, recording or otherwise
without the prior permission of the copyright holder.

*The publisher works with the financial assistance of the
Arts Council of Wales*

Printed in Plantin by CPD Wales, Ebbw Vale

THE *A*SSOCIATION FOR
*W*ELSH *W*RITING IN *E*NGLISH
*C*YMDEITHAS *L*ÊN *S*AESNEG *C*YMRU

Contents

Foreword

My thanks and acknowledgements are due to the editors who have allowed me to reprint some of these stories, but particularly to Reginald Moore, Robert Herring and Gwyn Jones, whose friendship and help have brought my writing to this issue.

Margiad Evans

Introduction

Short stories are like chocolate to me – I can't resist them. I sit down and gobble them up. (Journal, 13 January 1947)

Margiad Evans loved reading stories, but she did not always enjoy writing them. She set herself high standards and often worked on a story over a period of months or even years before she was reasonably satisfied. Although she had been writing short stories since her early twenties, if not earlier, *The Old and the Young*, her first and last volume of short stories, was her sixth book. It was not published until 1948, when she was thirty-nine years old. "When I'm trying to write short stories, my hand feels as if it were in a tight glove", she had noted in her journal in January 1944, when she was already working on some of the pieces that would be included in *The Old and the Young*. However, since this book contains some of her finest writing, any constriction that she sometimes felt the form imposed on her may in fact have been beneficial.

Like most of her work, these stories are deeply rooted in the countryside of the Welsh Border, in her beloved Herefordshire. So great was her attachment to that area that it is easy to forget that she was already nine years old when she saw for the first time the land that was to be her spiritual home for the rest of her life. She was born Peggy Eileen Whistler in 1909 and spent the first ten years of her life in Uxbridge and Gerrards Cross. It was in 1918, when she was nine years old, that she first experienced the strong pull the area was to have on her, when her father took her to visit his sister, Annie Lane, who lived on a farm called Benhall near Ross-on-Wye. The child did not want to leave and was grief-stricken when she was not allowed to stay. But in March 1920 she went to live with her aunt at Benhall for a year, together with her younger sister Nancy. This proved to be one of the most formative periods of her life, and is evoked in much of her published work, including the stories in *The Old and the Young*. The following year the Whistlers bought a house called Lavender Cottage at Bridstow, a short walk across the fields from Benhall on the western bank of the river Wye, and this was the family home until 1936.

Lavender Cottage was Margiad's anchor until her late twenties, a place to which she regularly returned despite spending long periods away from home in a series of short-term, unskilled jobs. This was her base when her first books appeared: the short novel or long short story *Country Dance* (1932), followed by three full length novels, *The Wooden Doctor* (1933), *Turf or Stone* (1934) and *Creed* (1936). The first three are set in the countryside around Ross, which she usually calls Salus, and *Creed* in the town itself. When Lavender Cottage was sold in 1936 following the death of her father, Margiad Evans went into partnership with her sister Nancy and their friend Helen Blackwell, the daughter of Margiad's publisher, and for three years they ran the Springherne guest house at Bull's Hill, a couple of miles south of Ross. When the lease ran out just as the Second World War was beginning, Margiad again moved from job to job. She worked in a munitions factory, as a housekeeper, and with the Assistance Board in Hereford, returning between posts to Ross, where her mother had been living since the family home was sold.

In October 1940, Margiad Evans married Michael Williams, whom she had met whilst running the guest house. His father, a Pembrokeshire man, was the vicar at the nearby parish church of Walford-on-Wye. During the first months of her marriage the couple lived at Brickhampton, near Cheltenham, where Michael was working on a farm, but in January 1941 they moved to a cottage called Potacre in Llangarron, a village about five miles south-west of Ross-on-Wye and close to the Welsh border. Here again Michael Williams worked on a farm at first, but in 1942 he joined the navy and from then on for increasingly long periods Margiad lived alone in the cottage. Despite the many pressures which the war imposed on women, this proved to be a more fruitful period for her as a writer than the previous few years had been.

In the late 1930s she had started 'The Widower's Tale', another novel based in the Border country, but had not managed to finish it. As she had already received, and spent, an advance for it from her publisher, Basil Blackwell, and was unable to pay the money back, she had to offer him something else instead. One form of writing that had not defeated her during these years was the journal. For years she had kept a journal, part record, part safety-valve for emotions, part literary work-book. Now she put together from this material her *Autobiography* (1943). This was not a conventional autobiography but a remarkable account of a spiritual journey from turmoil to calm and maturity, achieved through minute observation of the natural world with which she lived in such close proximity. That journey was facilitated by the recovery of childhood memories and with them the kind of inspired vision of the world that children possess and which is usually lost in adulthood. This process, she felt, was linked to her marriage, which had brought her the emotional calm and stability which had been lacking in her previous relationships, and allowed her to find her true self. She was happy because "I have got back", she wrote to her husband a month after he went into the forces. "Strange that the most adult experience in life should make me as I was in childhood – as I feel I was intended to be ... You and this country together are my essence" (14 August 1942).

Now she was able to write again, though not in the same way as before. Her novels had been written rapidly, almost frenziedly, for once she began to see clearly the shape of her narrative she would work day after day and late into the early hours of the morning, fortified by cigarettes and black coffee. To revise the resulting draft and make a final copy would then take her no more than a few weeks. But her circumstances had changed. Then she had enjoyed a fairly leisurely existence, with her father's pension guaranteeing a certain standard of living. Now, however, money was short and Potacre more primitive than Lavender Cottage or the Springherne guest house. As well as having her own home to run she had to expend much of her time and energy in her garden in order to grow as much food as possible, and in the early 1940s she also often took casual work on farms in Llangarron. It was impossible to secure the protracted periods of peace she needed for writing a novel, so she had to turn to other forms of writing which could be fitted in to whatever moments she could snatch. Editing extracts from her journals and bringing them together to form *Autobiography* was her first priority, but once that was behind her, although she continued to keep a journal, she concentrated on more imaginative work.

Poetry was one kind, and by the end of the war she had enough to put together a volume, *Poems from Obscurity,* which finally appeared in 1947. But she continued to write prose as well, turning to the essay and especially the short story. The advantage of these three forms was that being briefer and more concentrated than a full-length novel, they could be drafted in her mind before being set down in writing. In fact in many cases an idea for a poem or story would present itself while Margiad Evans was occupied in physical activity. Often very strongly visualised or "realized", to use her own term, these ideas, sometimes with key phrases or lines, might be recorded in her journal in the evening, in the hours between supper and bedtime. Later on, when the poem or tale had formed itself more distinctly, she would work on it late at night, gradually pulling it into shape. Once a story was completed she would send it off to the editor of a periodical or anthology in the hope of earning some money to supplement her small income. Several of the stories included in *The Old and the Young* were first published in this way.

Apart from her journals, our most valuable sources of information about her work and, indeed, her life in general at this time, are her letters to her husband. She wrote to him almost daily while he was away in the navy, and her letters fulfilled a dual function. They maintained the bond between husband and wife as she recounted the details of her own existence and all the gossip of the neighbourhood, but they also took on the function of literary workbooks. Although they were obviously not revised and were often written in some haste between other tasks, they contain many fine passages of the kind found in her published work, especially in her poetic evocations of nature through the changing seasons. Moreover, it is in these letters that she often first recorded the material that went into the making of the stories in *The Old and the Young,* whether it was just an idea for the core of the narrative, a detail of description or a story she had heard locally. This means that it is often possible to tell exactly when and how a story came to form in her mind, and even to identify the origin of certain details or strands. As time passed and she reported to Michael Williams her progress with the writing, the gradual evolution of the text into its final form was chronicled and beyond that her attempts, both successful and unsuccessful, to have it accepted for publication in a periodical or anthology. It is from these letters that we learn that in some cases, notably 'Thomas Griffiths and Parson Cope' and 'The Lost Fisherman', the ending was substantially rewritten after submission to an editor but before publication. Since the only surviving manuscripts of any of these stories are final drafts or fair copies, Margiad Evans's letters to her husband, together with her contemporary journals, are the only sources to throw light on her way of working and the genesis of *The Old and the Young*; their importance, therefore, cannot be overemphasized.

They reveal that a number of the characters and incidents in the stories can be linked directly to her own life. In drawing on her own experience in this way Margiad Evans was continuing a practice which can be traced back to the early days of her literary career. Although only her second novel, *The Wooden Doctor*, is overtly autobiographical and seems to be closely based on her journals, all four of her pre-war books are undoubtedly a reflection of her inner life during the 1930s and represent unresolved grapplings with questions of personal identity, sexuality and religious belief. In *The Old and the Young*, however, the relationship between the self and the text is different. This more mature work still reflects personal experience and concerns, as we shall see, but it is far more out-ward-looking. And whereas in *Autobiography* she had been drawn out from introspection into contemplation of the natural world, here she reinstates human society into her vision, presenting a more rounded view of life.

Some of this material is drawn not from the present but from those childhood memories which she had repossessed in the writing of *Autobiography*. Here again, in 'The Lost Fisherman' and 'The Old and the Young', for example, she draws on her idyllic recollections of that year spent on her aunt's farm when she was eleven years old. They also inspired many of her meditations on the nature and uses of memory, reflected in 'The Boy Who Called for a Light' and 'The Old and the Young', where a sight or incident in the present opens a door onto the past. Not only does this reveal the mysterious link between the adult and the child he or she once was, but it brings back into life those who have died in the inter-vening years, dressed as they were then, dancing the same steps.

The role of the writer as memorialiser of the forgotten was one that had always interested Margiad Evans. In her first book, *Country Dance*, she names and gives expression to a woman name-less and silenced in a tale told in the Border communities, and her 'Ballad of Mountain Vowr' in *Poems from Obscurity* similarly explores the nature of story preserved in oral tradition in a rural community. Stories she heard in Llangarron during the 1940s now provided a rich vein from which she could mine material, and through them both individuals and a whole community and way of life are vividly depicted.

One of her most important sources was her next-door neighbour, Mrs Ellen Saunders, a superb storyteller, who in her rich Herefordshire dialect regaled Margiad with both up-to-date gossip and stories of earlier times. People and events sprang into life as she spoke, her gestures and facial expression heightening the dramatic effect. Other neighbours and occasionally relatives provided further tales or became themselves the models for certain characters. The foundation of 'All Through the Night', for example, was a story from her husband's family. A particular place – a house, for instance – often suggested not only the setting but the narrative itself, hence the very strong sense of place and atmosphere that pervades all these stories. By comparing the finished text with the raw material noted in her letters and journals, it is possible to see at work the process by which she developed a story around a central idea or image, adapting and reworking repeatedly anecdotes, narrative and descriptive detail, or even dialogue, from different sources. Anything she witnessed or experienced while in the middle of working on a story might immediately be seized upon and incorporated, giving a new twist or detail to the narrative.

Although many of the stories are concerned with the re-emergence into the present of memories of the past, both distant and recent, some of them reflect contemporary concerns as well. 'The Lost Fisherman', for example, depicts the effects of the Second World War on an individual, a family and a community, whilst 'The Ruin' explores the problem of readjustment for a couple when the husband returns after long absence in the forces. It could be said that these two stories provide a riposte to those patriotic reviewers who criticised *Autobiography* for not referring constantly to the war, but it is unlikely that this was the motive for the choice of these subjects, if indeed "choice" is the appropriate term. Often ideas presented themselves to Margiad Evans with such clarity and power that she was impelled to respond to them.

Once a story began to gestate, however, she accepted that it might be a long time before she reached the end: "My pen traces paths. I'll walk over the hills of peace for on the far side are my stories", she wrote in her journal on 22 July 1944. Sometimes, even when she knew exactly what she wanted to write, she could manage no more than a paragraph a night; at other times she was too busy or too exhausted to write more than a brief entry in her journal and a letter to her husband. As a result it took her a few years to assemble the stories in *The Old and the Young*. Apart from 'The Wicked Woman', which dates from 1933, all them were written between 1943 and 1946, while she was living at Potacre.

Originally she had intended to use 'The Lost Fisherman' as the title for the collection and her reasons for deciding on 'The Old and the Young' instead are not mentioned in her personal papers. But perhaps by the time the book was published, three years after the end of the war, she felt that to have as the title-story one so firmly rooted in the events of 1940 was no longer appropriate. Certainly the present title is a better choice, for it reflects more closely the subject matter and themes of the collection as a whole, since so many of these stories are concerned not only with the relationship between the old self and the young self, but also with that between the youngest and oldest members of the community. Children and older people predominate in the world she depicts, and between them there is a deeper, easier understanding than is possible between parents and children. The old and the young share a similar vision of the world, seeing beyond the limiting mundane reality perceived by adults of the middle generation.

It is evident from the stories themselves that Margiad Evans had a strongly visual imagination, through which she saw distinctly the people and places which she described. Nonetheless, it was important to her that her word-pictures should be complemented, or even reinforced, by the addition of line-drawings at the head and tail of each story. Twelve of these illustrations were also incorporated into the design of the book-jacket. Margiad Evans drew and painted all her life, and in her teens she had favoured art rather than literature as a career. In fact her only post-school education was a brief period at art college in Hereford. When, in her twenties, she began to concentrate more on her writing, the visual representation of her subjects remained important to her. All her published prose works before *The Old and the Young* had included at least one illustration by her, under her real name, Peggy Whistler, and she had designed dust-jackets for books by other writers as well as her for her own novels. Although she was not entirely satisfied with the decorations

13

for *The Old and the Young*, they give some indication of how she herself visualised the subjects, settings and mood of the stories.

By the time *The Old and the Young* was at the press Margiad Evans was planning a further collection, and again she proposed to illustrate the book herself. It was to contain twelve stories, of which six survive, all but one, 'A Party for the Nightingale', unpublished. But her plans were thwarted by the major upheavals in her life in the post-war years.

In 1949 she had to leave Llangarron. The house where they lived and the farm where her husband worked were sold and for a while they had to live with relatives. At last they found a new home, a cottage at Elkstone near Cheltenham, and seemed on the brink of a more settled existence, but then disaster struck. They had only lived there two months before Margiad Evans suffered the first of a series of major fits. Shortly afterwards she found that she was pregnant, and her daughter, Cassandra, was born in 1951. Her priority now was to write about the onset of what was thought to be epilepsy, and in *A Ray of Darkness* (1952) she gives a moving account of how she came to terms with her illness and its implications for her child. The following year her husband was appointed to a teaching post at Hartfield in Sussex, and Margiad, on top of coping with her unpredictable illness, now found herself exiled from that Herefordshire countryside which she had loved so deeply and which had informed virtually all of her writing in the 1930s and 1940s. In the years left to her until her death in 1958, she continued to write when time and strength allowed, but sustained work was difficult. Her last book was a collection of poems, *A Candle Ahead*, published in 1956.

Although she was unable to complete her planned second volume of short stories, she continued to work towards it, as the surviving unpublished examples show. Moreover, she was still noting down any likely material. In December 1950, in a letter to her American friend, Winifred Ellerman (the author 'Bryher'), Margiad notes how her own pregnancy reminded her of a typical example: "the story of a friend's grandmother, who, learning she was to have her twelfth baby, went up to the granary and knocked the oak cradle to splinters with an axe." Such nuggets would be recorded and saved up, but in the event she never had the chance to use them.

But even if the raw material of her stories, in terms of characters, settings and narrative, was usually derived from her own experience, the possible influence of other writers on her style and technique should not be disregarded. She had read widely from childhood, and after leaving the high school in Ross when she was sixteen she followed her own inclinations rather than sticking to any prescribed canon, borrowing and buying books as and when she could. Her tastes in fiction were eclectic and in the 1940s ranged from Jane Austen, the Brontës, Tolstoy, Thomas Mann and Flaubert to Le Fanu and the romantic stories in *The Woman's Weekly*. While she was living at Llangarron she subscribed to two literary journals, *The Welsh Review* and *Life and Letters*, which introduced her to a wide range of contemporary writers, as well as publishing her own work and commissioning book reviews from her. She had strong likes and dislikes, and voiced them without inhibition in her letters and journals. She was less than complimentary about Virginia Woolf's short stories, for example: "I am beginning to think that all women write alike, as though they sit on a flowery carpet in a warm private beautiful room", she told Michael Williams (28 September 1944). Katherine Mansfield fared little better: "Sometimes [she] is so profoundly good – at others she doesn't seem to *know* and puts down bathos – an awful sort of tripping drivel like a young green girl" (letter to Michael Williams, 27-8 November 1944).

Her mixed feelings about these and other English writers may partly stem from Margiad Evans's attitude to London: Bloomsbury drawing rooms were a long way from the muddy fields and outside privies of Llangarron. She enjoyed trips to London and meeting people in the literary world, but she did not take that life very seriously and was always glad to return to the less glamorous life of the Border country. It is understandable, therefore, that the writers who earned her unconditional praise were from outside the English metropolitan circle. The American author Eudora Welty, born in the same year as Margiad, was one of her great favourites. Her stories about working people in disadvantaged rural communities in the southern states of America, told in a superb literary style, appealed strongly to Margiad Evans, who felt that they possessed a "power and fury" lacking in Katherine Mansfield's work. Eudora Welty may perhaps have had some influence on Margiad Evans's stories; certainly there are stylistic affinities here and there between the stories in Welty's *The Wide Net* (1943) and, for example, 'The Old Woman and the Wind' in *The Old and the Young*.

But she also greatly admired several Welsh writers writing in English, such as Glyn Jones and Gwyn Jones, who depicted people and communities not very different from those central to her own life. None of these, however, could match for her the Welsh-language writer Kate Roberts, whose work she had read in English translation. "One thinks of Kate Roberts and drops the pen!" she wrote in her notebook in October 1953. "Kate Roberts, the only classical writer today: whose beauty is without fussiness, whose tragedy and comedy are integral ... who is a genius". Margiad Evans's story 'The Ruin' is the closest in spirit to Kate Roberts's work, and may in fact have been influenced by her.

What attracted Margiad Evans to the writing of Kate Roberts, however, were those very qualities evident in her own work. Like Kate Roberts she wrote directly from her own experience of a woman's life in a small community, using her intimate knowledge of that world as a context for revealing the universal human condition. Each story is a microcosm, or, to use Margiad Evans's own words on the dust-jacket of *The Old and the Young*, "an attempt to put the tree back into the nutshell". It is true that in her stories set in the North Wales quarrying community, Kate Roberts was writing about the place in which she had been born and brought up, whilst this was not the case with Margiad Evans. But the Herefordshire countryside had been her only home since she was eleven, despite periods spent working away from it, and in Llangarron she lived a life in many ways similar to that of her neighbours. The fact that she was a writer, and sometimes dressed eccentrically by local standards, set her apart from them, but her existence like theirs was dominated by physical work, the elements, the seasons and wartime stresses and shortages. As *The Old and the Young* reveals, she also shared their taste for gossip and stories.

This collection also shows a deep sympathy towards people of all ages, backgrounds and peculiarities, from the eccentric gardener in 'Thomas Griffiths and Parson Cope', the cheeky small boy in 'The Boy Who Called for a Light', or the giddy young girls in 'The Old and the Young', to the practical, elderly housewives in 'Mrs Pike's Eldorado', and the gross, oboe-playing, chip-frying Miss Allensmoore in 'A Modest Adornment'. Whether country people or town-dwellers, Margiad Evans depicts them with all their quirks but never lapses into caricature, for they are drawn not with condescension but with a love stemming from close familiarity and understanding. Their personalities and feelings are conveyed with great delicacy, especially through the restrained but effective use of dialogue. The Herefordshire dialect could easily have been overdone, undermining the dignity of her characters, but, apart from indicating their social background and material culture, it is used above all to express their thought processes and the interaction between them.

In her review in *Life and Letters* of *A Summer Day* (1946), a volume of Kate Roberts's work in English translation, Margiad Evans noted that her stories "are as narrow in scene as they are wide in inference. Her writing has a seamless beauty, a deceptive quietness which draws upon the intuition of the reader for its final effect". There could be no better description of her own stories. *The Old and the Young* sets Margiad Evans amongst the finest short-story writers of the twentieth century and its republication is long overdue.

Ceridwen Lloyd-Morgan

The Wicked Woman

LORENCE MORGAN was close on sixty, had never done anything much amiss in her life that people knew of, and yet she was like Satan inside.

It was a sickly-hot night in July about half-past eleven; Frank Evans and his wife were getting to bed. Frank Evans kept the "Harp".

He had just stretched himself out with his sharp features against the turn-over of the sheet, and Elsie was combing her hair. The window was closed, a lace curtain drawn across it; the candle was burning down low on the washstand.

"Frank, I heard summat!"

"So did I. Somebody's yelling outside. Put yer 'ead out an' see what 't is."

Elsie opened the window, and a voice came up from the garden: "That you, Missus?"

"Yes, it's me. What d'you want?"

"Tell the Boss I wants un."

"What's the matter? Tell me first."

"Old John's got in the pond. I can't do nothin', an' 'e's making such a funny noise. You tell the Boss t'come."

"All right."

Elsie turned round. Frank had heard; he was already putting on his shirt.

"You run down to Morgans' and follow me to pond. It's Williams, ain't it?"

"Yes," said Elsie, sticking pins in her hair; "you'd best take the 'urricane lamp, Frank. There's a moon but it's washy. Was Old John 'ere to-night?"

"Ay ... 'e was."

"You didn't let 'im 'ave too much?"

"No ... couple o' pints o' cider. I watched un down the garden. 'E was all right, hardy as a buck. We shan't get into trouble."

They hurried downstairs. The dog, tied to the settle in the tap-room, got up excitedly, but neither noticed him. Frank unbarred the door and Elsie, her round figure trembling with energy, put the hurricane lamp into his hand. Its light struck across the slate path

19

to the scraffy patient man leaning against the gate. It was Tom Williams, the lame postman.

The two set off as fast as they could go, the lamp flashing its radiating beams on hedges and trees. A few drops of warm rain fell on their faces. They climbed a stile and followed a damp path through the woods. Williams told how he had heard old Morgan groaning. As he had left the "Harp" before ten o'clock, he must have been in the pond nearly an hour and a half.

"'E must 'a slipped, an' the banks bein' so steep, an' 'im so old 'e couldn't get out."

They heard the groaning while they were still a couple of hundred yards from the pond. Evans ran on ahead with the light. The pond was at the end of the wood, skirted by the narrow path.

He looked down the steep sides, standing between two bramble bushes and holding the lamp out at arm's length over the water. The light revealed a terrible head with closed eyes and dropped jaws which appeared to be floating on the turgid water ... John's breathing stirred a ripple, and his beard was like weed. Evans saw a taut arm, a stony hand, grasping a protruding thorny branch in a desperate death-grip. He would have thought Old John dead but for that fearful groaning breathing which shook his livid lips.

Williams came up.

"Catch 'old o' the lamp," said Frank, "an' 'ang on to summat. You've nobbut one leg, so you've got to use both arms. I'm going down."

He slid into the water. There was three feet of it, and two more of black slime which poured into his boots. He could not unclench John's hand.

"Got a knife?"

Williams set the lantern down and felt. He passed Frank a strong penknife and Frank cut the branch. Old John sank over sideways against him, so that for a moment he thought they would both go under. He found his feet.

"'Old up the lamp, you bloody fool!" he cried frantically, his hands under the old man's armpits. "Stretch out yer arm and get 'im somewhere ... 'e's dying, we shan't never get 'im out!"

Williams, who was filled with terror of death, the black water, and the night, clutched the bank and the lamp with one hand, and stretched the other blindly towards the horrible group in travail.

"Look what yer doing! God above, this ain't no game," exclaimed the bitterly toiling man below.

Williams caught hold.

"That's 'is beard. Dost want to break 'is neck? Ah, give over, you aren't no good. Give over, give over, give over ...."

Williams shifted his grip. Frank wound his arms about Old John's body, heaving, twisting him in the mud, like a big root that must be plucked up.

"Now, *pull!*"

The moon shone out full on their demented activities. At last, with a vile sucking sigh, the mud relinquished Old John.

They half-rolled, half-pulled him up the bank, and laid him on his back. He was still breathing. The mild light of moon and lamp mingling showed a ghastly figure glistening with black ooze, utterly inert: it was that of an old man of eighty, dressed, as far as could be made out, in two black woollen cardigans, corduroys with yorks, and heavy nailed boots. His grizzled beard fell across his breast.

Williams lifted one leg; it fell back with a thud on the ground.

"Like a bit of 'ardwood," said Frank, who was a carpenter as well as host.

The two men, harsh-featured in the lamplight, stooping over the dark mass on the ground, began pulling and jerking it into erratic life. Frenziedly, and then more rhythmically, they raised and lowered the arms. They rubbed the heart. In the distance another lantern wavered. Another moment and a man and woman joined them, out of breath, and staring: the man was Old John's strong, sullen son, Mark, stiff and tall, inclined to stoop; the woman was his wife, Florence, a big woman in a print overall with her sleeves rolled up.

She stood looking down on her father-in-law, holding her arms away from her body, swinging her head. Neither she nor Mark attempted aid.

Frank burst out again:

"Ain't yer going to do nothing? Ain't yer brought nothing with yer? We got to get un 'ome, ain't we?"

"We ain't brought nothing. What d'yer want?"

"'Ave yer got a barrow?"

"Yes, we 'ave."

"Well, go an' get it. Put some bags and straw on it."

21

Frank spoke as he worked. The sweat was rolling off his forehead. The lame man helped him like a good one.

"Where's Elsie?" Frank shouted after the other two.

"Gettin' out blankets."

"Trust 'er!"

When the wheelbarrow came, John was lifted on it by Mark and Frank. There was a handful of hay at the bottom, and one sack thrown over the edge. Williams put his flannel coat under the old man's head. Mark hesitated a moment, then shed his and pushed it under his back.

Old John's legs scraped the ground, jolting stiffly like a new-born lamb's. Frank and Mark took turns to push him; Williams walked beside the barrow holding the lamp. When Mark was fetching his breath, Florence brushed close to him, inclining her mouth to his ear:

"If he do die, there'll be an inquest. That'll be bad for Frank .... Dad was drunk. They get 'is money off 'im ...."

The evil insinuating whisper ceased.

At the stile John revived for a moment as they were lifting him over. Florence looked into his open eyes.

"'E bain't dead – 'e bain't dyin'! My God, if 'e saw!" she thought.

Old John's eyes closed again.

Elsie and Mark and Frank put him to bed. They laid him between blankets with stone jars of hot water to his sides. Elsie gave him a little brandy – not much, lest it should choke him. Then Florence had hysterics. It was two in the morning before Elsie and Frank got back to the "Harp". Nobody thought of getting the doctor. Old John's breathing had eased.

They woke at seven. Frank was so exhausted that he could hardly move his arms. Through the iron bed-railings he saw Elsie putting on her petticoat.

"Where are you off to?"

"Morgans'! I must find out. I'm not a bit afraid of anything they can say even if they *do* have an inquest; I want to find out 'ow 'e is."

She ran all the way to the Morgans' cottage. Florence spoke to her through the window:

"'E be fine, thanks, Mrs Evans."

"I might as well see un now I'm 'ere."

Florence thought: "I'll be terrified to the end of my days o' what 'e'll say." She called down:

"There's no need. 'E's gettin' up."

"I'm comin' in," Elsie said.

She climbed straight up to Old John's room. There was he, sitting on the edge of his bed, pulling on his best trousers.

"You'd best get back to bed," she exclaimed. Then she left him. He went round to the "Harp" for breakfast.

"It beats me 'ow *you* got to 'ear of it," he said. I don't remember nothin' after thinkin', 'I'm alone an' not a soul will come this way.'"

"You mid easy 'ave died."

"Yes."

Thomas Griffiths and Parson Cope

**T**HOMAS GRIFFITHS awoke feet first, rubbing his two big toes against each other. Consciousness steeped his legs and trunk slowly, before he opened his eyes, and finally stretched his arms.

It was a red sunrise. The wall at the bottom of the bed was a map of scarlet quivering threads within and over which were separated spots of ultra-light, shuffling like leaves.

Thomas rolled out of bed. Into the flush and fleece of morning struggled the shadows of an old man dressing himself.

He was in his shirt, fishing for his trousers under the quilt. He pulled them on anyhow, bunching them unfastened in his left hand, as barefoot he went mumbling and groping down his windowless stairway to unbolt the door.

Pushing his face out, he peered disconsolately at the wild and daring daybreak. He could not tell whether it was cloud or glow that reddened the dripping garden.

"Bin r'ining," said Thomas, buttoning his trousers. "Bain't a-goin' ter sing be 'a?" he asked a robin which whished out of the woodpile on the wall, puffing out its geranium breast. The robin was silent.

"What do tha s'y?" Thomas asked a snail which stubbornly and searchingly was creeping down the door. The snail was an old friend: it used to hide under the latch in wet weather to escape drowning in the overflow from the spouting. Thomas looked again at the sky, then stooped and very gently tapped the snail's shell with his thumbnail, as if the creature were a weather-glass. The snail cowered, withdrawing its horns.

"Hasn't tha got eyes? Look at that tempestuous sky. Turn round. Be g'wing wrong w'y!" The snail's horns appeared.

"Tchuh! be daft? Have tha breakfast and be off to work. It we'ant r'ine, I'll be bound," answered Thomas for the snail.

"Oh, wean't it?"

He edged his feet into his boots, feeling the cold, damp crinkled leather with a groan. Taking his "dentures" from a turned-down jam-jar on the windowsill, he fitted them in, chumped the tricksy teeth once or twice, yawned, and tuned them up for the day with a couple of fingers. Then he looked round for signs of overnight mice. His back kitchen smelled like a burrow. In a corner on the copper lay a heap of mole-traps. Onions and snares hung from the beam. Thomas went out into the garden and washed his face with a cabbage leaf. The trees were fast asleep, their branches helplessly sunk in their beds of moist air.

Suddenly, from the black ivy that hid the ruined mill-dam, a flock of sparrows exploded into the morning. A dozen flew to the water-butt, twinkling and disputing. They began to bathe in the dark-green water which, the butt being askew and off one of its bricks, inclined its dial towards their crisp little bodies. The frisk of the drops, the garland of play round the butt's rim, fascinated the old man. They were the deliciousness of morning, its hunger and alertness. His blue eyes brightened. He spat with appetite, turned round, and went in again decidedly. If it had rained he would have stayed at home and spurted the potatoes, but as it was going to be a nice day he would go and get on with the digging at Parson Cope's.

Half an hour after, as he was walking over the fields, the sunlight formed. The weather is the good gardener's sharpest tool, and Thomas was a good gardener.

"It's a fallow d'y," he would say as he kneeled sorting his shallots or cleaned his lucky old gun.

To-day was a doing day. He could feel himself digging in the Rectory garden, smoking his pipe. He stopped to light it, leaving the blue smoke in the bright air floating alone, like a transparent island.

"All the s'ime," said Thomas, rolling the burnt end of the match to a smooth point in his fingers, "all the s'ime they taties, them do want spurting." He stopped short, feeling for a moment the doom and trouble of those who exist alone on their two hands. Never, never, could he stretch out, touch and take all the ripe labours. Always something waiting, something left behind, even something neglected. In that moment the morning aged. Down the bottom of the valley the cows were being turned out. An old man with a collar of white hair, of innumerable gossiping occupations and eighty grudges, was driving them. He was tugging a chain over a gate-post. Becoming aware of Thomas Griffths, he stared. First his eye woke, and then it went to sleep in the stare. A long blackthorn staff he clenched under his arm.

"Morning, *Mr* Griffths-the-Mill," said the enchanted cowman.

"Morning, Sammy. Nice d'y."

"Ay. Where be you g'wing?"

"Rectory."

"Oh, ay," the old man sighed. "'Ow be Parson Cope?"

"Middling," Thomas admitted. "Queer," he added.

"Oh, un be queer, be un? Hee, hee!"

"Well, if him do be in un's right senses, I bain't."

"Ay."

"Eh?"

"Any road, him bain't alone," said the old man. He shook his head. He spat into the hedge. He whetted his thumb on the blackthorn. Thomas watched him lower it and slowly dig the point into a mole-tump. At last he heard words. The old man spoke, as it were, in the surly character of his friend the snail.

"Seventeen grandchildren and three great-grandchildren I 'ave. We was ten to feed at once at 'ome, but now us be gone from 'ere. Us be gone. But listen. I do know what I be saying. Bain't 'olesome to live by yerself."

"I be 'olesome," cried Thomas indignantly.

"Ay? 'Oo says? 'Tain't as it should be. 'Tain't like *me* any road. Queer be un? Well, like master, like man. Good d'y."

The old man began wanderingly to climb the hill, prodding the mole-tumps as he went. Thomas walked on his path angrily, trying to escape from a sense of blame and unease which was like a memory of something unfinished, thought out by himself. He was sensitive about living alone. He hated to be discussed. He felt shy of himself, shy of the being who lived in himself. That old bugger!

"A' do talk like a book," Thomas raged. "Like master, like man!"

Parson Cope was in the bathroom. Water gushed out of the pipe as Thomas went round the back into the garden. He peeped. Up there in the little window the parson was shaving. He turned sideways, his neck stretched thin, his cheek lathered. His long nose pecked at the mirror.

In front of the Rectory was a square lawn divided from the lane by a sandstone wall. Four lime trees grew out of the close quiet turf. Double green gates of solid wood, carriage width and seven feet high. A haggard shrubbery. A drive up to the porch with its grey steps and pillars. There was scarcely space for a trap to turn and branch off to the stable yard, but if a wheel so much as grazed the lawn Parson Cope had an "attack". When this happened, resurgent noises, apparently detached from the parson, tumbled about the hollow house. Sobs in the attics – but the parson was in the conservatory. Cries and lights, buckets swilling, rags being wrung – but the parson was sitting lampless in his owly study. There was at the Rectory a paddock and an orchard also. The kitchen garden was at the back; it had a wall which was hidden in ivy – the beautiful flowering kind with the slender leaf. Through the middle ran a wide path, box-edged and weedless, with skilfully stunted fruit trees. Short paths cut the garden into tidy plots each in season showing its rows of vegetables, wigwams of beans and peas, its dahlias and sunflowers propped on tall canes with flower-pot hats.

It was a beautiful garden. Nobody but Thomas worked in it; the attacks settled that.

He fetched a spade and began to dig. He dug carefully from the wall to the box edge, plodding down the weeds with his boots and turning under only those which were harmless. His jacket, which held his tobacco-box, matches, and other, after-dinner pipe, hung from a pear branch. The thrushes and blackbirds gazed at it whenever they thought of the worms Thomas dug up. He smoked all the time. The wind, passing him, went away with the swirling blue breath of his pipe. The wind would jump suddenly down into the garden and shuffle the yellow ivy leaves out of the side-paths – it was early spring. The frail shells of some grey crocuses were just opening. The sky looked through one blue eye.

When Thomas had worked for about an hour he heard the back door open. That would be Margery with a cup of cocoa and a piece of cake in the saucer soaking up what she had slopped over. She was always hurried, because her youth was indispensable to Parson Cope and his elderly, sluggish housekeeper, Martha Lane. Sometimes when she was hardly half-way to Thomas he would hear one of their voices, and then she would put the cup down on the path making with her free arm an oath of a gesture. Thomas pitied her; and she called him 'Uncle', as all the friendly people did. She confided in him. If Parson Cope dropped a pencil, Margery said he wouldn't stoop to pick it up. No, he would ring the bell for her. And he would never think of putting a piece of coal on the fire or drawing a curtain.

Thomas looked up. No, it wasn't Margery; it was the reverend himself. "Toadstools instead o' mushrooms," muttered Thomas.

By the crocuses Parson Cope stopped to cough, bowing over them his tall, coarsely made body, clad in deepest, gauntest black. He clasped his hands behind his back, walking deliberately up and down the path, ignoring Thomas, eyes fixed at the level of the roof.

Thomas sucked and bit and dragged at his pipe. His smoking became articulate.

Parson Cope had on an overcoat and round his neck a blue-coloured scarf which resembled a woman's shawl. On his feet, large and blunt as Thomas's own, he wore elastic boots, one of which was unfastened. He blew out his lips, and each time a gust struck him his expression grew sourer and more offended.

Gradually his ups and downs became shorter, and then he stopped.

"Good morning, Griffiths. Rather wet for digging, isn't it?"

"Be 'um?"

"I should have said so," snapped the parson, stepping over the box edge.

"Got to be done, any road."

Parson Cope walked up the slippery trodden slope and leant his back against the wall.

"I feel my heart," he said.

Thomas was silent. A white nose such as the reverend had to-day might mean he was really poorly. It was possible that later on there would be a trip in the shandrydan to the chemist's or the wine merchant's. Parson Cope slipped.

Thomas took the pipe out of his mouth. "Look out. Don't tha go standing on thic glimey ground. Tha ool slip and down tha ool go."

"Nonsense! I'm quite firm on my feet."

Thomas plunged the spade into the earth and turned over a rosy worm.

"Do you bury the worms, Griffiths?" cried Parson Cope anxiously. There was a look on his face that Thomas feared. He was grave for hours after thinking of it, lest he himself should at times wear that same shocked and lonely expression of trouble.

But at that moment Parson Cope slid down. There he was sitting with outstretched legs showing the soles of his boots with some straws stuck in the wads of mud under the instep. Looking stupefied, struggling to incorporate some reaction to this physically new aspect of the earth, the Rector sat silent, and silent also was Thomas, having ceased to dig. From somewhere out of the ivy there fell, very softly, a little bowl of grass and horsehair, once a bird's nest.

"Well," cried the Rector at last – "well, Griffiths! What are you going to do?"

Thomas considered. "Bain't 'urt, bisn't tha?"

People said truly that he was a queer old man by himself, but he was at his queerest with the "reverend". They quarrelled all the year round, yet existed in and out of each other's minds as easily as a couple of mice using a mutual hole.

"No," said Parson Cope, "certainly I'm not hurt."

"Ah," said Thomas, and he laid hold of the spade.

"Help me up. Help me up this instant."

"No. Tha fell down, and tha can pick thaself up agen."

"Griffiths, it's damp!" the Rector said, holding out a pink polished hand.

"Sit on six penn'orth o' coppers, then."

At this Parson Cope did battle to his feet. Thomas did not stop work to look at him. Presently he heard the glass door clash. Resting his foot on the spade, he wiped his forehead with a red handkerchief rolled into a ball. "Bury the worms ... likely life!" he muttered. "Tell tha what, Thomas Griffiths, one of us be mad, and it bain't tha. One o' these days them ool be coming to take he off to the as-y-lum."

Thomas ate his dinner in the yard, sitting on a log in the sunshine ... two great jam and bacon sandwiches thick as mill-stones, cut from the ends of a round tin-loaf. He chewed doggedly, spitting the plum stones into the woodpile. "My jam be good, but next time I must riv out they stones. Them do muddle me dentures," he thought. He looked absently at the blackened stems of some frosted nettles, rustling in the dead logs' crannies. Flies hummed by the coach-house; a very early bee darted out of the stable door. Margery came and set down a cup of coffee by him. 'Here's the *Gazette*, Uncle, and don't you hurry over your dinner. Him's asleep.'

"Ay-eh?" He was unconscious; he had dozed.

"Him's asleep," repeated Margery. "Did you hear a row? Mrs Lane have fallen downstairs and she have drunk all the whisky and gone to bed."

"Gone to bed, have she? What do you think of that, now? Well!"

"Ah! The reverend, he says you've got to go to Salus, see."

Thomas looked up sharply. He didn't see Margery's quiet face. He saw a small, sparkling picture of himself driving the shandrydan through the gates ... an instantaneous flash of pleasure showed him every particle of the moment – the turn-out complete even to the knots in the whip-lash which danced in the socket. He felt himself jump out, undo the iron hook which fastened the gate – crash!! He was driving off ...

"Margery, woman, why don't tha go to get married?" he asked suddenly.

But Margery was running off already. "Married!" she shouted. "I don't know anybody."

By and by Thomas went and rapped on the study window. Parson Cope's spectacles glittered against the dark old glass. He flapped a book down on the floor.

"Well, Griffiths?"

"A be come to tell that as I can't go to Salus to-d'y, reverend," said Thomas. "I do want to finish that digging while it's set."

"It's too wet for digging, I tell you."

"Bain't. Ah be drying off nicely. And I do want to tidy up gi-arden edge a bit. Don't think I've got time to-d'y, sir."

"But I insist! Mrs Lane has fallen downstairs. She thinks a little whisky will do her good and there's none in the house. Not a drop! The decanter is quite empty and so is the jar. I don't know why I keep servants. They have nothing to do at all, and yet they let us run out of everything. Scatterbrains! Chatterboxes! Useless parrots!" screamed Parson Cope.

Thomas winked. Down came the window. Up it flew.

"Popinjays!" cried the parson. "Poisonous peahens!"

Thomas caught Joshua, the dun pony. Joshua came grudgingly to the shafts. His knees were crusted with dirt, there were burrs in his witches' mane. The greasy blinkers hid his cunning eyes with their hay-coloured lashes that flickered maliciously. Disgust, hatred, and contempt those eyes expressed for Thomas and the shandrydan and all work.

But for Thomas heavenly happiness, to shut the green gates, to grip the reins and hear the wheels grinding down the sandstone lane. It was real! The moment had come. He puffed and he grinned, he looked sidelingly and asquint at their shadow, flowing so quietly along the bank, complete and detailed even to Joshua's ears pricked up among the foxglove leaves. He threw his head back and breathed up to the pigeon-blue sky his happy sensations which seemed to float above his buoyant body in long shallow flights. His feet on the front seat and a rein in each fist, he drove through his cocked knees, jerking along under the hedge, humming 'The lark in the clear air'. The whip wriggled in the leather horn. He heard lambs and rooks, jays and woodpeckers and singing thrushes, and the voices of men starting the season off with a push in the fields.

A hedge-cutter, hung up on thorns like gipsy rags, called, "Out agen, Uncle?"

"Ay, out agen, and nothing to p'y," answered Thomas blithely.

Reaching the town, he took a long look at the market clock in its stone cupboard. He stopped to set his watch and then drove straight to the wine merchant's, drawing the shandrydan carefully into the gutter with a forewheel in a grating to ease Joshua.

"We are out of whisky in jars," said the manager.

Thomas scratched his hair under his cap. What was to be done, then? Like as not Parson Cope would say whisky in bottles was poison.

"Will the reverend know the difference?" he asked.

"It's exactly the same whisky, I assure you."

"Tha hasn't a jar as tha could pour it in, be chance?"

"I'm afraid I haven't. But there's no difference. I don't see what's the trouble," the manager urged.

"Tha don't see. That be it – I be telling tha – Parson Cope be pe-cu-li-ar. 'E do p'y a girl pounds a w'ik just to pour whisky from jar to jug and jug to cut-glass. Like as not 'e'll 'old a meeting for less nor whisky in a bottle."

The manager shrugged his shoulders. He looked at Parson Cope's ridiculous shandrydan, scrolled fore and aft, and at Joshua lolling in the breechins, with his nose on his knees. Then at those queer, hard, prejudiced country eyes with their childish problem unsolved.

"Try," he said.

"Done. I ool tek a bottle. One, mind," Thomas agreed.

And the bottle, wrapped in white paper, with a twist at the top like one of Mrs Lane's curl papers, was thrust into his pocket.

For, thought Thomas, driving home, if the reverend didn't want the whisky, he would have to return it. Another trip, maybe.

The sun was low now, and the light was what Thomas called "weavy", meaning that it threaded his sight with hedge-woven beams. He blinked, and keeping his head low saw the brightness on his eyelashes. The banked fields looked steeper with the shadows climbing them; the breeze touched the highest catkin branches as with a taper. Thomas listened to the wheels, and for the hundredth time thought how he would like to own Joshua and the shandrydan. Perhaps when Parson Cope died there would be a sale. But suppose he didn't die? Suppose he got "put aw'y"? "Him be getting queer. That's it! Ah, him ool be going from here one d'y. If him was a poor man him 'ood be in an 'ome already. A man like me would. Ay! Be a lucky thing the parson be daft and not tha, Thomas Griffiths-the-Mill, a rare lucky thing it be."

It was thickening to sunset when he got back, with no moon, and a mist coming out of the trees. Thomas unharnessed Joshua, talking to him.

"Him bain't a bad owld feller, the poor owld gov'nor bain't. We'll go agen Friday, and if I don't get thic jar then I ool pitch into that jawing manager chap. Ah, poor owld parson, poor owld reverend, 'ow I do 'ave 'e on! Soft 'e be, and quick I be. Ay, quick – all me wits I 'ave, all in me 'ead, all to manage. Damn tha, Joshua boy, get over. Well, there you be and off tha goes."

He slapped Joshua on the quarters and watched him trot into the orchard. The sun was gone: there was dew on the iron bar which fastened the gate – dew that stained his hand with a rusty band.

Parson Cope was standing on the steps, waiting. He had a newspaper, and he had wrung it in his two hands like a dish-cloth. When Thomas saw this he felt a little frightened. He heard somebody sobbing, and a light was fanning a bit wildly through the house.

"'Ere you be," said Thomas, hoisting the bottle. But Parson Cope said nothing.

"Tek owld, will tha?" Thomas entreated. He began to explain: "Them hadn't no other. 'Tis only for a d'y or two tha ool 'ev to wait. I ool go agen Friday. Come on now, reverend."

He held the bottle up again. Then he shook it. Then he lost his temper.

"Tek you," he shouted.

Parson Cope's arm shot out, and then he seemed to snatch it back into his black body, grasping the bottle. Almost before Thomas had heard the crash it lay shattered, smashed against the iron door-knob. The pieces lay, little fragments of glass in shining curves, turned up to the dusk – light on the stone. In the bright twilit sky the owls twittered ....

Round the back, where Thomas was gathering his tools, the kitchen lamp shone out on the lawn. No cup of tea to-night. That was young Margery crying. Thomas felt for his pipe – it would last the way home.

"Be a regular owld fi-end," he whispered. He was tired, and he didn't want to come here any more, even for the shandrydan. He would go home and throw some wood on the fire and have a look through the *Gazette* again. And he'd take a bit of that rabbit for supper.

Pipe in one hand, matches in the other, he stood thinking.

"Damme, rabbit bain't in the pot!" he said at last.

He had forgotten. Here he stood, dreaming, and his supper not even paunched, hanging on a nail in the shed!

"Mad as parson," he muttered – "mad as parson you be after all, Thomas Griffiths."

How it happened he never could tell, but having lit his pipe, he threw it away, and put the red-hot match in his mouth. Tranced, he stood, sucking his burnt lip, staring at the smooth tongues of the laurels in the lamplight ....

"Daft you be. If anybody had seen thee do that them 'ood *know* it. Time tha was owld Thomas. Time to stop, time to stop, when tha do go stuffing tha trap with lighted matches."

The fleeting echo of a piping voice filled and flowed over him. "Hee, hee," it laughed, "'tain't 'olesome. Like master, like man!"

Thomas drew just one long breath of grief. "Best 'ide," he muttered, "best 'ide it while I can." He took up the spade. Down to the bottom of the garden he went quietly.

He buried pipe and tobacco-pouch close under the yew summer-house, where the old mulberry hid him from the house. At the same moment, Margery, on her knees beside a famishing candle in a saucer, was gathering up the broken bottle from the step. Thomas started heavily for home. The feeling of the dewy earth in the dusk touched him like a youth he would never regain. And yet there was something triumphant trying to find its way out of the darkness. A comfort? A retort?

When he came to the spot where he had met Sammy in the morning, he stopped and saw that it was night.

Darkness – the silence of the eyes ....

He waited.

All at once – it came!

"Eh? If Parson Cope be mad and I be like 'im, I be like a *gentleman*, any road. 'Night, Sammy," said Thomas beginning a long uphill laugh.

He could afford to be like a gentleman, whatever the gentleman resembled.

"Yes, and I can go along ter-morrer and pick up me pipe and 'bacca."

It was a queer thing, but as he said that he seemed to hear a window fly up, and a voice screeching:

"Griffiths! Harness Joshua! We must have whisky. Mrs Lane says she must have whisky."

"'Ow, reverend? In a bottle?"

"How! what does it matter to an old woman, *how*? Jugs, jars, bottles, acorn cups! Harness the pony!"

Nature has its own agenda
lost / late help

The Old Woman and the Wind

I N her grey, blunted garden, with the gutterings of the long slidden turf mounding about her, old Mrs Ashstone was stooping over her broken crocuses.

"Maybe I can rise them up," she was wailing as she touched their bruised cold petals, "maybe. But what's the use when that old wind'll only blow 'em all flat agen?"

They were her only flowers – just the one clump of ochre yellow sheaths growing under the cottage wall as close and thick as if they were in a pot.

And even them the wind had smashed as it had smashed everything else. The porch, the fence .... Mrs Ashstone had nothing pretty or hospitable to look at; nothing but the rocks that broke out of the quivering wire grass, and lay about like sheep. Wind! Mrs Ashstone growled, *wind!*

The air was stiff with it – solid and encroaching. Wind more than age was dwindling her sparrow frame. Sometimes it felt as hard and narrow as churchyard mould; others it was like being cuddled by a giant. Wind, always blowing, roaring, pushing at her and her cottage, shoving her out of her place, pouncing on her hair. Cursed wind, too big for the world.

Look how the grass was bending! That melted bank had been a stone wall once. And the stumbling gusts that harshly rocked her tiny body. And the flattened smoke coming down round the chimney's neck in wisps like her own hair. How she hated it, oh how she hated it!

Mrs Ashstone straightened her spine slowly, pushing her knuckles into her knees, her thighs, and then her hips. "Ah! Ah! Ah!" she groaned, "if only I could get away from here I shouldn't get old so fast. A nice soft little place in the village now, like what Mrs Maddocks has. Or Mrs Griffiths."

Mrs Ashstone was seventy-one. She had little to think of after living alone on her hill for twelve years except her own bad luck. She was not stupid, but so ignorant that she imagined "Mrs" to be a common Christian name and the marriage service a sort of second baptism. She had forgotten that she was called Annie. Mrs

Ashstone, Garway Hill, she was, and there she stood with tears in her eyes, stroking her crocuses and wishing for a pathway, box-edged, and a little orchard with a clothes line. It was the hour of evening, which seems made solely for the first slender winter flowers. The shadowless January twilight enclosed and shaped each contour with leaf-like distinctness. The tiny cottage, slapped with limewash, was built under a single flake of rock. Some bloomless gorse bushes and pale bracken patches, that was all. There was no living feeling, but only a heedless and violent solitude.

Under the slurred turf lay half-buried a few heavy stones. Swept and seamed by each gust, the old woman toiled up and down the frail track she had worn from her door to the gap in the mound. Each journey she brought a stone. These she laid round the cro-cuses, lifting their golden pods: "There, now, if the sun shines, they'll open in the morning," she said when it was done. Then she raised her face menacingly and flapped her fist. The gesture seemed not hers but the wind's. "Keep off," she screamed. "Keep off 'em now. You go down there and break off some of they great el'um trees." She went to the step and rested against the door, arranging her dim dress and apron, gripping them down at the knees with fierce self-conscious modesty. She had a little screw of hair on top of her skull, a screw of nose curled upwards like a dead leaf, and small, clutching yellow hands that were always chasing the flying and broken things floating in the wind's wake. Somebody said she looked as if she were forever catching feathers in the air, and it was true that she did.

She turned to face the valley. The soft sound of it was going underground, but up here it was coming a gale. She could feel it in her heart. Every breath seemed too big for her. Her eyes followed the downward path to the village. Ah, it was always still there, always blowing here. Below the oak trees, where the round winds whisked the dead leaves in figure forms, the quietness began. Warmth, sounds, birds' voices. Up here she had to listen through the wind, but after the oak tree was passed things found their own way into her hearing. Voices, footsteps trickling from cottage to cottage through the peaceful lanes ....

It had been like that this morning. There she had stood and stroked her hair. She'd lifted her face and smelled the sky as if she were smelling at a flower. A flock of birds as fine as dust she'd seen.

Then she had gone on down, cruel rage and cruel envy in her mind, tears in her eyes. Mrs Griffiths's daughter had cancer, they said, but Mrs Griffiths's front path was ruled between primulas and violets. The sunlight touched the dark-green box bush.

"Good morning, good morning," the ninety-year-old woman had nodded cheerfully. Well, Mrs Ashstone wished her no harm, for her son carried the coal up Garway. But, oh, the meadows, the gentle river at her garden side, made tired flesh drag with longing. Old Mrs Ashstone had passed on, not answering the human greeting, but hearing the water's poem, the crow flock's rustling over the elms.

Mrs Maddocks, she was hanging out washing – sheets, Fred's shirts. This time it was Mrs Ashstone who stopped. Under the hedge, wide open in the grass of the bank, a constellation of celandine shone at the sun. Five of them, shaped, she noticed, like the Plough. She put out her torn, black foot. She wanted to kill their beauty. But she closed her eyes. The sunlight was red through the flesh. And then she had a vision. A white willow tree in a red world. It was an effort to raise her tired lids. Mrs Maddocks was slapping each garment out in the air. She was standing aslant, empty wash bath on her hip, the breezeless sheets a white screen for her shadow.

"There 'tis!" she cried in triumph. "But will it dry! Bain't no wind." Would it dry! Mrs Ashstone sneered to herself as she fingered a twig in the hedge. Would it dry, and the sun gloating on the orchard! She pressed her lips together and walked on quickly.

When she came out of the shop some impulse took her up the steps to the churchyard gate. She stood there eased of some of her misery, for it relaxed her just not to hear the grind of the wind. She waited for the hatred to return and help her home. Her feet were on a cracked stone, her hands folded on the dusty gate, when old Captain Ifor and Mr Brewer went by below with their sheepdogs and retrievers, talking.

"Good day, good day," the Captain called. "You down from your eyrie?"

She blinked at them mockingly, fumbling with the old spoon latch, clicking it with her thumb, her face expressing only a kind of humiliating wistfulness. What was an ar-ry – and what had it to do with her hill? So she turned her back on them. "One day I shall lie here, and none to prevent me," she told herself. Up there, where the greyness roamed the bracken, was her home, looking from where she stood, like a white pebble that a boy had flung out of the river. Later on she trod her way upwards with her groceries and a bucket of shallots Mary Maddocks had run out to give her. They were very heavy, but she stopped to gather a handful of bracken, bending the canes over and over to fit her small grate. The climb made her tremble. The wind took her breath and threw it away as if it were nothing. "There's no mercy, no mercy," she began to whimper, feeling her hair blowing awry, and her knees clutched invisibly.

That night old Mrs Ashstone had to bolt her door against the boulders of air the wind rolled against it. The latch and bolt jigged with each solid blast: the glass in the window rustled, a beast roared in the chimney, and a wet black mark like a footprint appeared under the door.

She looked at it. "This is a rare storm that brings me such a visitor," she said.

The rain tumbled down the chimney on the flames.

"My fire's scalded," she said.

She sat down on her fender and began to unravel the shallots. Suddenly, letting her hands fall, she called: "John? John Ashstone?" she thought a voice had spoken to her aloud. She wasn't afraid. She had many voices inside her, but fear had seldom spoken. Her mind turned and talked to her often enough. Yet this had sounded different. It had come in the gale, now all but through the walls, now backing away, moving it seemed with and among the freakish screams, the lumps of wind, and the long dragging sounds that hung back along the earth.

A slate crashed. "Mrs Ashstone, Mrs Ashstone!"

Mrs Ashstone stood up. "Be you my conscience?"

"No."

"Then be you my stomach?"

"No."

"Then you must be the roof going?"

"No. I'm the wind. And you're a witch." And the roaring rose all around the room, like heatless flame.

"You may be the wind, but I'm no witch."

"Yes, you are."

"I'll pummel ye," said she. "Leastways I would if I could see ye. But all I can see is black cobwebs a-shaking in the chimney and soot in the lamp. I never was no witch."

"You've lived alone, and that makes a woman a witch."

"Oh, do it? Well, be that your footmark?"

The wind laughed and the sound was like stones leaping in a quarry. Then it seemed to fade, and when it spoke again there was only a tiny distinct vibration, like embers tinkling and creeping when a fire is left alone.

"Come outside and look at me," said this sequestered voice. The gale at that moment stopped; it was flat calm.

Mrs Ashstone stood on her doorstep, looking to the south-west, where a low black toadstool of cloud gloated over the hollow. She gazed at this evil web in silence rubbing her little hands. In the doorstone dent lay a handful of starlit rain.

The old woman shook. She waved her fist and shouted: "I don't like you. Get away, wind, ugly thing you be!"

The cloud was nearer. Around it the stars shone as in tender piety. "I cannot abear that thing," the old woman said, and she went in and closed the door. But the voice bent itself round the chink before she could thud the bolt: "Where shall I go, where shall I go?" it uttered shrilly and rapidly.

"Go?" screamed Mrs Ashstone. "Go anywhere. Go down the village and blow down all they great el'ums and rookeries and Captain Ifor's peaches. Haven't them had peace all these years?"

Her words were repeated, but slowly, as a lesson is read, meditatively, engraving the stillness. Then there was silence. She was alone. Her fingers hovered about her ears as if to catch meanings in the lamplight. But she heard nothing except clock, kettle, and mouse. She felt that she lived in these stirrings. Thoughtfully she went to the cupboard, took down the sugar-basin and flipped a mouse-pill out of it with her thumbnail.

When she opened the door again before going to bed she noticed that the darkness had a strange sallow smell. There was a faint wavy noise. She strained to hear. "'Tis like the weir!" she said staring. On the hill it was as still as mid-summer, with the sheep cropping the hushed mounds. She saw a star sinking slowly as if someone were lowering a candle to the floor. The old woman put out her hand to catch it ....

In the morning, looking under the sunrise, she saw the empty floods and the river winding through their vacancy. Red as copper, the dull waters showed seaweed-like patches spread upon them. These were ricks of hay and clover and corn which the wind had lifted and carried away and dropped furlongs from their foundations.

Mrs Ashstone dropped her sticks and ran away down to the village without lighting her fire or even so much as lifting the lid off the bread pan. When she was past the oak tree the breeze fluttered like a flag in her face, but it made no sound at all. She ran into the 'Street', holding her left wrist in her right hand, and then she stopped and listened.

Slates were lying on the paths, trees were down, with their roots that had burst the sod, washed bare of earth, and strange sand bars and pearly pebble beaches rippled across the lane.

Most of the doors stood open on the tightly-furnished rooms, but nobody stood looking out. It was so quiet except for the cadaverous murmur of the flood that she could hear the puddings snuffling in the saucepans.

She ran on round the bend. Then what a sight! The river had cut the village in half. It had felled the bridge, and was rushing over the road fifty yards wide, and rough and red as a ploughed field.

On the side where Mrs Ashstone was running the slope was abrupt and the houses stood clear above the torrent. But on the far side old Mrs Griffiths's cottage was four feet deep, with a broken door and the green velvet furniture floating in the garden. In the greatest danger was Mrs Sate, the baker's wife, at her second-floor window with her baby up against her cheek. For the river divided from the flood at the corner of her chimney wall, and with enormous pressure split into two, islanding the cottage, with the cage of its partly-demolished porch clinging to it like rubble.

Mrs Sate was shouting wildly to the people who stood by the water. They did not seem to listen, for they were all telling one another the story of their night. They had remote incredulous expressions on their faces because they could not go to work. The children were crawling out as far as they dared along the broken bridge stones. Captain Ifor was there in a mackintosh cape, prodding the water with his stick. And Mrs Maddocks, shouting at him, her white cotton bosom overlapping her folded arms. And many others.

"'Twere more like sunset than sunrise, so wild and lonely 'twere," Fred was saying.

Then they all turned round, hearing old Mrs Ashstone running. Her footsteps sounded intelligent, as if they brought an explanation. But the old woman was rushing towards the river without any idea, her arms stretched before her as if she wanted to prevent the waters. She ran right up to the end, and then pulled herself up. She put out her foot and gently paddled her shoe in it. Old Captain Ifor cast her a glance, and then once more plunged his stick in it.

"What I do say is it's come to something when your own roof's blown off you and you're the last to know it," Mrs Maddocks was screeching at him: "Sitting there mending Fred's shirt I was, and not a notion in the world what was happening till he comes in. 'Mother,' he says, 'do you know the roof's lifting up and down like a rick-cloth? For God's sake,' he says, 'come out and see'."

Mrs Ashstone looked at her, and angry as she was Mrs Maddocks politely included her. But a voice that might have spoken out of the group itself, so monotonous and undistinguished was it, began to recite:

"Mrs Sate, she be s'ying as she 'ev nowt with 'er for sus-ten-ance but 'alf a pork pie and a crust. And her the baker's wife! Charley, 'e's been at the bakehouse all night. What ool 'appen I can't think, for 'er can't swim to 'e, and what be good o' 'e swimming to 'er? And there bain't no boats in this village."

"And all the telephone wires are down. I've tried and tried," said the Captain.

Mrs Maddocks raised her stern voice again: "Whose fault is this, I said, when I'd seen. Eh? Who won't do the repairs? Eh? Who? Captain, you can take the key this minute if you've a mind, for I'm not a woman that will live under a roof that's tied on me head with wagon ropes as this one be this minute. All me furniture's out." And she handed the key out from her armpit where she had been hatching it. The Captain took it gingerly. Mrs Ashstone turned her eyes across the water. She stretched out her arms, and it seemed to her she was stroking the faces in the upper windows. She wanted to say something, but the waters and the gossiping stopped her frail words. Her face was beautiful.

Just then, on the other side, a man came running down the slope in a greatcoat. It was Charley Sate. He threw down the coat by the water's edge. He was in vest and pants. Round his waist he wore a scarf, and tucked into it were two bottles of milk.

"Ah, brave fellow, brave fellow," clucked the Captain. "Many waters cannot drown love. Besides they're going down. He'll make it."

Charley thrust out. His jaw was like a knot under his ear. He seemed to look into all their faces and to live in the look. The current knitted itself round his neck and his separated hands, walking, as it were, before those dark and frenzied eyes. He plaited his arms in with the water, weaving all three.

In a few minutes he was safe on the shed roof, lifting up a little window under the chimney. Mrs Sate's face vanished. Every one shouted and a little boy dropped a flat stone with a ringing splash.

Captain Ifor nodded: "Well done, well done!" He propped his stick against his shaking knees so that he could clap. This made him recognize the key. Mrs Maddocks was crowdedly cheering with the rest, and for the first time the old man saw what was in his hand: "What's this? A key?" His eyes settled on Mrs Ashstone – eyes like smoky glass. "Want it? She doesn't. Mary always makes up her mind by accident, but when it's done, it's done. You're more pliable. You have it. Get you down from that eyrie of yours."

Mrs Ashstone was no longer beautiful. Her body had dropped that direct expression. She stood twisted in an attitude of crooked secrecy before the Captain, and between their two silent figures flowed a little eddy of air, as it might between two trees.

She shook herself, as you might shake a clock that is stopping, and the slow tired look of secrecy was gradually transferred from one old face to the other, as though by reflection.

And so Captain Ifor and Mrs Ashstone stared silently at each other.

To him it was suddenly revealed that she was not like other old women. At least when you thought of an old woman you did not think of anybody like this one. Old women in the imagination are all alike. But old Mrs Ashstone was nothing you could imagine. She had a child's distinctness, he thought, yet she looked enfeebled, as though in her old age she saw the world by candlelight.

"Won't you have it?" he said.

She shook her head: "I have a friend up there. One that do know where I was born. To live with me."

42

"A relation?"

"Nearer than that," she said. And then shyly, and, as it were, *wonderingly*, she took a peppermint like a white button out of her pocket and tossed it in her mouth. She turned away and walked slowly up the road, her feet leaving little quiltings in the thin red mud where the nails in her soles stuck. Under the oak tree she stumbled over the wind as if it had been a dog asleep. It circled round her, blowing a wren out of a bush.

"Well?" it said out of the grass.

The old woman sat down on a stone.

"If you was a bettle I 'ood stamp on you," she scolded.

"Oh!"

"Some of them people have been kind to me."

"Then why didn't you take the key and go and live with them?"

She considered this question as if it lay on her lap with her hands. After a pause she said quickly, "*You* didn't ask me that – I asked myself. I can't hardly sort you out from my thoughts," she said, "even when it's quiet like here. I bain't got the *use* of a lot of people and voices. I bin too long on Garway. Down there I couldn't hardly tell whether I were glad or sorry. I couldn't seem to *hear*. And that's the reason as I don't want to change my ways now. I do like to hear even the mice in me cupboard, and the cockroaches, I'm that curious and learned. I 'ave got used to them. I've worked with people, not loved them, and now I be done with work I do want to be shut of 'em."

"It can't happen again," said the wind.

"Nor I don't want it should," said she, rising and beginning to bend over the crackling bracken.

Into Kings

ARRY was five. He simplified everything. And he couldn't understand why such a tiny cottage was called a castle. Peewit Castle. He asked what a peewit was, and they told him it was that bird up there. He shook his head. Kings, not birds, lived in castles.

The name was written over the door. Mr Lackitt had painted it in the kind of thin white paint which is used for signs reading "Licensed to sell tobacco" over country porches. The coarse-grained, twilight grey wood showed through the letters, and the two words were divided by a stop about as big as a dumpling. The Lackitts lived in the Castle. There was Mr Lackitt, Mrs Lackitt, and somebody his mother called Miss Lackitt. She was strange. Harry remembered them before he went to sleep. He had a minute, vivid memory of the kind of smells they had – white roses, velvet dust, fur, and onions. He neither lived nor remembered in sequence, and life and his dreams appeared without season. He was a busy visionary.

The cottage was in a turnip field, close to a wood. Mrs Lackitt's brown, loosely and knottily knitted shawl was like bark. When she was in the raspberries, it caught on the big grey and green leaves, and pulled out behind her like a tent.

Mrs Lackitt was a tall, strong old woman, who folded her arms. Her eyes were black, but in the middle of them shone a diminutive light, like a vigil. She wore a blue apron. Her husband was older. He was usually down at the bottom of the orchard where the trees strained away from one another in order to keep apart. He kept pigs. The Lackitts didn't seem to live in their cottage, but to lead a brisk outdoor existence round about it among their livestock.

Harry went there nearly every day. They didn't mind; they were fond of him. The old man seldom spoke; but he used to bend down his silent face and blink at the little boy, and he did this so funnily that it was pleasanter than words.

The leaves were falling out of the trees. There was a golden sloping wind. The great loose-leafed elms held the gusts and then let them out with a high over-your-head sound. Mrs Lackitt knelt in the lane beside a crock, gathering acorns from under the oaks for the pigs. Harry felt the fine mesh of the mist closing round his warm cheeks.

He picked up a dead crow with bald white elbows of bone.

"Is this a peewit?"

"Let un alone, dirty boy. That's a Johnny Crow. They hens 'ave bin pickin' un." And Mrs Lackitt got up stiffly to shoo the hens out of the orchard with her skirts, for, she said, "They don't lay because them do pick at the cider apples."

"Come, and I'll give you something nice," she said. She took his hand and led him down the garden to the raspberry canes.

"There," she said. She let the wet berries roll from her palm into his. She shook the rain clusters off the sticky leaves and sprays and made a lapping noise with her lips.

"Mrs Lackitt, these raspberries don't taste of raspberries."

"What do um taste of, then?"

"Raspberries and water."

The old woman grinned. She liked talking to the child. A son of hers was buried in Scotland, a daughter between the mists of mountain and sea. Half-gipsy, it comforted her to tell someone about her youthful travelling. In those days her surviving child had been as others. Then she had gone to be a servant. One day, after market, a drunken gentleman had taken her up in his trap. He flogged his horse; it had bolted and flung the girl out. He was unharmed, but she was crippled for life. She sat all day by the fire poking it with a stick viciously, as if the flames were a nest of adders. She looked terribly like a little old man. Harry was afraid of her. Only once he had spoken to her.

"Are you lonely?" he said. It was a word he had heard used for grief. And then softly and profoundly: "Do you wish you were the only person in the world?"

"Go away," she gruffed at him, clutching her stick.

"There, there, boy, leave her alone," Harry remembered Mrs Lackitt pulling him away and whispering. "She bain't reely cross, but her'll never be right again."

After that he looked at her secretly, wincing from her notice. Her face was as though worn away by thought, its expression of disdain and privation never changed. She couldn't turn sideways, but she could bend forward to strike at the fire. She used to do this about every five minutes unless she was asleep, or carefully pinning on a board the skins of moles that Mr Lackitt trapped. With their pallid mauvish membrane and the thin red-ink veins, they looked like tiny maps when she had tacked them down. They were dried and wrapped up in newspaper, and put under the cushion until she felt she wanted to count them. Sometimes she would throw a whole lot on the fire.

Harry could remember the beginning of his visits. At first he used to go with his mother, holding her hand. They went for eggs. They stood in the porch, and Mother passed the basket over his head. Mrs Lackitt took it inside, and they waited, Harry trying to push the white roses back through the trellis. It was a long time before the basket was returned. Then his mother said, "How beautiful, Mrs Lackitt. How kind!"

Each egg was wrapped in hay. Pale pink, and milky, brown or golden, faintly mauve, he unwound them on the table at home. On the top lay a sprig of green leaves with a sweet lemony smell, and there was always one extra egg for him.

It was exciting, unwrapping the snuggled eggs. His fingers trembled – he felt they would go through the shell.

And now for years and years he had been coming by himself. Each day he came. Each day the Harry of yesterday seemed somebody else. He used to talk now of "when I were a baby".

Only one rule his mother made: he was never to eat anything at the Lackitts'. They were poor, with their invalid to keep. He never told her about the raspberries. It was November. The foggy trees leaked mist; the brown winds were visible with leaves. Yellow and tortoiseshell, grey and lacquer red, mahogany and gingerbread colour, they span and skimmed. Between the afternoons and the twilight stretched an hour of intense silence. The sun came close, as though listening. Harry's days went with him into his nights, filling the darkness of his drowsy eyes with the colours and the scenes. Only the words never came back with the other treasures. He began to be aware that he was a being – a *private* being, and that he need not tell.

Sometimes he seemed interrupted. His mother watched him sitting on the floor, his ruffled games abandoned. The toys, left so purposeless, looked startled, accidental.

"What are you doing, Harry?"

"I'm thinking about the Lackitts, Mother."

His mother coaxed him: "Yes, darling. They're very kind to you. But what are you thinking?"

"It's something they've got."

She stared. "What is it?"

But he was silent. He turned away his head with a peculiar, stately reticence. His new, gentle refusal amazed her. Looking straight ahead, he smiled, as if he had seen something pleasing and grand in a glass.

"I hope," she thought, picking up the vermillion engine which looked so extraordinarily like a real accident, "I hope this doesn't mean he's been riding that scurfy old donkey. He's such an *outdoor* child. The Lackitts are *very kind,* but ..."

It was rather as if the Lackitts' kindness had fleas in it. She wished he had somewhere else to go. She didn't know what to do with him in the afternoons. Oh, well.

What had happened to Harry was that he had seen a sign. It was one day when he couldn't find Mrs Lackitt. The old man was in the orchard, at the far end, gossiping by nods to someone in the lane. Harry stayed to watch the uncouth conversation for a little while, and then he ran back to the cottage. He pushed the door open and stumbled over the serge curtain into the room. The twilight inside came like a dimness over his eyes. After a moment in which he could hardly breathe for terror lest someone strange should be hiding among the furniture, he saw there was only the invalid.

An unknown animation was on her face. She might have been talking fast, but she made no sound. Her eyes were opening and shutting quicker than anything he had ever seen, and her mouth seemed to be talking. That was why he had thought there must be somebody silent in the room looking at her, to make her twitch back so wildly.

And then, going close in his bewilderment, he saw she was asleep, and it was the firelight moving on her mouth and her eyes. The firelight was giving her long dark eyelashes of shadow that rose and fell, rose and fell, shaggy and startled. Her whole countenance was panting. After watching for a moment, he ignored her. An apple rolled from her lap to the floor. With an involuntary snatch which seemed to escape him, he picked it up and bit it, his eyes rolling round over the fat apple in which his teeth were stuck.

He had never been alone in the Lackitts' room before. And it was a nice room, full of lovely things, shiny and small such as he could hold in one hand.

Gripping the apple in his teeth, hurriedly, because he felt his jaws meeting and the bite coming out, Harry first pulled up one sock and then the other. And then, restrainedly, as if he had but few movements to spend, he began to step round the furniture, touching, admiring, and lifting into a better light the collection of ornaments and trinkets. He thought the china boys, the vases and little boxes and cups upside down in their saucers, were so pretty, so very wonderful and valuable. There was gold paint on the boys' hat-bands and on the cup handles, thick stripes of it ending in little shiny stick-out roses which he fondled with a realistic delight. Indeed, those old cups were really charming and lovely, and so was the large leaning wall mirror of gilt on wood. It was even older than the china, and not dusted so often, and the golden patina was dimmed and softer, from the fine ash dust and the smoke in the airless room. Two rounded pillars wreathed with formal moulded rings, and a ribboned and feathered galaxy at the top framed it. Into its grey misty glass it gathered all the strays of light there were, reflecting them as still flashes whiter and brighter than the fire. To look into it was like looking at the sky through a wood where colourless clear shapes are cut out of the black-brown branches.

With the poetry of all mirrors, whether sixpenny or Sheraton, it seemed to reflect not only light, but *stillness*. The quality of abiding-ness which poverty, closeness, and use had given to the chairs and tables was compacted in the mirror into a tilted but solid peace. In the glass even the clock pendulum seemed to wave more slowly. Harry turned to look at it, and was puzzled by the quick way it really jerked against the wall. Harry's self went sideways into the glass, which stood on a low chest of drawers. He could see himself down as far as the belt of his mackintosh, a little boy in a green sou-wester.

Pleased and somehow proud, he stretched his arms with a strain-ing of stiff rubber folds. Turning his palms from him he looked at his dirty little hands still red from playing with the rusty wet gate. Opening and shutting his fingers, the thought of how much he would do with them when he wanted to begin occurred to him happily.

He felt his shoulders, the top of his head, his breast, and saw himself repeating the touches. There was the beating under the hand that pressed, but dimly he understood there being no heart to thud in the glass.

Forgetting she wasn't there, he turned to ask "Mrs Lackitt, why –?"

Quietly, outside, with regular pauses, the rain ticked into the butts. The fire sighed and settled on its nest. The shadowy eyelashes no longer flickered fast on the invalid's face, but a delicately formed darkness like a hand lay across her forehead.

The boy, with his face literally almost upon a magic moment, gave two quick gasps. Indeed, whatever the simple explanation, the chance was amazing, that he should have been the one to meet it. But this was all that was, in any sense, preternatural, though the glimpse was exquisite and perfect in its way.

A cheap round shaving glass had been put down on the crochet runner. It was a softened magnified reflection of one gilded wreath that looked from the angle of Harry's height like a beautiful crown .... Exactly like a crown. Into Harry's eyes came the uncovetous rapture of the child who for the first time sees royal gold.

He didn't connect it with fact. Instantly, the likeness of a crown, suggesting glory and glorification, became part of the Lackitts.

Harry saw the orchard; and walking in it, strangely altered, and yet the same, were the Lackitts, crowned and wearing trains. But the invalid was out of it.

Hadn't he always wanted to know why they lived in a castle? It was the greatest of marvels, the most delicious answer, that went straight, it seemed, and struck into his breast, into the beating of his heart which burned up like a fire of raiment and jewels and gold. The most real of stories seemed about to begin. He saw Mrs Lackitt as queen with a great yellowy ring around her brows. And driving her, in the little black tub, Mr Lackitt, the king. Poor drab old Nellie the donkey disappeared, and in her place in the shafts trotted a circus pony with red harness ....

He didn't believe in the crown, any more than he believed that the excited heart he could feel was alive in the mirror. Yet, like the heart, it existed *outside*. Perhaps, yes, somewhere?

He turned. The invalid's eyes were wide open and fixed on him with a gentle, mortal glance. It was as if Miss Lackitt had woken up someone else, and Harry ran to her, pressing his fist into her lap, deep into the rough little pink and black tongues of the rag rug.

"Whose – who – who?" he stammered, pointing, feeling as if his meaning were changing in his mind before he could settle on it.

He could feel how calm she was. It was strange when she put her hand out and touched him, how quiet the gesture was.

"Why, wasn't you asleep then?" he asked, surprised.

"Come and sit on my knee," she said; but her arms could only make gaunt hard movements, and she had no power in them to lift him, controlled as they were by her warped spine.

"I ate your apple," he mumbled, atoning. But she made no answer. He was astonished that she should be crying.

He would have liked to have said something, but shyness made him hide his face.

"Why, look at that now!"

It was Mrs Lackitt's voice. She stood in the doorway, her husband crowded up against her. She was holding a bucket; and he had two dead fowls by their legs. They both peered and stared.

Mrs Lackitt had been feeding the livestock. Chaff had blown into her hair and her eyes, and clung to her clothes. She set the bucket down with a rattle. Mr Lackitt pushed by her as if to go into the lean-to at the back, but he paused in the middle of the room with a perfectly blank face.

Harry didn't understand their silence. Mrs Lackitt lifted the corner of her shawl and wiped the rain off her face. Harry thought she, too, was in tears, but it was only the trembling of an old restless lament that went over her features.

"Mrs Lackitt!" he cried, "Mrs Lackitt."

But he couldn't tell, after all. It was something he could only have himself, to keep and to question.

After a moment Mr Lackitt decided to move. He shuffled into the lean-to and threw the fowls under the sink. Then he searched along the shelf for his pipe. He was the only person of the four to whom nothing could possibly have been otherwise than as it was.

wonderful
scarcity
calmness
native authority
man
minute detail

People of his Pasture

T HE sun had gone in for the moment and the north-east wind was briefly dimming the hills and hollows with sleet. Any one standing close to the mill wall could have heard the lapping sound of the ivy leaves as they ruffled over one another in the sudden storm. They would have seen, too, how the mealy mortar, ages old, was crumbling on the dark green leaves and falling on the sprouting nettles, freshly springing from the whitened and cankered logs thrown against the wall after some tree-felling years ago. And how the bent and broken straws had stuck in the swirl of the ruts, showing that the passing earthquake of a wagon had jolted that way not long before. An apple-tree stood within the wall with a rotten halter hanging from a branch which the children used to swing themselves over the brick-hard ground under the buttress. Once there had been a garden where now was only daisied grass and a path enclosed in iron hurdles. Now the only flowers were the white violets lying like sleet on their leaves, and along a broken border of stones, some browned wall-flower bushes and plants of God's hand. But a child was playing by herself quite happily, tossing her careless body up on her hands, kicking and counting as she turned her cartwheels.

"One, two, three, four!" she shouted as she whirled. She was trying to go across the grass from the play-worn tree to the garden seat without toppling. She counted four for each cartwheel; but suddenly, as if realizing that she would come to the end of her secret limit of numbers before she touched the seat, she stopped, thinking breathlessly and biting her finger.

"I know!" she cried, "I know," and she was off again. "One" – cartwheel – "Two" – cartwheel – and with twelve she tumbled against the seat and kicked its arm. She sat up and pointed her finger. "Boom," she cried, "boom boom! You must die when you're told." Suddenly she smiled – only she knew what deliberate thing she saw hovering before her.

And when the small soft petals of the sleet began to fall on the grass, she ran to stoop from them under the buttress, her blue mottled hand bent back against the stone, close to her ear. She was

51

listening to the sweep of the squall and the March budding branches swaying. The apple-tree seemed to inhale, to change: she listened as if her smile had alighted on a distant recognition while she kicked its stubbed and lacerated trunk with her shabby-toed shoe. She thought she heard a hint of animals at play, running, leaping on squirrel paws. Then the icy wind slowly relaxed, her hand fell to her side and the light edged round the back of the storm.

"One, two, three," she began again. Her hair was in plaits, tied with white tape. She wore modern blonde glasses but no warm clothes. Only a shrivelled faded dress – faded but of a queer fierce blue, full and torn and short, with patches of damp dirt on it, like a cheesy wall. As she careered carefully across the grass she seemed to become tiny in movement and far away like a stampeding calf or a galloping pony seen a long way off in relation to the vast inherent motion of a landscape.

The mill wheel was not working. The water under the span bridge lay low, submerged as it were by its stony, muddy bed and the ooze where the sheep drank. On the hills around this solitary house shone the astringent green of the March pasturage, dotted with ewes like silver-grey puff-balls. The lambs lay in the angles of the steep fields waggling their huge ears as if teased by the pointed cold: the ewes nibbled, their little knees butting foward, their chewing mouths making a faint nervous noise. Plovers, black and white as moonlight, turned above them. And that was all. The sky was smaller than the land, and the land was one great pasture, one loneliness so large, so lost as to stir a kind of abstract pity. Such clouds as crossed it seemed to do so piece by piece, huddling their shoulders from the blows of the hills. The house, half mill, half farm, with its wretched, bald garden, was positively alone, by the path of the water. Nor did any other homestead, barn or shelter show itself within view. As the wind leaps into invisibility when it leaves a wheatfield, thought left the mind at those horizons. The sun crept out again casting a thin unsettled shadow from wall and tree. Among the hill contours, hollows were left vacant in suspended, colourless light. Colour and depth were washed out by an elemental formlessness, a chilly and radiant blankness. Lower down in the green slopes and the mist blaze of sun rays the figure of a man trudging with hurdles, strove against wind and hillside, crossing and recrossing distance as unheeded as the child playing in the garden; bowed, the only example of humanity, he worked as if he were the only saviour of the land, its symbol and its sacrifice.

The girl sat down to button her shoe. Close by her foot, enmeshed in the grass roots, lay a rusty penknife. She tore it out.

"Oh, it's here. I've found it. Our mam, I've found your knife," she shouted. She looked up quickly to the shut house and the cold, chapel-shaped windows.

"Chop, chop, chop," she muttered, and wantonly, with grunts and the thin hillocks of her shoulder-blades slipping about under the torn dress, she slashed at her shoe button. Then she heard a sound. She threw away the knife. A boy was getting over the iron hurdle – someone she had never seen before. He came striding up, not seeing her. She sprang up and with a quick suspicious glance, full of fright, ran with her flopping shoe round the back of the house.

The lad was panting and in a hurry, red with running. He rushed up the straight path in strides shorter than leaping, longer than running. In the grain of his flesh under the scarlet flush it could be seen he had a calmer, more constant bloom. He jumped up the steps, frightening a hen which reeled away under his feet, squawking strenuously as she fled into some bushes. Seizing the iron knocker, pocked with rust, he sent a blow flying like a missile into the groaning house. It seemed to bound from wall to wall inside: he heard its echoes being distributed and dealt out to empty rooms as he waited. For an instant he forgot why he had come, listening to them, feeling the country, the humourless stare of the windows. Turning round, he laid a rucksack down on step, jostling the paint-box and water bottle inside. He was a thin boy, perhaps fifteen years old, or a year or two over – it would be hard to say. He had bright young enticing eyes and hair; his mouth was charming, and there was power in the dark-coloured gawky hands which hung by his sides, clutching themselves into fists. He jammed them into the pockets of his worn overcoat as he waited. His eyelids fell, showing the dark brown lashes. But no one came: only a long gust from the alders, rustling by the bridge. The door was faded: on its panels trickled rivulets of white flakiness, like lightning's tributaries where the shell-thin paint had cracked away.

He banged again, and again his brown lashes lifted, revealing his thrush-clear, expectant gaze. This time he heard footsteps, shuffling, a twittering cry, a sharp murmur .... The door opened, swept across a woman's face by a hand level with her brows. She leant there, a figure bowed and fruited, with a baby on her arm, a child in her skirts. Pressing the baby to her cheek she demanded shrilly:

"Well, whatever's the matter? I saw you coming across the field like hell in the night. My husband 'ood tear you in pieces if he'd a-seen you running them sheep like that." In the passage a draught groaned, blowing her skirts out. The waist-high child, a black-haired boy, beat them down, clinging to her thigh.

The lad on the step spoke quickly. "I'm sorry. Are those your husband's sheep?"

"Yes," she said grimly: "they are. Some of 'em."

"Then I've come to the right place –"

Surprised, she glanced away and back to his face as if startled into remembering there was no other –

"There's a sheep that's ill. Dying, I think. I'm sure she's in terrible pain. Couldn't somebody come?"

"Where?" she asked, contemptuous, furiously rude. And she walked out on to the step, craning her head, bending forward with a movement which scorned him for an ignorant meddlesome nuisance and a *stranger*. He saw her hand under the baby's arm half hidden in its woolly mufflings – a thin thumb and a wasted wrist with wrinkling veins like an old woman's. The wind blew across their faces like frosted leaves, and the baby blinked its queer little milky blue eyes where all its silence lay exposed.

The boy, whose name was Daniel, pointed. "There – right over there. You can't see. On the bank in the corner, lying down. She's, she's – all swollen. Blood on her. I tried to give her some water but she wouldn't drink –"

He stopped, bewildered, sensing a blind hostility and scorn. He was unknown to anybody in this country, nothing, the son of an architect staying on a farm four miles away. The woman, the child he had hardly noticed in the garden, they had a peculiarity: it was as though they had never been looked at. He felt her rage though it was incomprehensible to him. It was as if he had foolishly insulted her. How? How could he have done? Surely it was a dreadful thing he had run to tell them? He was sure he would never forget the sight of the dazed and dying animal lying quietly in its calm agony in the corner of the field. They must do something – bring her into shelter – help her – perhaps shoot her, it had been an awful sight; the plight of the ewe had filled him with horrible pity. The spaniel, Blackie Dog, had barked at her, but she hadn't lifted her head. Her long neck was stretched on the ground, her motionless, wide eyes were staring. The eyes were so hopeless, toneless from suffering, their strange gold and black stare remote from all sympathy. He had put his hand on her head, instinctively; the mossy feeling of her skull was still in his fingers, and he could see the purple swollen teat like a monstrous fuchsia flower lying between the small hoofs – the tangled blood ....

"You can't have seen!" he exclaimed. The little boy began tussling with her pocket. "Stay quiet, will you!" she said, putting her hand away from the baby down among the child's black hair. He went limp against her, grizzling: "Mam, mam."

"Yes," she said impersonally, not regarding him, "I've seen. Thank you for calling, though."

She backed into the doorway again, the group shuffling before the boy's astonished eyes as if about to dissolve there for ever.

She didn't appear to understand.

"But – but –" he said, "you *can't* –"

"You're a stranger, aren't you? Well, leave things alone."

He felt the brutal shock of her words go through him. For an instant he thought she was going to shut the door. But for some reason she seemed to hesitate, to hover at his eyes. Holding the door as she had before, near her face, she waved it slowly to and fro, with a kind of quarrelsome grace, as a fan is used.

"We've got five of them bad," she remarked; "there isn't much we can do for 'em. It's something they get after lambing. Garget they call it. Something goes wrong ... it's been that *cold*. That one you've seen – we've amputated a teat. But we've had two die already. It can't be helped."

Her manner was softening to the pleasure of talking. Suddenly she smiled, swaying on the door. "We do our best to keep 'em ticking," she added.

Daniel seemed to hold her gaze on him by physical force. He stooped before her; the dark brown, neat eyelashes touched his flushed cheeks: there was a curious sneer about his lips and his jaws were moving slightly and nervously.

The woman lifted her eyes to his modest face: "We do our best," she repeated. She began to glance about, turning her head alternately from the sound of the wind to the black-haired child's stifled whining. She had the true, rare sloe eye, so different from the hard black gipsy stare – beautiful eyes, oval and candid, the pupil seeming to mist the whole iris with its oblique indigo bloom, the brows following the shape of the lid in a faithful curve. But they were rather bloodshot and seemed to overlook what they rested on by miles and miles.

She sighed. She looked almost imploring as Daniel's gaze rose: the vacancy, which was all she could see in the fields, had left its loitering reflection in the lines of her mouth. She didn't hold it open, but it looked as if one day she might.

The boy was feeling a browbeaten fury which appeared in him like smouldering shyness. He at once abominated the woman and wanted to placate her. He could not believe in her attitude; he thought she simply could not have understood. "Look here," he began. He stopped. He didn't see the human eyes – he saw the ewe's with their queer yellow veining ....

"What sort of a dog do you call that?" the woman suddenly asked. He turned and saw Blackie Dog slithering under the hurdle.

"A cocker," he said impatiently.

"A cocker, is it? I suppose it makes it more valuable when you know – when you can call it something?"

"I ool drow a stone at it," said the little boy, flapping his arm.

"You dare!" cried the mother.

"Please," said the boy passionately; "*please* can't something be done for the sheep?"

"Huh!" the woman tossed in despair. She shoved the child away from her hip. He began to cry, drearily showing a glazed and mizzling cheek, and she pulled him close again, fondling his shoulder.

"Listen, you think we don't understand," she said violently, "but we *do*. We do know how to treat sheep. That's the way we're brought up hereabouts. My husband isn't cruel. No, he's not a cruel man. He does all he can. He's always with the sheep. He was over that way this morning with the corn and water, a-looking at that ewe you saw. And he's away now back up yonder after something for 'em. What with one thing and another the man's always from home. He can't do no more. Mortal couldn't, not if they were people. Always, always off."

She laughed.

"Why, good gracious – why, he never parts with one if he can help it! He says this old ewe, she may get better. Times they do. We must just wait and see. But mostly they die. Yes, they usually die, ewes do, with the garget."

"But she's *suffering!* Couldn't you have her killed?"

"You mean destroyed?"

"Yes."

"Why, no," she said in a tone of the strangest innocence and amazement. "You see she might recover. And then it would be waste, wouldn't it?" She stretched out the hand with which she had been caressing the child, and to his surprise laid it timidly on his arm.

"Ewes are valuable," she said gently.

Daniel moved backwards. He absolutely recoiled from her without disguise. Why was he afraid of her? Why didn't he shout at her, abuse her and her brute of a husband? Worst of all he hated her cunning gentleness, her touch. So this was what country people were like! Well, they were hateful: he had always disliked their way of shooing and booing at animals, the furtive grouping of their glances, their secret, wanton love of gain. He thought of that phrase, "a holiday in the country", with its attractive associations for town-bred persons. Flowers in the garden, lambs in the fields ....

In that instant he happened to look up into her face, seeing it with the instantaneous recognition of intense feeling. He saw that she was lovely. Done with all prettiness, she was beautiful. He turned away his head, it was more than he could bear – Somehow, with some piteous, hidden emotion, she was reproaching him, and his rage and humiliation turned to anguish.

Quickly he turned from her eyes.

"Good afternoon," he said stupidly.

"Wouldn't you like a cup of tea?"

"No, thank you."

Half-way down the path he suddenly shouted over his shoulder: "What's your ewe worth? Her wool?" He hurried on. His remark pursued him and he in his turn felt he had been cruel. "Ewes are valuable," he muttered. Hand on the hurdle he paused. What

57

extraordinary admission was his mind refusing? Confused, he waited. He would not look, but he knew she was there.

She faltered: "Can you tell me the time? Our clock stopped this morning and we haven't a wireless."

"Yes – no. I'm not sure. About three," he stammered. The quiet baby was staring at him, the black-haired child kept frowning and looking about in angry bewilderment.

"It must be more. I'm afraid I don't know exactly. I *started* at three," Daniel added, getting over the hurdle. He plunged into the boggy track among the ruts swerving to the bridge, the cloven cattle prints deeply sunk and filled with light brown water. He looked down and saw a picture – the shepherd forcing his narrow flock before him, through the corridor of the bridge, wagons hillocking over. Clearly the mill was no dead thing. Whatever life there was on these hills would have to converge here.

It was no good. He had to turn. She was standing outside the hurdle, the baby slung on her hip, struggling to pull her hand away from the child's. He couldn't see her face, but her short hair was parted at the back by the wind and flowing two ways. At the sight of that hair, watered sleek by the wind into two thin weeds, panic rose in Daniel; he seemed to feel his body turning pale. And yet he went back to where she waited, facing him now with hot red cheeks and lowered eyes. For a moment he said nothing, then he asked her if she could tell him a short cut to the farm where he was staying. He told himself that he couldn't pass the suffering ewe again.

"Yes," she said. "Oh, be quiet," she screamed to the little boy who had lain down and was kicking and yelling on the grass. "Yes, there is, if you walk to the top of the hill. Wait a minute. I'll come along with you and show you."

"No, our mum! No, no, no!" the child was shrieking, with sobs and blind face upturned.

"I can find my way, thank you." He was shaking. Once more he started away. Behind him he heard the screams of the child, frenzied and maddened: "Don't go, don't go. No, no."

She was beside him. It was like being asleep when you could hinder nothing, the boy felt. The child was screaming appallingly now. She might never have heard him. Side-long, Daniel saw her feet sliding in the mud, in askew trodden-down shoes, floor-worn and thin as burnt paper.

"Oh, I say, your feet! Don't come!"

They were close to the bridge. He was pressed against it. He thought he had some warning, but it was too brief for him to think. In a gasp his body seemed to become two bodies and one being. An uncontrollable one. An arm was round his neck pressing on his breath. Strange glimpses of colours he had, of a woman's neck minutely seen, with the fine encircling lines, the faint pores speckling it. The woman was kissing him! She held him imprisoned and she seemed to be kissing the astonishment out of him, pouring her kisses in between his bones. He struggled violently at the end of her lightning, fighting her off. Between the crevices of the embrace he could feel the wind blowing on his face and hands. The experience was like a tree toppling, branches, clouds, heavy rain falling ....

Suddenly, close to his own, he became aware of a pair of listless little blue eyes. At once he ceased his resistance. So strange, so horrible even, it seemed that the baby was making no cry. And then it had got into his arms, and he was free, and looking over its head at the mother.

"Here, take hold," he said after a moment, quite gently.

"I wouldn't have hurt you, I wouldn't have hurt you!"

She opened her hands which had been clasping her face, and held them out: "There are days when I could scream and scream and scream," she gasped, "days when I could go mad."

She was sobbing. The boy picked up his rucksack and pelted away up the hill. She stood still, watching him go, and when he was out of sight she gave one little moan and then walked slowly back to the other child. He followed her as far as the granary steps. She went round to the back of the house, not looking for him nor at the baby. Quietly, with a blind, intent inward look, she took a kettle up from by the back door, filled it at the pump and went indoors to get the tea ready. She seemed to move and to be totally unconscious of anything. Up in the granary the girl and the black-haired boy were playing. Standing on the dipper on tiptoe, one plait unravelled like a tassel, the girl was poking her finger under a rafter. She was feeling for a bat's nest. Her dress was ripped further than before and across one shoulder trailed a crawling grey cobweb.

"Dust," she proclaimed.

"Make it rain – ay Marge's s'all us!" the little boy was saying. He chuckled and threw a handful of bouncing peas on the boards, and then slowly fell into the cool sliding heap of peas and oats, sneezing and laughing together ....

The boy Daniel was not far away. On the top of the hill he had met a view of all the hills, and a darkness which was stillness. A cloud came and covered the wind; and he sat under it on a gate feeling it round his shoulders.

Softly, as if it had been a woman's, he was feeling his left hand with his right, softly, stealthily stroking it and wonderingly learning the making of fingers and knuckles.

Only in his sleep had he ever been kissed by a woman.

The experience had made a stranger of his body. When he got home the first thing he would be certain to do would be to look at his face.

He thought of it. But there was something else in his mind, some peculiar association of ideas too vague for him to bring together. Yet his eye searched the hills for a figure which was not to be seen, instinctively, as if the man he sought would bring to the incidents of the afternoon an undiscovered association.

But there was no one. And in scanning the horizon, his gaze forgot its purpose. There was no one, and nothing, words, image, recognition, none of them came, but only a breeze which went snuffling along the ground, like a hand searching for something hidden or lost in the seamless grass which was the same, every-where, near or far.

The Boy Who Called for a Light

HEN I was a lad I'd a passion for moonlight nights .... Particularly the winter moonlight. It seemed as if I couldn't resist it. I'd whisk out when Mother was in the back kitchen and run up our lane and wait under a big old pear tree that hung out of Parry's orchard. There I'd stand till my nose was frozen, looking up and around me at the bright, transparent sky, listening to all the sounds in the night. The tree was old: it bore little hard pears with a strong rind, and its leaves of a dirty pale green spotted with brown turned completely black in the late autumn. The moon was so bright I could see them singly and there were little and big silences that were yet all of a piece and cut short the stirrings of the earth. Sometimes I was out there late enough to see the frost glittering on banks and brambles; and then, running home, my boots would rustle the grass and the ice in the ruts crunched like broken glass.

Then our mother would collar me and give me a tap on the top of my head with the thimble on her finger, which I hated. She called it "thimbling".

"Where 'ave you been, Derry? And what did I tell you I'd do to you? Eh?"

"Only out the back a bit, Mum," I'd answer.

Our mother wasn't very nesh in her language when we were young: "Bloody liar," was what she would say. "Well, what did I tell you I'd do! I said I'd tan your bottom and send you to bed, didn't I?"

Sometimes she would and sometimes she wouldn't. I've heard her say to Dad that I was so little it broke her back bending to reach my behind with the hair-brush. I was very small: people shook their heads when they looked at me and muttered that I only grew downwards. But I was naughty. When we came to the village I was only three and Perritch the grave-digger expected to bury me he told my mother; but before long he'd changed his mind and said I'd live to be a hundred if he didn't take the skin off me first.

"You!" shouted my mother with her elbows turned out, "you couldn't take the skin off a rice pudding!"

"Him's a chastisement," said Perritch.

When I was caught at my mischief the only way out was to cry, and as all the other children were twice my size they wouldn't touch me. With the first simper of tears on my face I can remember the way their hands would drop off me: "Don't hit Derry – he's such a little thing ...." How often I heard that when I'd tormented some of the big boys to the point of blows. Somehow there was always someone to say it. I dare say I saw to that myself.

But I was a nervous as well as a daring lad. I loved the moonlit world but I was terrified of the real whole dark. It seemed to me it buried all my senses, and I noticed that on dark nights there were never any echoes. Bell practice sounded different over the fields, sheep bleated thick and guttural as if they were choking. On a dark night the wind frightened me. It was not a shy, darting fear but a powerful, mature terror, shapeless and senseless. Only since growing up have I found even approximate words for it. I never thought of defying it for one moment, as a child does his playful, wild, pet fears that he feeds, fosters and caresses in his privacy.

School was two miles from our home. Of course, we all used to play about the village; but when the days were short I'd only linger when I was sure of having company on the way back. That wasn't unusual though: generally three or four of us used to go wandering home together, climbing the banks, kicking stones, snatching apples and flowers, listless or quarrelsome or merry. For there were several families in the lonely cluster of cottages where we lived out in the fields, down an oozing lane like a cutting, with moist shade and the flat green leaves of hazels spread between us and the sun. The wild strawberries! The tussles with bramble, burr, and dog-rose – the fights we had! Our mothers cobbled and wrangled over the wounds in our faded clothing; our fathers patched our boots and swore. Well, that was the way home, and the queer thing is that after the first, the first one you remember, there's never another, not even when you're a man, married, with your own children, living somewhere and going to work yourself. That one way you ran with your brothers and sisters and your child mates goes through your life, right back to the beginning, to the overcrowded table and the pink glass sugar bowl. It remains, a contrast to all others; like the old china when you go to buy crockery. You always see those first smudged garlands, those saucers, that thick cloam infant's plate that went down the family and ended as the cat's.

I'd no idea of remembering that much. It all fits in so that it is difficult to take out the pieces I need. I seem to be back there in the moon-blanched lane, standing under the tree, hearing the sounds drop out of the sky, falling clearly, with a starry stillness and shapeliness on the fields of hills. Words, footsteps, bells swarming and beating off each other, owls and the clawing, scratching sound of twigs in the brittle tree. I listened so keenly that the moments froze into an hour, rubbing my numb finger nails on my jersey. And then I'd run home and mother would say I looked as if I'd been eating white eggs. What woman ever says things like that now-a-days? How I wish they did, but they aren't so countrified.

Every night at nine o'clock she took the mat in. It was the best mat, not for boots, for we had to step over it. But she would slap it against the wall with a bang that shook me in my bed. She always did it, and she always said the mice were waiting outside at night for a chance to get into the light. So she bolted the door and we had go out through the back kitchen where we burned no lamp. What woman would go through such a performance these days? We used to picture a row of mice outside waiting, my brother and myself. To this day I shut my door when I turn on the light. There is an idea somewhere in my mind that as a young boy I was some-what like my mother's mice .... I had an elder brother. He worked for Gregory, the farmer next the church. Father was an Insurance man, in his way an intellectual, and he would have liked my brother to go on learning after his meagre education years were up. But ambition on Sammy wasted away like a candle in a doorway and to Gregory he went. I had his company home from school when he thought of me, otherwise I walked with Hubert and Nelly. Hubert was as much of a nuisance to everybody as myself, an astonishing person, a little racketeer and a gambler. We had different tastes in devilry, so when we were together we were usually negative.

But I'd another passion besides moonlight. Now I come to it, it seems to me a peculiar one in a child of eight. Or anyone. It was more than a passion, it was an overpowering temptation. I used to go and knock on people's doors. Oh, not to run away, like other children! No, I don't know for certain why I did it. I have a very vivid memory of walking up those cinder paths and waiting after I'd knocked, in a kind of concentrated friendliness, for the door to open and someone to smile at me and look – well, *pleased*. Nobody ever did. They used to shout: "Who's there? If it's Derry Painter go away and don't bother me. No, I won't lend you anything."

Because for something to say when they *did* occasionally open the door, I'd ask them to lend me a bicycle-pump or a paper-bag.

There was one elderly woman whose door I never had tried, though there was only a railing and a bit of wallflower bush between the cottage and the school lane. She used to whiten her step twice a day, and it was so clean, to step on it I felt would be worse than getting into bed with my boots on. A plump, white pillow of a doorstep, with a soft looking dent in the centre. And a bootscraper and an iron door-knocker. Not that I couldn't have reached across to rap, but Mrs Owen had a way of saying "little monkey" that cured me ... it seemed far stronger than "bloody liar" to me when she said it with her thick underlip stuck out, in that severely gentle tone. She always wore a velvet hat. I can see that hat now and her thick body standing erect to talk to me. I would have liked to ask her why she had the silver brooch of a shilling she pinned in her neck band but my heart skipped like a dead leaf when I saw her looking at me, as if challenging me to play the naughty boy of the village with *her*. She had caught me picking my nose.

"Derry, that's a dirty thing you're doing. What would your mother say? She don't know you do that, I'll be bound."

"Yes, she do."

"And don't she stop you?"

"She do do it, too."

My friend walked on without another word, joggety, jogging down to the village with her basket and milk tin over her arm. We used to call her Kicking Kate from her tricksy gait. But I didn't call after her. Her scolding had given me an instinctive trust in her. And so, somehow, I was always saving her door for real distress.

Mr Gregory, my brother's boss, had a cart shed on the road near the school. I used to play in it and wait there for my brother who left off work at five o'clock. Hubert and I would scramble over the carts until someone bawled to us to be off to our teas. We climbed on the rafters and we used to lift the big stones in the corners, spying for rats. Chains doubled, hung in loops from the roof and through these the shafts were pushed to keep them off the dirt floor. We sat on the shafts, sliding our bottoms on the sweat-sleeked wood, and scuffling our feet against the pink, dry ground. There was a pond near the shed covered with yellow elm leaves and I can remember them blowing in on us one squally day, and what a drift of them I found in a wagon ....

One dusk I was there by myself. Hubert had told me to wait, but he didn't come, neither did I see my brother. Instead I saw Mr Gregory's face looking in. It was late. So late I daren't go home by myself, and he was startled at the sight of me.

"Why, w-w-w-why, why, boy, what be you a'doin' there? Bain't you afraid of the visions?" he said. He was a small, chattery-limbed fellow who wore a soft hat squashed down on his face under which stuck out a pair of tusky eyebrows. He had the stammerer's mouth and features, always jumping and jarring. He came in and laid his hand on the tilt of a cart, and standing there, his pallid twitching face lowered over his arm, he began talking to me about the "visions" he'd seen: "Hundreds of 'em. Hundreds. But don't you be afraid of 'em. Th-the-they d-don't see you. They-they don't sp-sp-speak, do 'em? Never. You can't tell, boy. They look l-l-like any other m-man you mid m-meet on the road. H-h-how be, be, be you to tell?" I guessed he meant *ghosts*. His stammering increased my horror. It was impossible to answer him. Speech with him was chaos: "Once, once I left a c-c-c-collar here. But w-w-when I came back for it, it had gone, gone. The visions h-h-had m-moved it, see? C-c-collared it. In f-f-fact, I never, never-n-never found it." He was laughing. But his conjuring hands were making horrible empty shapes in the air. The whole of reality was being bewitched from me by those fingers. I gazed at him, listening and staring, it seemed, with one combined sense. In another way I saw our Mum turning up the lamp. The house stood there in the trees, the door shut but the windows bare, hollow with the light it screened, like a lantern. With all its yellow windows! ... And I wasn't there.

Mr Gregory stooped closer. He said the Cobblers' Point, the bridge I had to cross on my way home, was haunted. Oh yes. Did Derry know that? No, I said, blinking from the hairy feeling his closeness gave me on my eyeballs. He shook his head at me and I shivered under the whisper of the dry leaves blowing on the road.

"Oh, yes, it ter-t'is. Oh yes. I've he-he-heard them myself. F-f-fellows hedging. Heard every sound they made-made. S-s-s-stake cutting. Axe and h-h-hook and beetle. All. H-h-heard them driving 'em in. And d-d-d-dragging, dragging the browst. What, what d'you say to th-that, boy? You'd run, ay?"

Did he mean to terrify me? I don't think so. I may be wrong, but I don't. He was frightened himself. It was perhaps *his* passion, being frightened. But I ran. I have never forgotten that night, never lost one single detail. There were streaks of wet in the road and the twilight had a grey sheen. It seemed to come between you and everything, you couldn't see a tree or a hedge *near to* however close they were. The stuff of which the shiny dusk was made had distance in it. And though it was a still evening, the dead leaves pounced ....

Well, I knocked and knocked on all the doors right the way through the village. Either they didn't answer or they bawled, "No, I won't lend you anything. No, we haven't got a light. Go away and don't bother us." I was the boy who had shouted wolf all right. And then at last I was at Kicking Kate's.

Kate hadn't pulled her blind down. I looked at her light through my tears. A lamp was burning, and the yellow panes looked thin as a bubble, bulging on the darkness, shining out on to the step, the cat's head scraper, the wallflower bush. Suddenly the blind came down. The darkness was like a clap of thunder overhead and my tears hung coldly on my face. I daren't knock. The blind rolling down like that on me – it was as if she had heard me; come and gone away from the window, cruel, triumphant, probably laughing under the silver shilling brooch. I thought of the mice and wondered with that strange detached curiosity of a child whether they felt as poorly and desperate as myself. Then I turned and looked at the dark dusk of the valley crossing my way; it seemed to me I could hear the echo of my own footsteps smacking across the bridge. With a sickly, propitiating smile, I chirped:

"Mrs Owen." Nothing happened. Kicking Kate was rather deaf, moreover she was loudly humming a hymn. I could hear her dragging furniture and presently the vigorous hissing of a scrubbing brush on flagstones. "Oh, Mrs Owen," I sobbed. The hissing stopped. Loud suspense, and then faintly Kate's voice:

"Who's there?"

"It's me."

"Who be that?"

"Derry. Derry Painter."

"Oh – ho!"

She opened the door. I stood very still, but my voice was trembling: "Oh, please will you lend me a light to go home?"

"Well!" she said. "Oh. So it's Derry. I know your tricks, young man. What be you a-doing out at this time? What've you bin doing? You ought to have bin home hours ago."

"I was waiting for Sammy, and he went home without me."

"I haven't got no light," she said, in an astonished way: "Why should I 'ave? *I* don't go messing about after dark. As I say, what's the use?" And she dragged me into her cottage. I remember the fender was full of feathers – little white rings. She had scrubbed the floor in front of the fire and it glimmered with wet light.

"Well," she said again, sitting down with her hands on her knees and her heavy red lips pouting with cogitation.

I sensed that she meant to help me and I cunningly admired a white chrysanthemum in a pot.

"It ought to be on a grave," I said. "A lovely big grave. Wouldn't you like to see it there, Mrs Owen?"

"Oh, I *would*," she said; and then she added gloomily, tossing her head towards the flowers: "there's them that do say they die indoors. Mine don't."

Did she mean humans or chrysanthemums? My own impression was that people did die indoors, since I had seen coffins carried out and been told that dead people were inside them. So there was a pause. "It's awful down there," I said at last, "the floods have been up and we can only go along by the hedge, holding on. I think I shall fall in without a light."

"I haven't got no light as I told you *be*fore. And you ought to be off home. As I say, your poor mother. She 'asn't got no con*trol*. Where's her con*trol*?" remarked Mrs Owen, puzzled and musing.

"She do hit me sometimes," I remarked, to cheer her.

"Oh, she do, do she? That's good. Nothing like it." Mrs Owen spoke as if whippings were something nice and tasty that every little boy should rightly enjoy.

I wouldn't answer. It seemed she didn't mean to help me after all, so to put off going I looked about me. There were spider-shawls in the curtains and the nests of flies: the lamp-chimney was sooty, the fire was moulting papery feathers into the fender. The first step to Mrs Owen's hearth was by far the cleanest ....

Looking at the clock I saw that it said nearly seven. Kate's eyes climbed to its face: "Yes, that clock do lag a bit."

My fear was reviving: in my shirt I could feel my heart pattering and crying, "You're cruel."

But suddenly Kate got up and began pulling down her sleeves and putting on a big coat.

"It can't be no wetter yonder than in here, hardly," she remarked, just aloud, glancing at that part of the swilled floor on which it seemed she had sloshed a bold shadow. And putting her hand on the lamp, holding her face over it, she blew out the light. I can't tell how she did it; it seemed as though she inhaled it – but I see her – her crinkled red face, her quaint lips shutting on the brightness that streaked up the glass, and then the blackness of her body leaning across the sleepy fire.

"Come along, young feller," she said behind me, pushing me out of the room.

Outside it was darker, much darker. The night had a sound of its own; and this sudden airy hush was as the strangest reprimand to me. The drifting, pausing, misty breeze sounded like a hundred distant trees, like the trailing of waning ghosts. Somewhere a dunness in the dark grey sky might have been the dawning of the moon.

Kate grasped my hand in her pulpy one, high up against her bosom. We stepped out, over the brink, into that thin watery sound, the air frilling round my face like a pure stream curling though the raw flood-smelling night.

The walk was an impression of moving quickly among a succession of barely-separated glooms: a grey touch of water, a bank of stars shining weakly and I have a picture of the world that night. Cobblers' Point lay at the bottom of two hills. I told Kate how Tom Gregory had said it was haunted by hedgers, but she only snorted, though actually she stood still in the middle of the road to do it, as if it were important. "Bah!" she said. "Booo-er," folding her hand round mine tighter and tighter, finger by finger. As for me, I found I wasn't nearly so frightened of Mr Gregory's "visions" as of meeting a certain old chap with a forgotten memory, an idiot man Hubert and Sammy used to torment, who would sit often under the alders trying to wipe sun spots off his clothes as they swerved on him through the leaves. The idea of this figure was a night-time dread, a day-time pleasantry. "I've been robbed, robbed!" he'd cry and shake his watch when Hubert would ask for the time. And then he'd stare round the sky and say, "That and that and that ..." and point after the gusts of sparrows that blew over the bushes ....

"Ghosts?" said Kate suddenly. "I don't know. Well, I've seen many a ghost in a live person, as I say. Yes. I've looked at them and I've thought: summat don't fit with you, mister. You'd better scoot from 'ere, or maybe you'll never get away from us. Maybe we shall keep you for ever."

"In the churchyard, you mean, Mrs Owen?"

"Yes," said she seriously.

Oh, it was black under the trees going up the hill! I thought of the stars. Darkness was like a noise to me. It could keep me awake, or rouse me like a nightmare if it fell on me abruptly while I was asleep. No light ever woke me; but sometimes when a storm put out the moon or Sammy suddenly doused his winter candle after dressing, I'd start up with the loss. Then I'd see the stars in the window. I've seen wet seashells since, wincing in the sun glitter, and they always put me in mind of our starry window and the cautious sound of my brother's footfall going slowly down the stairs.

Kate had seen a ghost once she told me. It was a very simple story about her dead brother. They had always lived together, he working on the same farm as Sammy, for Mr Gregory's predecessor, she keeping house for him. In the war 1914-1918 he went to serve abroad and died in Mesopotamia of pneumonia. One dusk before the news came, Kate met him pushing his bicycle through the Old Quarry. She exclaimed: "What, you've got some time off, have you?" He didn't answer, only looked aside and when she got home he wasn't there.

"When the telegram come they'd no need to tell me," said Kate. "I knew. His name be on the Memorial ... Henry Prosser. You look. You can read, I s'pose?" A sigh seemed to settle down in her – something seemed to satisfy her. She stood still: "He was a good brother to me. I never *could* dig ... my back just won't stand it. And I never had to."

We were walking over the rotten stubble in the field that banked above our lane. The water in the draining furrows was just visible: the wind spooned us from behind towards the pear tree and our breath was like moonlight in front of us, shapely in the air. The moon was going to rise: away, the young owls were crying their kitten calls in the elms. I liked the tune of Kate's voice and the way she talked to me without stooping. I liked everything about her. And yet, when I left her, I did it without thanking her or even saying good-night. When we came to the break in the hedge where we children used to slide down into our lane, perversely and without a word, I just tugged my hand free and went ....

Glancing back at her as she leant far out of the hedge over the darkness, like a clubbed tree, astonished no doubt at my rude act – glancing back, as it were, from the present time, it seems to me that there was a certain incompatibility between Mrs Owen and adventure. That she really belonged to morning, village shopping, faithful living and the admonishing of all little boys, chickens and stray behaviour, her figure, as I remember it, was a sure indication. And yet some odd gay talk from older women who thought of middle-aged Mrs Owen as a girl; there was, I believe, something about her dancing and wearing Parma violets she'd grown herself ....

I looked back again, but she had gone. I ran home. My brother was going out to meet another boy. "Our Mum gave *me* your supper," he said. She was standing in a split of light outside the kitchen door, her foot in the crack, running a knife round a dish rim and letting a dangle of pudding-ribbon fall on to the chrysanthemum bushes. I steered past her but she banged my behind with the dish and cried to me to get on in and go to bed. Our Dad was writing up against the chimney piece and the table was full of a meal.

I don't know why I wasn't howling but I wasn't. I felt full of achievement and triumph, running over with friendliness ....

"What've you been up to?" my mother asked curiously. She had come in after me, shut the door and was turning me round in the lamplight. My father was scribbling. I looked at her. I felt a smile coming over my face; and before I knew it I was giggling and boasting.

"I had old Mother Owen out to-night, I did, and I made her come all the way home with me nearly."

They weren't the words I'd meant to say, they weren't what I would have liked to say. They sprang out of me like an animal out of a trap, and I couldn't put them back. Kate had opened her door and befriended me: she had spoken to me as nobody else in the village would have thought of speaking and I had wanted to make a paean of it, because I felt that she was better than all of us.

Directly our Mum laughed I understood what a horrible thing I had said. But she didn't laugh for several moments and during those instants I felt only a child's uncertainty and bewilderment as to what he has caused to happen unwittingly.

Her silence and our Dad's were two opposite things. Because they were too surprised to speak, there was a pause, like a phrase growing. Her mouth twisted as if her lips were itching, but our Dad's face was very quiet as he shut his book and dropped the pencil in his pocket.

"Good gracious, Mrs Owen!" gasped our Mum. Then she began to laugh. She sat down to the table and hid her face in her tight black arms, and roared and sobbed till the lamp flared.

"Don't laugh at him, Missus! He's wrong to talk like that."

Mother couldn't stop, but she turned and looked at him affectionately. "Oh, shut up. I be bound to laugh. Mrs Owen!"

"Be quiet," our Dad said, low and quickly.

She took no notice; her laughter dragged mine out of me, for when Dad said "Be quiet" so fast and quietly it sounded like "quack-quack" to me. But I stood between them, hollow and burning with shame. If there had been another pause I might have made a wild amendment, although in a dim way I understood there was nobody there to say I was sorry to. It was Kate I had wronged.

When our Mum's laughing began to stammer itself to an end, Dad said, "You're out of your senses, Missus. Derry," he said to me, "you're a traitor. You'll never have a friend in the world. This boy'll never have a friend ...."

"Nonsense. He may be bad, but he's not so bereft as that," retorted our Mum, slapping jam on a crust of bread: "Now, Derry, take that upstairs and get to bed." Her laughter, as generally happens, had left her wan and short.

She pushed me through the door and left it open for me to see my way up. But I couldn't eat. I was crying. I put the crust down on the chair and crawled under the quilt.

In the night I woke up with a marvellously clear plan. I would go and wake our Dad and speak to him quietly and tell him how much I liked Kate and how she liked me too. And in the morning I'd knock on her door to thank her.

I climbed over Sammy's body; but my feet, which were still walking in sleep, wandered to the window and I looked out under my hot eyelids, gropingly. The sky was a strong steel-blue, the moon was clear, the stars shone in hollow squares and pyramids and the reverberating silence of the empty fields touched my ears like the cold air. It was that time of unfamiliar night when the known skies are so reversed in space that they become part of the unknown. I wondered why I was there and what I had been thinking and dreaming; and I tumbled into bed again and felt the warmth indistinguishable from oblivion. In the morning, I remembered but made no confession. I could no more take back my words than return and find Kate where I had left her, leaning over the lane, watching me turn my back on her.

And when I met her, like her dead brother, I'd nothing to say to her. Not a thing.

The Lost Fisherman

 MILY came flying down the steps, glaring at a piece of paper in her hand.

"May have time to get the tape," she muttered. She let the scrap float away, and ran down the street. It was quiet and warm and empty; the only person in it besides herself was a woman in black ringing a door bell. The church clock was striking five behind the roofs which were only a little lower than the tops of the huge chestnut trees: from the churchyard stole the green scent of the sward, the coolness, lightness, peace, of the petal-dripping trees.

But round the market hall trampled these strange crowds that the small townspeople were getting so used to; hot, bewildered people, burdened, with a dazzled look on their faces, looking for hotels, for lodgings, for rest. Some of them were sitting on the stone stairway, with their suitcases; some were eating, and some with their hands loosely clasped were staring downhill into the blue-grey hollow of the town. Many more would be queuing at the bus stop, the cafés would be full; there would be forms being signed in all the sash-windowed offices just as if the whole population were suddenly going to prison or to law or something. For last night London had had another heavy raid, and the three o'clock train had come in at half past four. Emily bought the tape from a country girl who was blind in one eye, and selling buttons instead of looking after her father's poultry. She was sagging on the counter.

"Are you done in? So'm I."

They had been to school together.

"Lord, you can't believe it," said the girl, heaving herself up on her elbow: "poor souls – there's any a host of 'em. God knows where they'll all sleep to-night. It must be *awful* up there! Has your sister come away?"

"Not yet. We wish she would. Keep on writing. Mother's terribly worried."

"She must be. Yes, it's terrible with children ...."

Emily nodded. She wondered if Annie and her family were still alive; if they still existed. Any moment they might not. Any second – The flashes when the truth showed were unrealizable. It was vile and horrible and terrifying, and yet unreal. Thinking was a physical, aching disease trying to conquer another disease – that of not thinking. Allow yourself to be injected – submit to noble advertisements. Save, work, smile. Be poster-educated. London was being struck and struck and struck again. Annie and the children lived there. Patrick was a prisoner. England was close, how close, to invasion. Patrick, Patrick.

She came out of the shop and looked at the town hall clock. Slow by the church chimes, she noticed. The white face with its hands like an enormous pair of scissors, what did it mean to her? There would always be only one time now on it. That was because she had been staring at it when she held the telegram. A Prisoner of War. A quarter to three. Queer. How did the telegram come to be in her hand? She would never quite remember. Her mother was away: and she had felt, "This joy isn't mine. I carry it."

There was a word *widow* and a word *motherless*, but for the condition of a woman who had lost her son there was no simple expression. Childless was false; a woman whose only son was dead was more his mother than she had ever been: she was as secret, as filled with mystery as when she and her child were one being, only this time she carried his whole life and death – she was the mother of his death.

Emily had gone into the telephone-box. Her mother's voice said, "Yes, dear?"

"Mother, good news. Hold on to something. Patrick is a prisoner."

Faintly the voice: "Emily ... Emily ...."

Now the town hall clock meant that hour. But sometimes these days when she looked at it she thought there was always time for grieving. Yes, always, Emily said to herself, turning round. Not for touching your love, or for seeing or being aware of the landscape you lived in, but always for sorrow.

Down the hill she plunged into the spinning people. The smell of war was the smell of a herd, weary and swollen footed. It wasn't the dead, but the driven, the sweated road, the shambling herd.

To avoid the direct but choked way home, she dashed up a narrow side street, one of the oldest in the town. Years before, a few cottages had been demolished. The walls still stood lodging in their niches the flying weeds of the fields, the winged grass which owned the earth, the nettles of gardenless places. Dandelions were in bloom and seeding, their bare wicks standing stiffly whence the flame had blown. There was the quiet intense odour of wallflowers in sunlight; and out of a doorless doorway two white butterflies lurched as if a breeze had puffed them out of the enclosure.

It was May. Oh, why did that still concern her? What was so urgent that it would not wait until the war was over to be beautiful again? Could you pull mankind like a burr out of your heart? But Emily stopped, swaying, conscious of this other presence in the worn, cracked street – the presence which made itself felt from the trees in the churchyard, and from the sight of the hills from her window.

She happened to stop, and she happened to peer round the doorhole ....

The mumbled heaps, the smooth dirt and weeds, had been somebody's garden. It was worn to a gloss with children's games, but in the centre grew a lilac tree, its clusters faded to a bluish-grey, dropping their crumbs in the shade. There, close to the trunk in a rocking chair, a paper tossed over his knees, a man sat sleeping: he was quite unconscious. His powerful, innocent face free from eagerness, away from the frightening smell of people, he slept like a lad in a field, and Emily wished she might wait by him for a little while. She knew him, though not his name. She wondered as she turned away if he lived in that street – she had always wondered, though not in an asking way, where was his home. And what had made her stop? Was it the white butterflies, that had flown as though from his brain almost into her hand?

"Is there any news from Annie?" she asked, as she ran into the kitchen.

Her mother was at the sink, washing lettuce. She said there was no news.

"Mother, I've seen the fisherman!"

"Oh, have you? Do you know where he lives?"

"No, he was asleep!"

"Asleep?" sighed her mother absently.

"Yes, in a rocking-chair in one of Saint's Cottages."

"Well, what a strange place to doze in! I can't bear to walk up that street, it smells so bad."

"You couldn't smell the gas to-day. Oh mother – gas. We've had a terrific day. Two gas extractions and both fought like mad. Poor Mr Jones, I bet he's bruised."

"My dear child! you must be tired. Sit down and eat something. Were you all right?"

Emily had taken a temporary job as a dentist's nurse and receptionist, being quite untrained except in sterilizing instruments and comforting people. "Oh yes, quite," she said. "I stood behind them, it was old Jones got the kicks. I say, Mum, I think I'll ring Annie up to-night."

She was twenty-seven and was to work in the ordnance factory at Chepsford as soon as the real nurse recovered from an operation. Meanwhile she quite liked her work. She never thought about it after the day was over. It was that kind of job. Teeth, she thought, when handed about, were rather absurd: otherwise she had grown used to the white overall, the sterilizers, the appointment book.

But – seeing the fisherman! As she ate her supper and helped to wash up, everything else that had happened since the morning seemed ugly and monotonous. He belonged to a life that was neither tedious nor terrifying. If her mother had guessed the emotions that filled her, she would have said, Are you in love with him? No, no. It isn't *individual*, like that. He is something – he's part of something that's being lost. And I want it to come back. It's life. At least it is to me. Oh dear. Am I going out of my mind, or is my mind going out of me?

The house that Emily and her mother lived in was at the bottom of the town near the Co-operative Mill. It had stood for centuries and smelled of stone and mice and coal, and the spicy old beams which still had the bark on some of them. It was said to be the oldest house in the town. The street door had a large dented brass knob: when you turned it and stepped into the passage it was as if you came under the shadow of a great cliff, for all the sunlight was at the back where it fell into a tiny paved yard as into a box. A long narrow corridor of a path led past a wall with a fine flat vine, as ancient as the building, to a large plot of garden. Next to that was the Friends' graveyard which had in the middle a cedar tree. This enormous geni, so dark as to be nearly black, seemed dead to all sunshine and looked the same by moonlight as by day. The house was simply number 17, but to the older spirits of the town it was known by its disused and genial name of The Friends' House.

The room where they were eating their early supper was the kitchen. It was clean and orderly: quiet with polished brown furniture, and lit by the evening sun. The door into the yard, and the well lid in the flagstones were open, for both Emily and her mother liked the delicate, flashing reflection of the water which flickered about the imprisoned space. The ferns and vine leaves were still: flies wove the evening light into their loom, and there was a calling note from a blackbird in the apple tree next door.

Emily looked at the canaries swaying in the window; she gazed meditatively into the corner at the oilstove. When war seemed close, she remembered her mother had said they would have to move the oilstove. How she had laughed! But it had come true, and they had moved it, for the shutters wouldn't close when it was in the window. Not a pinch, not a leaf of light showed after dark now. Emily, glancing at the fuchsias in their pots built up on bricks, recalled how the lit plants were sprinkled on the darkness before the blackout came.

After they had washed up, she went and sat in the front room by the "town window". She was as glad of the shade as of a different mood. The mother lay on the sofa, her tired legs lifted high on cushions. She read the paper, her face grim and pale, frowning with anxiety. Emily looked at the chestnut trees behind the warehouse, and the clear sky. She could hear the blackbird singing, "Bird of Paradise, Bird of Paradise", over and over again, and then most sweetly, gently, "Come butty, come butty, come butty".

It was so small a town that ducks swam right through it on the brook. Jays and woodpeckers flew screeching over the roof, regarding it perhaps as no more than a large and stony shadow. The wind sowed hayseeds in the cattle market, and the gardens, even the scratchiest, were scented with their red hawthorns and lilacs. Everywhere one went one breathed them. And there was the river, and the silver-blue hills.

May, all of May, Emily thought, her arm resting on the sill, her body supple and pleasant. The shadow of their gable was falling on the road, and the sun was pouring gold over the pale blue sky. A slow, dusty echo tracked each footstep. But down here in the faded part of the town where there were no hotels but only poor men's lodging houses, they escaped the weary rummaging on the hill.

Slum games were scrawled in chalk on the pavements, women

looked at their neighbours' doors, and men in shirt sleeves smoked. The human beings, the trees, bathed in the delight of the evening. Children, grime painting scowls on their faces, sulky mops of hair in their eyes, squealed and squatted akimbo on their games, monkey hands on their knees.

May, May, May! The time of year when all is perfect and *young*. The hills were the same, the trees had the same roots, as when she was a child at Aunt Fran's. How long the grass must be! She could feel her toes combing through it, aching with cold dew, the snapping of a clover head in a sandal buckle. She could see the white billy-goat chained to the stone roller. How many horses did Uncle Donovan say it would take to move it? All of them – ten horses. Ten horses in the stable ....

Her mother got up and went out. Emily lapsed on. The women came and seized the children; the doors shut, the air grew purer and more and more transparent, as if for silence to shine through it. At last Emily thought of the river, shining smoothly under the mist, on those early morning bathes. Why did it all seem so near, and closer every day, and yet so irrevocably saddened? If one person dies, the past is altered. Uncle Donovan was dead. People she had loved were dead. When you were young every one was eternal. Her eyes moved, and she wondered at her emotion on seeing the sleeping man. She almost laughed. Yes, people would say she was in love with him. She laughed at the ridiculousness of her being in love with anybody. She couldn't be. And the fisherman – he wasn't like the others. Their talk had been casual, never cautious. They had never seemed to meet for the first time. In fact, although she could remember their first words, they never had "met" any more than animals or birds meet. He was – what? An atmosphere in her own soul. Something more than a mood which was increasing in her.

"My dear, I wish you'd go and ring up Annie." Her mother was looking in. A flush was on her cheek and neck, streaking her thinness. Emily knew that this meant great nervous endurance. She jumped up and said she would go at once. Suddenly she shivered. She had to put on her coat.

It was quiet now, growing dusky. She had sat for a long time waiting for her call to come through. The mirror with the lettering on it was sinking into the shadow of the wall, the smoky voices in the bar were thicker. Suddenly someone shouted: "Do with 'im? Give 'im to the Jewish women, and tell 'em to save something alive for the Poles." There was a guttural laugh, a hoarse shuffling of tones, and then a blending again. Emily leant on the weak little cane table, the ice cold edge of a slippery magazine touching her hand. Her heart beat in the long suspense and she sat with her eyes fixed on the telephone hanging in the corner by the door.

Presently the house emptied. There was a shambling noise in the street: the landlord looked in at her, rubbing his bare arms:

"Not through yet?"

"No."

"Want a light?"

She shook her head.

"It's cold in here," the landlord said, buttoning his cuffs, and he went out closing the door, leaving the shutters open. The moonlight fell towards the window sill, creepingly, like a hand edging on to the keyboard. A twist of breeze made the hem of the white curtains writhe.

"There must be a raid on. I'll cancel," she said to herself. Five more minutes passed. The landlord had gone back into the smoking-room. He was crumpling papers, talking in a petulant undertone with louder bursts of sighs and yawns. A woman spoke sharply, "... this time of night?"

"She's trying to get London."

"Oh! Well, I've locked up –"

The telephone rang.

"Annie?"

"Yes, Emily – you've had my wire?"

"No. Nothing."

How cold and queer the air felt! And those old magazines with their odour of linoleum –

The receiver spouted words, all unintelligible: it whistled, it gurgled and was hollow with some deep resonance, like a dry pump.

"To-morrow – to-morrow," it shouted.

"All right," she yelled. "You're coming to-morrow. Is there a raid on?"

"Not 'alf," said Annie's voice in a little space which it exactly filled. "It's not too bad yet but I must get ready to take the children down to the shelter. There, did you hear that? Christ, I hope it's not going to be as bloody awful as last night."

Emily heard her call, "All right, I'm coming." It was as if a prompter had spoken for the stage, a half tone, sibilant, expressionless. Then she seemed to have hung up. She went out into the passage and tapped on the hatch.

"Finished?"

"Yes, thank you."

The man looked at her as she paid. He stooped, then reached up, and then once more framing himself pushed a little glass towards her. "Come on, Miss, drink this. I know you won't tell on me." He winked, but his face was concerned: "It's bad up there."

She drank. The blood bristled in her cheeks, she leant against the wall, not because she was overcome, but because for the moment she was concentrating so intensely elsewhere that her own body began to slip sideways. She could see the skies. And those unseen, immeasurable arms which human beings carry folded in their breasts, reached out – out – out to fold back the menace. She stood in this state of extended will, her spirit a vaster version of her physical resistance, for about a minute, and then went out, carefully shutting the street door.

"Emily, how long you have been! Was it all right?"

"Yes, Mother, perfectly. She's coming down to-morrow."

"Oh, thank God!"

Her mother was in her purple dressing-gown, holding it round her throat, her eyes peering over the light of a tiny lamp she held, with a globe like an orange: "There was nothing happening?"

"No, Mother."

"But why hasn't she wired?"

"She has. I don't know why we didn't get it. I must just go and finish emptying those drawers."

"It's a pity you didn't do it this evening. You ought to go to bed. I'm glad we've arranged things."

For days they had been discussing receiving Annie and the children. There were only two large upstairs rooms, and the mother wouldn't think of using the attics in case of incendiaries. She would share the great brass bed with Annie, and the two little girls would have Emily's room. Emily was to go every night to sleep at Aunt Fran's farm – about a mile away from the town. It was a gentle level

walk, by the river: she would love it. It was the possibility of returning to Aunt Fran's roof perhaps which was making such a vividness
among her memories of her childhood when she had lived at Ell
Hall for a year.

Electricity was expensive. The two women lit a larger lamp and
went upstairs. In their dressing-gowns and soft shoes they fanned
from corner to corner, Emily bending over a trunk, her mother
absently touching the walls as if she were planning certain movements.

At last she sat on the end of the sofa to unroll the elastic stock-
ing from her bruised and swollen veins. "Jamie's cot *there*?" she
murmured. She got up and touched the wash-stand.

They moved it: somehow they both wanted to complete everything,
to move into their own new positions as far as possible that night.

They continued their soft, hushed midnight work. Sometimes the
boards shook under the grey-green carpet, and the young starlings
stirred startlingly in the chimney. But at last they were in bed. The
black-out curtains of heavy sage-green serge were left across the
mother's window in case she might remember anything she might
want to collect in the night. But Emily pulled hers back; her sash-
window looked towards the garden and the faint irridescent colours
of a moon cloud. There were the vine leaves and the path leading
to the moon and the cedar tree. She lay on her side facing them,
her hair all pushed into a heavy sensation at the back of her head.
Her hands burned with the restless touching of the day, but at last
they were alone.

The night was the ghost of the day, as the moon was the ghost
of the sun. And the fragrance which balanced in the window was
the ghost within a ghost, neither retreating nor advancing, but
fluttering outstretched and withdrawn like a breath.

She didn't sleep. Her eyes refused to close over the dream in her
brain. 'Planes drove over; and it was as if they were seaming
together long strips of sky. But when they had gone the wavy stillness of the night still clung about the leaves unchanged.

She began to see Annie in the shelter, the baby on her lap, and
the little girls in the top bunk, peeping tearfully over the abyss.
Guns, bombs, barrage, and then the screech of a 'plane being
drawn into the vacuum.

She sat up suddenly, and drove her head between her knees,
embracing her body with those amazingly powerful thin arms: "All

this! Oh, what a pity I can't go to sleep because then I get there, I get there ...."

She rocked, and then driven to stillness crouched in a knot, surprised at her dry voice. Her eyes felt as if they must work, must see everything; not seeing anything, she was reduced to their corner in her flesh.

Unexpectedly she saw. What she saw was the fisherman's peaceful face, asleep. She had started up at the shelter scene, but now she lay down again and turned her face into the shelter of her hands, lined, as it were, with chilly, green grass. She found she could array her thoughts if she couldn't release them.

When you were out-of-doors your body became the touch, the texture of the world, with all its fluid airs, plants, waters, wind. The wind's flesh crept against yours, and the grass clothed the prone body with its feeling of openness and closeness.

She saw the river meadows, the little red bays in the bank where the turf had slipped into deep pools, and bendings where the river bent, the narrow green path rubbed into the grass. Across it lay a fishing rod. Sitting precariously on one of the jutting turfs which was dead and brown fibre, was a man, feet braced against a lolling alder limb. It was March; he wore a belted raincoat, but he had thrown a scarf into the tree. She was walking towards him: as she came closer he turned his face and looked quietly at her. And then suddenly, but not as if it *were* suddenly, they were speaking to each other. This happened quite often until six weeks ago, but as an image she retained none except the first meeting. She knew that of all the faces she had met, there was none at all like this one. It was secret, if candour can be secrecy; it could have been knowing, but she had never seen it when it was. Very dark shining eyes, oval, olive cheeks and chin, a smooth skin. They couldn't resemble each other physically but she felt as though each of them sent the same lights and shadows up to the surface. She walked on guessing, "I can look like that." For a few weeks every time she walked that way she met him, and then one day, not. She didn't see him again until she looked at him in the weedy rooms of the ruins. But she was sure they had understood something instantly, perfectly, and for ever. They were friends. And in their perfect familiarity with each other there was incalculable individual solitude.

She smiled into her hands. And this time it didn't feel as if she were roaring with laughter in the middle of everybody's despair. It felt as if she were talking to the fisherman about the curlews and watching the male bird go round and round the sky, calling and searching. The fisherman always made her think of the bird, the hills and the river, and not of himself: he recalled to her a beam of the true meaning of freedom and fulfilment: with him or thinking of him she became again the real Emily who used to swim across the river in the early mornings, who was free, whose being absorbed and radiated the harmony of the countryside in which she was growing. Perhaps it was talking to him which had made her ponder so much on her childhood this terrible spring.

Sleep was like tears in her open eyes, sharp yet tender. She was getting there. Her mind swayed and she no longer knew herself as separate and conscious. The room was the linen room at Aunt Fran's where she had slept, with the dark brown cupboard at the foot of the stairs and the dull leaded window, like a pattern of muslin in grey and black with another pattern of twigs shadowed through it. She remembered how coarse seemed the texture of the sky seen though the thick glass .... She was looking up at the candle Aunt Fran was holding, floating in its haze, blinking .... And then the room was gone and she was sitting on the garden seat watching her aunt's fingers as she split filberts open with a silver penknife. They were sitting under the Wellingtonian and the air was full of the scent of resin. Aunt Fran was saying:

"Your uncle and I are very fond of you. You have always been good with us."

It was evening. Children were shouting; a vast splash of light over the west meadows dazzled through the trees. She put out her hand to lift the basket from the grass when suddenly she was awake and knew there had been an eruption of sound which she hadn't heard. It was like a silent explosion which shattered the perfect sphere of rest in which she was lying, and it was the siren.

The mother woke up convinced that she was young again. Her husband was alive: he was with her in the dream; she was married to him but they were being introduced. She woke, talking; part of her speech still seemed to be joined to her, but part had vanished.

"The wind was so lonely last night with the window bare that I went to bed early. It seemed so long since I had been playing the piano and talking ...."

Then she heard herself say: "Beethoven."

She lifted her head: "Where's the cot? Where's Jamie, my little Jamie? Annie! Where are the children? She struck a match. She was awake now: "Emily, Emily ...."

She could just see the empty corner where the washstand had been.

Emily came in: "I don't hear anything, do you? It must be Bristol again. Or Gloucester." She was smoking and seemed tenuous with sleep, her body clinging to the support of the wall.

But as she came wavering round the big double bed, the mother moved to put her feet down, and seeing that unhappy blue and white flesh hovering to reach the floor, a pity and an anger which she could never have mentioned caused her heart to make something like a gesture in her body.

"Don't get up, Mother," she begged: "It can't be anything else."

"I hope they don't bomb the bridge," began her mother. The bridge was very close, carrying the line across the street where they lived. Like a great many of the older women in this small town, Emily's mother instinctively regarded it as an exceedingly likely target – as indeed it might have been had the raiders ever discovered the whereabouts of the great filling factory at Chepsford. The groan and slow thunder of the ammunition trains was a part of their nights. "Lethal," the mother would murmur, and the walls would tremble, like the pillars of the market house when the tanks and dismembered 'planes came swerving down the narrow streets.

They listened, their chins lifted, their necks stretched. Was that a 'plane?

"Bombs!"

They looked at each other in incredulous silence. And there fell through the sky two percussions locked in each other's vibrations. Clash, clash – like cymbals, like lightning with music. Emily had never heard two sounds so simultaneous yet so separate. It was most beautiful, distinct, entrancing, the way the skies played for that moment.

No thud came. No blow. The quicksilver fled all over their bodies: in the silence they stared and heard the mice ripping at the lining of the old house, rustling and searching through the crowded pockets of its deep cupboards.

"Put out the light!" said the mother.

About ten minutes passed in darkness. Some soot fell down the chimney and they heard it showering in the fender. A bird squeaked. The hush was the suspense of thousands listening, an underground, underdark thing, conscious and of the earth.

"I'm going to look out of the window," said Emily. She saw fire on Hangbury Hill, red fire, crawling into the woods. She gazed and remembered how the birds and rabbits and snakes screamed when the heath was burned.

There were three bombs, they heard the next day. The man who is always present, no matter how outlandish the fact or the hour, described how he had seen them burst in the woods. He said the trees had writhed, there had been a kind of ashen light and the furrow in which he was standing had wriggled like a snake. He told the tale in the market square, outside the station, and in seven pubs.

Some of the strangers laughed.

"Well, damn!" they said. "Fancy bombs here! Well what next, I say?"

But some of the rich ones were packing already, having heard of the neighbouring factories.

To Emily the event of the bombs crowded into an already crowded day. She wouldn't think about them. The weather was clear, but there was something stifling in the air, something sated and flaccid. Through the warm swishing streets the scent of meadows and chestnuts in bloom drifted with the smell of the fire-blighted broom and gorse now scattering in slow smoke. She was busy: a great many patients were admitted, but there was nothing dramatic in this day's work: and as she sat eating her lunch in Mr Jones's conservatory, where somebody had left the hose dribbling among the legs of half a dozen wormy kitchen chairs, her mind returned again and again to that one generous year of childhood with her aunt. There was something then on or behind those smoking hills for her. One by one her passions were being lost, but this – this spirit of place, this identification of self with unregarded loveliness and joy – seemed, after a dormant cycle, to be becoming her life.

She sat breathing the green, double-hot air of the geranium-trellised conservatory, eating sandwiches and seeing Aunt Fran. Sometimes she was in her greenhouse, stretching her nose over the plants, with the perfume of the vine in all her movements, but most vividly she saw her at her bedroom window on a summer evening about seven o'clock. Emily saw her smiling and waving across the buttercup-yellow fields to the distant shallows where the naked town boys were splashing like stars in the burning silver water. "Look, look – I suppose we can call it summer now," the aunt would laugh. And it *was*: such summer as it had never been since. There she would sit, and call Emily to her to come and have her hair curled before going to bed. She held the brush on her lap, and the fingers of her right hand she dipped into a mug of tepid water before twisting each strand of hair into the rags. Emily could feel the slight, drowsy tug at her scalp, and the selected lock sliding through Aunt Fran's first and second fingers. The book she was reading aloud lay open on the dressing table among the silver things and the old yellow combs – *The Story of a Red Deer* ....

"There! Good night. And when you're in bed sing me a song."

"What shall I sing?"

"Well – 'John Peel' – or – 'The Keel Row'."

Her voice seemed to stir in her as she remembered, and she heard the air coming from herself as she crouched in the bed.

As I came through Sandgate, through Sandgate, through Sandgate,
As I came through Sandgate, I heard a lassie sing .....

The silent voice in her was physical now – she could hear it, feel it rising ... she never sang at The Friends' House; she liked to sing out of doors. She saw the leaves in the walnut tree, the wall where Esau, the red cat, sat in the dusk, she heard the owl, and felt the grain of the light fading in the room.

I heard a lassie sing.

Why did it all seem beautiful then? It couldn't have been, not everything. But no Emily nowadays would climb an oak tree to see if sitting in it would make her sing like a blackbird, nor listen to the notes with such an unaffected thrilling expectancy.

When her work was over she went straight home. A little girl in a red check pinafore, whose two hands had swallowed the door knob, was jigging on the doorstep, and peeping through the key-hole. Her laughter and that of another child inside was pealing out into the street. When she saw Emily she peeped up sideways under her arm.

"Hullo, Aunt Em'ly."

"Hello, Ann."

"What d'you think I'm doing?"

"I don't know."

"I'm looking at Diddle. And Diddle's looking at me. I can see her eye. I said I'm going to look *in* at the keyhole. Because I'm not often out in the street. Hullo, Diddle," she bawled, "I'm here, are you there?"

"Hullo, Ann, I'm he-ere," cackled a smaller voice, with bursts of chuckling. Suddenly Ann lost interest. She gave Emily a long stare that was cool, peculiar and consciously measured. And Emily felt shy of the child's sudden gaze and stooped to pick a red hair ribbon off the pavement. Ann triumphed, and yet was reassured. She broke up again into a small skipping, smiling creature.

"*We've* all run away from ole Hitler," she said cheerfully. "Mummy's here, and Diddle and Jamie. Did you know?"

She twirled the door knob faster, and the catch inside went clack-clack.

"I knew you were coming," said Emily.

"Jamie wasn't frightened. Diddle was. Wasn't you, Diddle, eh?"

"Ye-e-s," chuckled the child inside.

"Diddle cried. Jamie didn't. I'm going to open the door. I want to tell you something."

They went into the cool stone shadowed passage which was heaped with luggage and a pram. Diddle, a very short fat little thing, was squatting on the mat.

"Don't touch!" cried Ann anxiously: "This is the-wipe-your-feet mat, Aunt Em'ly. I put something under it. I didn't want to drop it. It's a penny. Here it is. Heads or Tails?"

"Tails," screamed Diddle.

"Not you – Aunt Em'ly," said Ann with jovial authority.

"Ann!" a voice called.

"She's here, playing pitch and toss," shouted Emily.

"Toss you for tuppence, Ann, P.Q."

"I've won, I've won. I always know. That's what I wanted to tell you. This is Tails," said Ann mysteriously.

"Tails," said Diddle.

"You look."

"Ye-e-es."

"You musn't look!"

"I muttoned look ...."

Annie appeared, slanting out of a doorway, lunging into an apron.

"Ann, for God's sake –" her voice was dry with fatigue. "*Will* you come and drink your milk?" she muttered, seizing each bland child. She was thinner even than Emily, her terse red dress tossed over the wind of her limbs. She held Emily's eyes for a moment, in her own an unconscious hardness and contempt for all things irrelevant to pure animal life – a look which was the mother's at times. Yet far back, there was a friendliness: "Hullo, sister, when there's a moment I shall see you ...."

"See you. See you. See you. No, you won't. I don't live in your eyes," said Emily to herself. She stepped out into the tiny stone yard; it seemed dull there – something was missing. Oh yes, the lid of the well was down and a great stone on it. The dark, ivy-green water was buried and all its flight of reflections.

"Emily," said her mother, draining the potatoes over the grating so that the steam climbed the wall like a plant – "Emily, fetch me that cloth, dear. I'm sorry there aren't any greens. I hadn't time to ... thank you. Perhaps before you go you'd get us some nettle tops. Poor Annie has more than she can do."

"Yes, Mother."

She could hear the canaries cracking their seeds with a tiny insect-like pop. It was so hot that the stones were tepid in the shade. The pods of broom and gorse burst in the sun with that wee minute crack, with only the linnet to make the stillness alive. Emily remembered, as if she saw the burnt grass and the sky above, the clicking and whirring world of heat. Upstairs the children being put to bed dropped a geranium leaf on her head and laughed in the bow window. She looked at her mother's amethyst beads and thought of the river. Under the drops and the silver, her mother's neck was patched with a scattered flush. Her love for her own children was all anxiety, only what she felt for her grandchildren was physical and enjoyable. She sat at the table straining not to interfere, not to run upstairs with kisses when Jamie cried, not to be upset by Annie's retorting voice. Annie, however, said less and less, and towards the end of the meal abruptly drew her chair back into the window and there sitting bowed with her strangely gnarled nervous hands binding her knees, cried wearily. Suddenly she seemed younger than Emily, younger even than her own children. And her attractive matronly little face which owed some of its beauty to work, but nothing to her everyday mind, became a rarer face – the real face. Seeing her crying, her breath jerking, terrified and childish, they knelt by her and tried to smooth the movements of her frightened body with their touches.

"He'll be killed. Oh Mother, Mother."

"No, he won't, dear. No, he won't. Please ... there," pleaded the mother.

"Yes ..." Annie cried; her tone struck them and they looked at her in silence. In the sunshine her shining tears crusted her: she smeared them from her eyes with her queer powerful fingers whose tips were like drops of coldness: "Yes. I can't live, I can't live. I don't know anybody here. I want Tom. I want Tom."

"Annie, darling, you've got the children!"

The temper of hysteria, which is so like mad fury, shook her. She stood up, crying out as she flew through the door: "To hell with the children! I shall send them all to school and go back to Tom."

The mother sat down, sighing. A slight breeze came blowing down from the garden and the vine leaves bent as though stroked by the dress of someone coming walking along the path. With that movement came the phase of evening, its entire separation from the day.

"What we shall do with her – what we *shall* we do – if Tom – if anything *should* happen to Tom. She told me before you came in – when she was quite quiet, you know – she told me he says she must be responsible for the children. She said, he said they must have *one* ...."

"Yes," said Emily drearily.

And now the seven o'clock train was in, two hours late, standing in the station releasing puffs of steam, and the light was beginning to bank against the trees and the yellow meadows. With a basket Emily was moving slowly along the coal dust path against a grey hedge of nettles, nipping off their tops with her gloved fingers.

Through the palings she saw the hurrying flickers of people with suitcases, bicycles, push chairs and children – all scuttering, like the pictures on the sticks of a fan which is shaken out and flicked back. The sound of their feet threaded past the new factory site where the hammering had ceased – the sound of their thin words, the tune of a stick being tapped out, towards the town, and three taxis shooting down the road. The greasy dark engine slid away: then came the pure smell of evening, the scent of sky and grazed fields, water and shadows.

She turned and put her basket down. She looked at two chestnut trees in flower, broad green and tapering blossoms balancing, that grew in a piece of willowy waste. The sunlight on them seemed part of themselves, and the flowers looked as if each one had been placed by a hand among the splayed leaves.

The birds sang. Their notes were always like echoes; as though one never heard the voice but only its reflection. The calls were the length of dark woods .... As they sang, thought Emily, in the rain outside the rooms one loved, where the fire was one slow old log charred like an owl's breast.

"I'd love to sit at a window and sew and look out at trees like that. For hours and hours and hours of quiet ...."

In that minute she realized that she had achieved the complete vision of her desire and her indifference. Her desire was peace and freedom – the wildness of peace, the speed and voicelessness of it. Her indifference was her duty, which she would do. Try to do. The spirit of life would be laid by for years of spiritual unemployment, that was a part of war. She glanced at the trees, their leaves drooping now in the sinking light. She would take with her their stillness: as she left them she said good-bye.

"If you neglect yourself you must automatically belong to something else. The State. There's nothing else to claim you ...."

Some quiet long task at a window looking out on chestnut trees in bloom. Sewing, writing poetry, or just growing older. Aunt Fran shelling peas, gathering raspberries. That kind of order, order not for its own sake, but for the wilder, more ecstatic rhythm which it imitated. Life's natural conformity to life, not to this warped form of death.

War has no seasonableness. No light or darkness, no true time but lies, lies, lies, to make the hands go faster.

She began to hurry, thinking of the clock.

Walking along the river to Aunt Fran's that night Emily met the fisherman. He came up the bank through the willows chewing a grass. She started when she saw him: she had been staring at the sky, all clear light, a sky which she seemed to have seen before but not on earth. As she stood wondering and unconscious, a dream of the night before came back to her with a feeling of distance and quietude. She remembered a kite bursting in space and two giant figures stepping down arm in arm and walking away, never turning round ....

The fisherman wished her good evening. For the first time they shook hands. He asked her where she was going; when she told him, he said that if she liked to walk back with him to the boathouse he would row her up the river.

"It would save you going all round by the bridge," he said. "Would you like to? I've got the keys."

Emily said she would love it, it was years since she had been on the water, So they turned and strolled along the bank. It was quiet and cool: they could smell the meadows up for hay and see the moonlight forming round the moon on the pale horizon.

"The moon looks as if it were made of thistledown," said Emily.

He looked at her quickly, and away at the water again.

"Are you fond of the country?"

"Sometimes I think I'm fond of nothing else."

They talked but seemed to give their minds to the river and the twilight. He went before her, holding back the bloom-laden sprays of hawthorn round which little moths were spinning their balls of flight: her legs were damp: in her flesh she felt the familiar chill of the fields at dusk and the clear wakefulness which often precedes sudden and deep sleep.

She was patient now, and at peace ... she saw his olive hand with the greenish tan on it, holding back the branches, and she wondered how it came to be that they should know each other so completely and yet so subtly ignore each other.

He walked slowly, his feet making a frail noise in the grass. Over the flowerlit meadows on the other side a shell of mist was closing. There was an exquisite clear coolness and spaciousness. Water under a root fluted like some stationary bird.

"I work at the factory," he said. "That's why I haven't seen you for a long time. I'm a charge-hand now."

"I saw you yesterday," she said, "in Saint's Cottages. You were asleep, though."

"Yes." His voice was expressionless. "I don't like little rooms in the summer. My shift's changed now. I shall be on days to-morrow."

She went with him dreamily, her mind full of vague emotion and one sharp thought, that she would never forget this, because somehow she also knew that they would never meet again.

The river was bent like a scythe, and on it a single swan sailed opposite the boathouse. Its whiteness was sharp, distinct, and its being seemed to cease at the water line, it made so little restlessness of swimming.

Inside the boathouse was a huge hollow rolling noise and a wooden banging. That too was familiar: clubmen used it as a skittle alley. While the fisherman went in Emily stood looking down at the deep ditch under the hawthorns where the water was concealed by the white floating petals. The smell of the bloom was like forgetfulness. She held a branch to her face, and when she released it it flew up into the tree with a battering sound like a concealed woodpigeon's wild shudder into flight. She sighed a deep sigh to give her heart room. The fisherman came out with a pair of sculls. They stepped down to the landing. A moorhen whirred the water.

"Get in," he said.

She walked steadily down the boat. She had a feeling as if her feet were breathing. Weeds wavered under the surface, darkness rose and clung. There was a sense of mist rather than dusk broken around them. The boat rocked and then poised itself into narrow balance. The river under it was taut and vibrant as a gut under a fiddler's finger ....

The fisherman pushed out, then all in one movement he sat down and opened the wide embrace of the oars. They glided to the middle and then upstream. They had only a short way to go, the river making less than a quarter of the way that the fields roamed.

Pausing a moment, drawing his fists towards his chest and bunching them there, he looked at her smiling and asked: "Can you row?"

"No," she said; "what does it feel like?"

"Grand."

He added: "I like to feel the oars bringing the tremble of the water up to my hands. They almost throb, you know, here and *here*. It's such a strong feeling, though – powerful –"

"Like electricity," she said.

"Ye-e-es. A sort of connection with something one doesn't know. You think a lot, don't you?" he suddenly asked, fixing his eyes on her.

"No," she said sadly.

"Well, you look as if you do. But perhaps you call it something else."

She dipped her hand, sank and floated it, watched its inner fingertips of round green pearls sliding mistily along under the surface. Dandelion seeds were drowning; all the stillness of the grey elf world was flowing and they were silent for a while, the banks piled on either side of this quiet corridor of water darkening its edges.

"I don't know, I don't know," she sighed in her thoughts.

"I often row up and down here all night," said the fisherman: "all night," he repeated to himself.

"Do you?"

He stooped again as if he were lifting the river on his back, and strokes sent them jetting upward.

"Yes. I love the river. To me there's nothing like it."

She imagined him at the factory all day and then out here, all night alone, never asleep, never losing sight of himself: "But don't you ever sleep then? Aren't you tired the next day?"

"No, I don't feel tired. You see I can't live my life among a lot of people all the time, and then just sleep."

She said nothing for a moment, laying her wet hand on her forehead. Then she asked, puzzled:

"How long are the shifts then?"

"Eleven hours."

He smiled at her. Emily tried to smile back, but her mouth felt as if it had been trodden on. There was an extraordinary solitude upon his face like that of a man who is standing away, right away beyond the last shelter, watching the lightning.

"My mother was a Frenchwoman," he told her abruptly: "but she wasn't a bit the sort of person you'd think. Not thrifty or tidy or anything Frenchwomen are supposed to be. I never knew what it was to have a solid pocket or a weathertight button on me .... I used to wander about the fields. I've got the habits of a tramp now ... oh, not the visible ones, I hope – no – but I can't stand houses simply because it seems you can never be alone in them. However –"

"I don't expect *a whole house*," said Emily laughing: "I like a *room* I can be alone in. And sit near the window."

"I shouldn't like a country without trees, though," she went on vaguely; "you'd feel like a bee in a glass hive. Was your mother scientific?"

"Good God – my mother!"

"Well, I think Frenchwomen are."

"Well," he said, "perhaps you're right. Perhaps she *was* scientific in her way. She liked growing flowers. White flowers – big white daisies – tall ones – I remember them all along our hedge, walking in the wind. Many a time coming home I've taken them for our white cat in the twilight. By jove, yes." And he pulled an oar out of the water as if it had a root, and looked at the end of it dripping.

"Smell the fields," he muttered, turning.

"My mother was a musician," said Emily slowly, "not one that anyone knew about – she just played beautifully and loved it. She wanted to be a singer, but her father wouldn't let her. Some other girl had failed. Do you know," she was leaning forward, looking down at her feet and clasping her ankles with her cold wet fingers as she spoke – "do you know, sometimes I think of mother all day, and what I'm sure was the happiest part of her life. It was when she was about my age. She had gone from the piano to the organ. Whenever she speaks of Bach she seems to remember herself then, when she was beginning to play his fugues. She used to pay a boy sixpence to blow for her. Just two of them on a weekday in an empty church ... her eyes shine when she speaks of it. Oh dear, I think of her then. It's unspeakably sad because one of those days she must have walked out full of ecstasy and never gone back. I seem to imagine her leaving her joy behind forever and then all the troubles and the hard work and the poverty falling on her. And then, I can't help it, I look at her face and feel heart-broken. Isn't it dreadful? I suppose it isn't – not when you think of war."

"I don't know," he said. "She got married?"

"Yes. And had four children. We're a poor substitute for Bach."

"I don't know," he said again gravely, thinking: "Bach himself was probably a substitute for – I mean he took the place of – some woman's single freedom. Don't you think so?"

"Yes. But we are nearly all bad," she said under her breath.

He was working the oar loosely, turning the nose of the boat towards the old sheep dip where she was to be landed. Glancing back at her, he demanded what she was thinking.

"I?" she said: "I was thinking we shall never meet again. I don't know how I know it, but I do."

"It's queer you should feel that, because it's very likely I shall be moved soon. Called up probably. I don't really care much where I go."

"Don't you feel anything?"

"Yes, I feel something.

"What?" she cried passionately.

"What?" he laughed, patting the water: "why, lost!"

The word seemed to sink down and down into the middle of the river. Her body felt light and chilly: she put her hand on the narrow edge of the boat and looked down at the shadow within the shadow of the reflected sky. A glow of yellowy green, precious light, *the light of darkness* as she saw it, lay on the level behind that they had left. On the top of the bank the enormous hemlocks spread distinctly, neither black nor green but a strange soft brown colour of darkness. This was the place. The current, with its go up or go down, would not let them think.

"Good night," she said, as the grass-swept boat thrilled against the bank.

"Good night," he said at the end of the swaying boat.

"Good night and thank you."

She jumped ashore. She stood on a stone. Hesitatingly he seemed to hover. Then came the clear plunge of the oars. The boat made a bias curve. She stared it away. From the fields the river was all mist, and the slight moonlight was only another kind of invisibility. He had gone. But she heard no stroke. He must be drifting down. He had gone and it was over and they would never meet again.

Emily bent and rubbed her feet which were as wet and cold as if they had been walking in the river. Neither of them had made the least individual acknowledgment of the other. It was from this point of view, the most inscrutable meeting in her life. And yet she understood what it might mean to each of them. Wasn't it the farewell to something each was feeling through the other? Wasn't that why neither he nor she could contradict her instinct that they would never talk together again? Was that too direct, too crude, an explanation? Wasn't it truly what it amounted to to-night?

She stood up, hooking both arms like wings, fists pressed against her, she fled down the tingling, tangled path, the pale yellow moon leaping about in the sky as she ran, the fragrance rising behind her from bruised clover, docks and nettles. In the home meadow each cow was lying still as a rock on the seashore. Her heart seemed to be vaulting in and out of a hole in her breast. A flock of ewes and lambs in the corner by the yard gate trembled on to their feet, shuddering like the echo of thunder in the ground as they shook themselves. The scent of honeysuckle was everywhere in the air as an intenser stillness. And now, the grit of the yard sticking to her wet feet like sand, she bounded up the steps – she was at the house. Weak, dazed, she leant against the porch. There came a pounding vision of machinery, of voices unbroken by silence, into her ears and her closed eyes. The future ....

She looked through the window into the room with its parasol of lamplight. Aunt Fran was asleep in her chair over her knitting, a candle in a brass candle-stick burning beside her. The dim gold shone through the tangled room and out on to the lawn.

Emily thought, "With that candle end I shall go to bed."

Solomon

T HE house is large, and filled with the green air of the trees. It has too few people in it. Sometimes, because each child had so many voices, nobody notices.

"But when we are asleep you'd think there's nobody here," says Thomasina.

"A hundred people could live here," says Ellen, and the other three cry hundred, thousand, million. Then they all forget. Except Barrabas. For him the million people tremble in the daylight. He sees them coming up the steps, all for some reason with the faces of old women, wearing spectacles, with little nobs of silver hair on their heads, and frightening smiles.

Barrabas is called that because once he stole the key of Mamma's little room and opened and ate a whole pot of cherry jam, and put the stones down the sink so that the water all came back. Knowing that he himself had swallowed many he waited for a long time for a flood to burst out of his mouth. When nothing happened the suspense was so awful that he had to go and tell somebody. Ellen was the one who thought of calling him Barrabas. His name is Albert.

Mamma has gone out on her horse. Papa has gone to the blacksmith's. Alice has scrambled all the dinner things on a tray and now, in the passage carrying the cheese, she makes them all go upstairs to lie down.

"Tig!" they cry on the landings. Slap, slap. Ellen and Thomasina run to their room, Griselda to hers. Barrabas goes on up alone to the next floor. He sighs and undoes the buttons of his boots. His door has a red mat in front of it. Standing on it he lifts his fist and gives a tiny soft knock, lifting his eyes as if someone very tall were listening on the other side of the door. Peeping, he enters the empty room on a groaning board.

He creeps on to the bed. How lovely it feels! Cool and sleepy. His naked feet nuzzle each other. He loves lying in this huge room where Mamma's harp stands against the wall, looking in the twilight like another door.

Presently his feet are still. There is left only a small clear spot in his head where all the world has shrunk. That fades too. His lips open, his head rolls on his shoulder, and he is asleep. The afternoon deepens. A white butterfly, its sails full of wind, plunges through the window. Barrabas wakens, whispers, and plays drowsily, moving his fingers close to his eyes. He pretends he is firing a gun at a blue-bottle in the corner. Then he begins to whisper a word. The word is "Solomon". He closes his eyes as he whispers, and then he opens them and looks carefully, longingly, all around the walls.

Solomon – who is Solomon? Nobody knows. He heard this heavy name he doesn't know where. Nobody picked it up but himself, nobody has heard him say it. Whenever he whispers it he is at home. He has places where it must be said. Nobody knows, nobody has heard. To the white lilies each one with a bee on its tongue he must say "Solomon's lilies". But nobody must see him speaking, not even Meffy as he trundles down the narrow path with polleny elbows, wheeling the barrow, the fork pronged into the manure, the red comforter Mamma knitted which he wears summer and winter tucked into the front of his neck. Solomon! The word articulates in some enormous still sound, all that Barrabas feels for the house, the park, and the trees and even the sky that he lives in. But not the people. They don't even remind him of that word, that figure which the word invites to be found one day or night. A calm presence it is as he imagines it, standing in a green or blue robe, with uplifted arms. If green the colour is a living softness; but if blue it's more wonderful still. There is no blue like it in his paint box – it is strange and full of meaning as the cadence of words not meant for him to understand.

Barrabas remembers Mamma telling them a Bible story about lilies and Solomon in all his glory. He sees not a king but the beautiful brick house, and the garden where the peacocks are dragging their trains like green branches. His mental eye switches from room to room, taking pictures of furniture and tall curtains. He hears Thomasina say drowsily:

"Were they *white* lilies?"

"I don't know. They were wild lilies, dear – the lilies of the field."

He interrupts, suddenly furious: "They *were* white.They *weren't* wild. They were *our* lilies."

"Albert dear!"

"You horrid little boy," Ellen scolds, "being rude to Mamma when she's telling us such a lovely story. Go on, Mamma. This house wasn't built, was it?"

"Never mind," says Mamma quickly and carelessly. Barrabas knows that Ellen wants to be grown up and like Mamma, but Mamma won't let her. She is too quick for Ellen. The more she tries, the faster Mamma changes. Sometimes when she throws her sewing on the table she looks as if she is throwing away Ellen. And when she gallops wildly from them all, flicking her hand back at them, Ellen will sigh, like Papa, and make a clumsy noise with her foot and pinch Thomasina when she says: "Will she come back soon? Oh, I do wonder if I shall be the first to see her coming!"

Barrabas is tired of bed. He tumbles out quietly. He will steal out quietly without Alice catching him, and look for Meffy to talk to. But first he kneels down beside the harp and pokes his curly finger into the gnaw of a mouse in the baize. He finds a string: a silver shiver climbs up the air like a geni, and leaving this whiff of music in the room, he runs out. But he finds Thomasina and Griselda and Ellen are before him.

"What are you all doing out of bed?" Alice wants to know. "No, I won't give you anything for your tea parties. I told you so. Make it up. There is that poor little Nellie never has anything to play with, and yet she's happy. You try it for a change; it'll do you good."

The black stockinged legs of the three little girls come twinkling out on the eighteen steps. Down they pour. The paved path is sunless and a straw hat hangs by its white ribbons from the wrought and embroidered gate. The children pause and open wide their eyes like animals who sense something different in their familiar field. The dappling day has changed, and the rooks flying look as if there is a load on their wings. In the air is a sweet close smell like hay and wool. The long hill uplands beyond the trees are dull and yet lit under the clouds.

"Griselda, have you got the sugar?"

"No, but I'm pretending I have."

"Alice *is* mean," mutters Ellen.

"I'm pretending I've got the teapot," screams Thomasina, and prances away ahead. "Anyway," she shouts, "it's silver, not an old kitchen thing."

Barrabas is left alone. It is one thing to go off alone, and another to be left so. Everything in him seems to have come to an end. The great cool, scattered room frowns under its tremendous moulded ceiling. There, over the piano, a rose is missing from the plaster bouquet. A champagne cork knocked it out when one of the family was married long ago. It was never put back. The house is all over such scars. Nobody can number what's in it or guess who dropped and hid the things they find. A silk purse with a black coin in it; the small, almond-eyed spectacles, the queer shrunken horseshoe Papa had carried to the blacksmith to-day which the girls had found.

Barrabas stares about him as if he could hear treasures crying out to be discovered. Then he goes very slowly out and down the steps and follows the others along the little path that has skinned the grass a footstep wide all the way across the Park to the river. A cloud is going and a cloud is coming. He walks through the stillness of trees and the brown, freckled butterflies, brown as toast, his forefinger squashing his lips against his teeth. Half way to the river and the stooping pink-and-yellow girls under the red tree, he turns and looks back at the house on its mound of steps, its soft Indian red like the streaks of ripeness on fruit, hardened and darkened by the valley of clouds hanging over the roof. He thinks it looks angry. Perhaps because no one has visited it to-day or yesterday. Again he murmurs soothingly, and runs towards the others shining in the distance.

The girls have made for the red tree by the waterfall. Round the blackberry bushes go little paths where the cowpats lie under swarms of glazy flies that have an iron brightness like nail heads. These vicious-sounding insects swarm like bees also against the bark of an oak and on the brick sides of the summer-house which is topped by a bell-shaped dove turret. Meffy stores onions there, and scythes and hooks and hackers. The year 1711 is written over the summer-house entrance, which like the garden walls is decorated with exquisite terra cotta tiles. There is silence, and the noise of the water and the shady singing of one bird.

The three dolls' cups and saucers which have been rattling in their box under Ellen's arm are set out in front of her in the form of a clover leaf. She is brushing the grass, looking for things that will do for spoons, while Thomasina carefully settling her empty hands, arranges the magnificent silver teapot and shrills that *she* must pour out.

"There's Nellie," whispers Griselda. "Can't she play too?"

Nellie is Meffy's grand-daughter, and she is lolling on the bridge

Minutae of life suggests diffkt issues + ways of life

dreamily fishing for a yellow foam dot with a bucket on the end of a rope. A green rock seems endlessly sleeking into the pool which is tortoiseshell with the first yellow shower of leaves.

"No," snaps Ellen. "She's been sent for water, the lazy little thing. Besides, we can't play with everybody. Miss Hachett says we're not to speak to her."

"But who told her not to speak to us?" Thomasina wants to know. "I believe she's asleep," she adds softly.

But no, Nellie isn't asleep. Suddenly the bucket gives a desperate jingle and the sun bonnet flops over the child's face. Her dark eyes glitter towards the tea party through her frills of hair.

Barrabas gives a strange scream of laughter like a woodpecker, and flaps his hands and sways as if he were wading. The stillness in the leaves shifts a little as if something mute and suffering had rolled over in the air.

"She hasn't nice manners at all."

"No," says Griselda sadly.

"Beastly," mutters Thomasina, for manners bore her. And handing the cakes they begin to talk about the dreadful day when Mamma spoke to Nellie in the drive. She said, "What pretty hair you have, my dear." But Nellie just shut her eyes tightly and never answered a word.

"An otter lives here ...."

Barrabas won't sit down. He stands by the tree which has no bark, but only long reddish-brown hair the same colour as the cows, and he strokes it and tries it against his cheek. He rests there, glancing, smiling, amused but apart, seeing in the place of the girls the three ladies they are imagining.

"Your hat's falling off," he tells Thomasina, who instantly puts her hand to her bare head and exclaims, "Dear me, my glorious hat," most earnestly. Barrabas walks round the blackberry bushes. Then he has another spasm of immobility and gazing. The girls are quarrelling.

"I found it."

"I found it."

"Oo, it was me!"

"Wipe your nose."

"I found it, and Papa says it's two hundred years old," Ellen insists.

"I know that," snarls Thomasina. It is the old horseshoe. Ellen is determined that she is the one who first poked her hand into the hole in the wall, when all the time it was herself, and Ellen is a liar. If Mamma and Papa hadn't been so pleased, Ellen wouldn't have cared. But Papa had gone on purpose to the forge to show it, and turning it over in his fingers, he had said everything in the house has history.

"I think it would be nice if Nellie plays too," yawns Griselda. "Tea parties are stupid and four of us could play something real."

"Really, Griselda, really, we aren't common children."

"No, but we're poor. Papa says our boots are too big for us."

The ladies hand up their cups and dust the places in front of them.

"It feels funny, don't you think?" Thomasina says, screwing up her eyes. "I feel an awfully long way off. I say, Barrabas, what're you doing?"

Barrabas's hand flicks, but he doesn't move, and answers in a voice that seems to come through the back of his head: "I'm listening. I'm listening to where all the little paths go to."

Then he sets off. Out of the skein of sheep paths that loops and curls and lies unravelled, he chooses the one that he thinks wants to go home. Everything he sees he imagines has its wishes, and now as he runs he feels he is taking back to comfort some small weak lonely will. But he is sorry he didn't dare to take the girls some cow pat for a cake. "That would be funny, funny," he joggles as he runs.

Cook is on the steps breaking off the heavy fruit from a tree that has torn itself from the wall. She puts two cool greengages into the crook of his arm. Barrabas laughs, "thank you", and turns to see which way the laugh went. He gazes amazed at some sky which is coming round the corner of a steamy cloud. It is a dark purple. And the doves have ceased to purr: and what he thought was silence half an hour ago was full of stirring compared with this deadness. He doesn't know, but miles away Mamma, rousing a dull wind, is galloping for home. She rides in a brown linen skirt, buttoned up the front, and swaying as she balances she presses her palm to her forehead. It's money, money, money. There's the beautiful furniture, but the shabby easy chairs are falling through, and the wan chintzes are more like faded weeds than flowers. But Ellen must go to school. How nice that will be for her! She will enjoy discipline and washing in cold water, and prayers and chilblains, and being the one away.

Boarding school. Mamma frowns. She remembers her sobs, her being downstairs in the dark, wrapped in a shawl and crying bitterly, bitterly weeping while they carry her box out into the winter morning. How *can* people who love you do such things to you?

The air is crowded with sultry, blinding insects that get in her eyelashes: she sees that the wild vetches have tiny black pods. All her children are in her face, of which she is unaware, though everyone who knows her sees that. How can she keep Barrabas, she thinks? No one so young should be tender, so remote. Children should be indifferent and movable, like John the eldest, who pretends not to, and perhaps really does not, like holidays. Barrabas, holding on to something all alone ... Mamma is happy, but it's a happiness not without its secrets and obsessions. A farmer's old man wandering round the lanes like a snail that comes out trembling to feel the approaching storm which is being milled in the sky, sees her galloping past, and says to himself, a blue-eyed woman beats them all.

It is dark, with the glassy darkness of an eclipse. A ring of lightning that nobody remarks dances round the earth. Barrabas turns round quietly in the silent room, thinking that something flew out the window. Suddenly his skin flickers lights and shadows. He has been in Mamma's bedroom where her frocks rustle. In a little while he travels to Papa's study, a huge stretch with a great wide open window on the garden. Feeling forbidden, not because he isn't allowed there, but because Papa's gun is propped, stiff and warning-looking against the back of an armchair, he sits down upon the carpet. At last, as he always meant to do, he remembers Meffy and runs out of the back door.

Meffy is milking, his yellow hands squeezing the cow's yellow udders. His face, with its enormous wrinkled buff teeth like broad beans when they are dried and show the black eyelits, is turned towards the bonfire which for some perverse reason of his own he has lit beside the back door. Rosa, the bitch spaniel, and Florence Nightingale, a greenish queen-tabby, have their eyes fixed on the bucket.

Meffy sits on a log only a foot high, sunk between his legs like a spider. Barrabas runs to him and spreads his hand over a patch on the old man's knee, a blue patch.

"Hal-o-o-o," he says, "Meffy."

There is lightning again, and Barrabas sees the shadow of the smoke climbing up the kitchen wall. He shakes his head to shake out the dizzy light.

"Tell me a story," he says.

"A story, ey?" says Meffy softly.

Solomon from the back is ponderous age. Compared with the façade it is earthenware compared with porcelain. The hunks of building, of coarse stone, are roofed with scabby tiles like oyster shells. The kitchens and dairies and pantries inside, large as they are, have only small kernels of space within the thick walls. This is the old house, and the story, Meffy's only one, is a part of it. It takes only a moment to tell, but a long while to think over. It tells how long ago people on donkeys came up to the door and bought the old Solomon, and all the trees, and the land, with gold that they carried in their hands. "People – the People," says Meffy. He means gipsies.

Barrabas wants to know, "Did Alice give them some bread?"

He has seen Alice giving food to tramps in skeleton clothes.

"Were they their *own* donkeys?"

Still Meffy says nothing. Barrabas looks anxiously away to the back door, and the low thunder seems the tremor of his own heart.

"Don't you remember?"

Perhaps the old man thinks he does, for a deep smile slowly gathers the wrinkles away from his mouth like two curtains that are pulled apart. And involuntarily he sees hanging on the nail in his cottage next to the bird scarer and the wooden cider bottle, the house keys left with them when the family goes away, as they always are. His memory is inseparable from the place. Yes, he does remember.

Barrabas turns from him at the beginning of a run: "I remember me," he says, lightly, carelessly. Just then Papa rushes into the yard. His beard is parted by the speed of his pace, his hat hangs on to his hair, and he grasps his walking stick desperately with both hands, across his chest.

"Where're the others?" he pants. Just as he hears their voices in the passage. The thunder has brought them to Alice. Papa bounds through them. Outside the forge talking to the blacksmith he suddenly and appallingly asks himself the dreadful question, where did I leave the gun? And for an instant confused and terrified, he

*concerned with
the self. inner
feelings*

has an impression as he pushes through the girls that there is either a child missing or an extra face among them. And when he sees the gun still propped up in the chair he snatches it up and looks at it as if it had just shot one of the children.

After a moment he raises his eyes to the window. The trees are faintly moving, but so silently that they might have feathers instead of foliage. His glance rests then on a pastel portrait of his mother hung low and intimately above the desk – a pink and blue face like a sedate china flower which never comes alive in any light. And then he hears Honeymoon's hoofs cantering on the grass. How dark it is! She is only just home in time for the sultry wind has come that makes the flowers crane over the path.

Mamma is laughing as she runs up the steps, but Papa cries, "Oh, my darling, you frighten me with your wild Irish riding."

"But Francis, *I'm* not out of breath. What's the matter?"

Papa goes over and pulls down the window: "We'll have our tea in here."

Mamma at the door says she must find them all first. She is gone. Or going. Papa's voice pursues her: "Why *will* you wear that hat?" She smiles into the space ahead of her, and going to the piano lights a candle there and carries it away. Papa pulls out a great handkerchief, cracks it in the air, and blows a groan from his nose, in the very middle of the room.

When Mamma rides she holds the reins in her left hand. It is with that hand she now lifts up the candle. The right one, the one that glitters to the children as she gallops, is raised slightly at her side as if she were denying something, or holding back a pressing thought. Up the house she goes, right to the top to the broad raftered rooms under the pigeons, where on a warm day their cooing comes through the roof with the scratching of their feet tripping and catching on the tiles.

What can be keeping up such a weight of rain she wonders, as she gently closes windows? The darkness falls across her light, darkness which is like the shade under a thick tree, sombre, woven of leaves and silent with silence of still tongues. The lightning is swaying in the air nearer and nearer so that often it is in a room before she enters. And then she sees it is not light she is bringing with the candle, but only a yellow smirch like fog.

She hears the voices in the kitchen, she hears a moan of thunder;

and her own shadow twirls about her as she turns. It's as though some loosened entity of the house were revolving wherever she moves, now dancing as in a cage, now fitfully concealed within her own body. The furniture, the lovely rooms with the wan curtains clinging to the walls like creepers, stand quiet, controlled, and yet articulate, in the opening and shutting of the lighting.

"All is not known here. All will never be known."

She crosses a floor and pushing up the top sash leans against the window frame, bending forward and looking downwards through the glass at the yard underneath. Terribly suddenly, as if he had jumped out of her heart, she sees Barrabas alone out there, stirring with a stick the lost jewels of Meffy's fire. For a moment she hardly recognizes him. That's what frightens her. Putting the candle down on the window seat, with both arms, she struggles to pull down the sash, but it won't move. She can only rattle it, and muted by the glass, call wildly.

"Albert, Albert!"

He doesn't hear.

"Albert, come in!"

Louder and louder, until she hears herself screaming as she knocks blows on the window: "Barrabas, O Barrabas, Barrabas ...."

He hears and raises his face, exposing to her in the white flash of light to earth, a look of the strangest prolonged expectancy, while with an amazingly soft rustling sound begins what develops into an immense avalanche of thunder.

The floor boards are still jarring as Papa finds her, fallen into the window seat, her arms over her face.

"Barrabas," she whispers. "Out there. It *is* our child, isn't it?"

Papa looks.

"My dear, there's nobody that I can see."

Barrabas has run in out of the rain.

Miss Potts and Music

PUSH away a bundle of letters, post-marked, slightly muddy. It has been wet for so long. In the orchard this morning the raindrops were no longer running off the slippery leaves: they were no longer visible but had become part of that dull, dark green glaze which is the old summer's surface. The rain had become part of the air, had disappeared and been absorbed into it.

And it still falls, at times heavily. It is a material then. In the bus I was thinking, why, you could almost build a house with it. Having observed this to no one in particular but unaccountably loudly, I felt mad. Well, there go the letters. Now, I can really begin to write if there's anything left over ....

But can I? Looking at those trees can I concentrate on this rather stately balanced article? Surely there is a child swinging in the branches? She – it is she – hangs and kicks her dangling legs: her long light hair held back by a band of ribbon, is woven like a cocoon among the three-cornered leaves. It *is* she whom for some reason I suddenly remember – Miss Potts? Of course not. The wind is between the lonely wet branches shaking them, and the low dark twilight is coming on cloudily, or I might think the flaxen moon made her hair. I think of Hardy's exquisite poem:

> My fellow climber rises dim
> From her chilly grave –
> Just as she was, her foot near mine on the bending limb
> Laughing, her young brown hand awave.

Many winds and winters are in those lines, which, like all real memories, hold much more of oblivion than remembrance. Not that Miss Potts was ever a fellow climber of mine, or as far as I know, anybody else's. In fact the question is, did she ever climb at all? That's what I am trying to decide.

But surely there *is* a child in the tree. Questioning the direction of darkness which is behind that tower of hustled leaves I ask, are you Miss Potts, are you dead, are you a success or a failure, what did you do at Weymouth and why do I remember you to-night?

If she is Miss Potts I don't see her often but I know that she lives somewhere up in Lindenfield outside the town, with her grandmother, her widowed mother and her aunt who teaches me music. Her name – well, it is never anything but Miss Potts to me and to all the other children who learn the piano from her aunt. It is in scorn of her isolation and her umbrella that we call her so. She wears white socks and she must be about twelve years old. Her cheeks are a round, sober pink, her fair, floppy hair is banded back, her mouth, not very originally, is a button, but a button sewn on very tightly. Precociously it has the pout and the quivering disdainfulness of an artist, for Miss Potts is already a solid instrumentalist. Her touch is formed. She is said to be a genius. I have not, at the stage when she might have been imagined swinging herself, ever heard her play, but at the time when the piano was to me a noisy bore, Miss Potts was said to use *both* pedals.

Of course, when we hear this we know we are hopeless. But that which is so sickening and altogether incredible is that she plays the violin too. The violin is her real forte; and yet as a second course she beats us all at the piano. Or so her aunt says.

Oh, how I hate music lessons and Miss Potts, *and* her aunt who looks an exact embodiment of somebody or other – or rather two somebodies as it has taken me years to realize. Combining Rossetti's Beata Beatrix and my own idea of Sherlock Holmes, I have the most perfect projection of her. A long, long throat, a big clever nose, a thin ethereal face with ascetic and romantic eyes, that was B.B.S.H. when I was ten. She looked a saint of music and her niece was her novice. But with her nostrils down on her fiddle she became pure Sherlock Holmes. Later on when I was sixteen I had another music mistress – a Miss Townsbridge, a black-eyed, hoarse, cheerful woman, who exercised the most amazing vocabulary of tone upon the violin, and who possessed a sheer mathematical knowledge of theory which made her a genuine mystic and initiate of her art. She used to do her shopping during my lessons and dump her damp bag of fish and watercress on the top of the piano where B.B.S.H. used to keep an unfurling rose in a silver vase. Miss Townsbridge used to declare that music such as mine required judgment at a distance.

I was going to write by that time Miss Potts had quite gone from my conscious memory, as she and Beata Beatrix, the mother and the grandmother had left the town years before. However, if I have forgotten her it must have been about then that remembrance revived with the letter I found and read about them being gone to Weymouth. That letter which has in a sense kept her continuous and connected the thought of her forever with wet esplanades and a snail-coloured sea ....

Why I thought of Miss Potts and my music lessons when I looked at the tree was because it is a birch. Birches grew outside the room where B.B.S.H. taught us. (Her name was Miss Amy Holman.) A pattern of tombstones, a diagonal path, green turf and the aerial trees filled the Georgian window. I can see those grey-green three-cornered leaves now. The room was up a flight of stone stairs, over a school. Outside on a long, ugly landing was a yellow pine bench where sometimes the next pupil sat with her music case and sweetie bag, kicking the wall.

Perhaps, too, my being in the orchard this morning unconsciously opened my mind to her image. Down there with the smell of the long grass and nettles and the horse mushrooms under old perry and cider trees the sense of an intimate past is always more powerful than anywhere else: under those trees my childhood grows over me; and to-night especially I can suddenly see myself with my friend Marian in my aunt's orchard.

We were feeding the ferrets which lived in a box nailed to a pear tree, Marian carefully holding up the saucer of bread and milk while I opened the cage for her to slip it inside. The ferrets stank and we were afraid of getting bitten: they undulated in their straw, and their sensitive, wincing nostrils and eyes opened and shut like stars.

Marian was the same age as Miss Potts. She had a large shining white face with clean open pores all over it, like the ostrich's egg in my aunt's bedroom. Her hands were red and blue and her hair cold-tea coloured and growing in a bunch over the middle of her forehead. She was my great friend because she was utterly different from me – tidy and quiet and concisely mannered.

"Mother is going to ask Miss Potts to tea," said Marian.

"Oh, Marian," I groaned. We all groaned when Miss Potts was mentioned.

Then I tried to envisage the arrival of Miss Potts and B.B.S.H. at Marian's father's shop. Would they walk up the alley under the barber's-saloon to the family door? Or would they, furling their umbrellas, step into the shop as if they were customers? I decided they would go to the door. I saw them with the little black coffins that held their fiddles, turning to look at each other on the threshold just as Marian's mother opened the door to admit them. But I couldn't see them going in. They would *not* go in. No, in my vision they would not. There, dressed for some reason as once perhaps I had really seen her, in a fine pale pigeon-grey dress with a soft white collar and a damson dark rose, stood Beata Beatrix with her peculiar ecstatic smile, holding Miss Potts by the hand as I had sometimes seen her do when they walked quickly across the churchyard to wherever they were going.

Suddenly I knew they wouldn't go at all. They were only *asked*. And I believe they didn't. I believe I can remember Marian muttering, "Too grand" when I inquired.

"Do you know what's going to happen to me one day?" I said, after we had fed the ferrets and pulled to pieces all the Jew's-ear fungus we could find: "Shall I tell you? One day *I'm* going to play the violin. I know I am! Better than Miss Potts. Miss Potts will sound awful after me."

"I bet she sounds awful now," said Marian.

"Ah, but you wait! This is really *going to happen*. You see. One day when I've been out all day, miles and miles and miles and I'm hot and thirsty and lame with blisters – I shall come to a cottage and I shall stop. It'll be an old man who'll ask me if I'd like a drink. And he'll take me inside. And there hanging on the wall –"

"Hanging on the wall ...?"

"Hanging on the wall there'll be an old, old violin, covered with dust. Nearly black with age and the strings broken. I shall say, do you want that? No, you can have it: I'll give it to you. It belonged to my grandfather and he's dead and I can't play it so you can have it –"

"But neither can you."

"I shall learn. I shall take it away and have it all my life and it will be in my grave with me, so there, Marian B."

"You always talk about being dead," cried Marian: "But what about Miss Potts?"

"Miss Potts! Oh, *Miss Potts*. Nobody'll listen to *her*."

I cannot see the tree any more. It's quite dark now, but out there behind the candles it is swinging the wind like a child on its branches. And what I wonder is – did I ever with my eyes actually see her in the birch trees? And again jumping off a tombstone, and running along the churchyard wall as far as the iron lamp? When I hear again her spirited voice – the only time I *did* hear it – passionately raised against us who were baiting her – "I'm *not* crying. My nose is going to bleed!" – I can believe that she did these things and I saw her. But who can tell me? I don't think I saw half of what I remember, and I may have dreamed or imagined it. Certainly it seems real. Terribly, noticeably real. But then so does the dark red car going swiftly along without a driver, but containing a man asleep in the back with his head on a white bolster. I feel that I saw that: it was the kind of car that generals used in the last war, but its reality never convinced any one except myself. I suppose it was one of those intense, psychic impressions very young children receive and isolate in their minds from time to time. However, don't let me patronize myself: at ten years old I had a good deal of penetration and independence. My reaction to B.B.S.H., for instance, was one of stubborn dislike in spite of her fascination and the atmosphere of admiring emotion she caused among some of her pupils and all of the grown-up people who knew her. Simply, the more they raved over her looks, her music, her cleverness and her brilliant ill-health, the more certain I was of her – what shall I say – her secret levity, her contemptuousness. And the formidable drive, the *will* of her. Nothing in fact that I should have disliked if she had let it be obvious. It was the sighing – the false exhaustion ....

One day she told me – I thought maliciously – that Miss Potts was playing the Moonlight Sonata. She was sitting beside me at the piano, her great coil of wistfully romantic hair falling down her neck. I asked:

"Why can't I learn it? I like it."

She sat up and stretched; her limp but beautiful body seemed to yawn: "*You!* Ha ha. My dear –" and she looked at me with thoughtful hate, "there are *immense difficulties*. You don't realize –" She sighed. "Constance is – well, she's remarkable."

And she spread her thin hands in the tenuous way she had ....

111

And then there was that dreadful music competition. We – the dozen or so pupils – all had to play the same piece. Miss Potts was the sure winner. Why she was included – but she wasn't. *We* were included, because she couldn't win without us. That was what we decided, anyway.

Ten girls and two middle-aged little boys waited outside Beata Beatrix's room that afternoon, quietly and carelessly playing Puss-in-the-corner. When we heard footsteps coming we flew and sat upon the bench. We giggled, we whispered as Miss Potts's grandmother arrived, as one by one we were called in to play. The game went on tensely; the cotton smell of our clean frocks mingled with the sharp one of glazed music rolls and satchels, the pattern of the piece now faint, now desperately bold, occurred and ended. I remember I hung out of the dull window and watched the swallows threaded in a double row on the telegraph wires, and the old almswomen in their tiny courtyards down below carrying their coal buckets into their doorways.

Miss Potts didn't sit with us. About half-way through she came. She wore gloves and she walked through us haughtily; and she knocked on the door. Then she stood, hand and forearm uplifted, posing complete indifference. It was easy. Her back was towards us.

But, oh, she would have made an artist! Why hasn't she? The tap, the listening hand – the feet a little tilted on the toes .... Lord, what hadn't those three women taught her! There was a giggle after the door had shut. Somebody said: "I say – the Light of the World!"

Slowly we nodded our heads.

We waited for her music. Until it came, we nodded, not looking at one another, but muttering her name all down the bench where we were now sitting: "Miss Potts, Miss Potts, Miss Potts, Miss Potts, go dots."

Down and up the length of the bench, her name went, like a scale of chords, the way of a ritual of magic. Separately we had all undergone the ordeal of Miss Potts, but now it was we who were unanimous ....

When she began to play I found no one to look at. And suddenly I wanted a face who would meet my eyes and my astonishment. For without premonition how could I have been prepared? *Astonished* – I was so astonished that I might have been picked off the bench and set down in the middle of the churchyard without noticing I'd moved. And my chest felt blank, not uncomfortable, but simply empty, as if I had no breath and no need to breathe. I had expected there would have been *some* likeness to our playing. Some recognizable equality. But there was none.

The piece sounded as if it had never been played before. Miss Potts might have been thinking it to me as she played it. It seemed as if I could see the arch of the notes in the air through the thick red panels of the door, definite and lovely as the swallows strung on the telegraph wires, but of some unknown spirit colour resembling white gold ....

As playing it was a boundary, Miss Potts and the grown-ups on one side, ourselves on the other.

The others went on muttering faster and faster. The spell was turning into a game. But all of my mother in me possessed me to listen, and when the music was over, to watch the door.

When it opened and she came out, I was more confounded than ever, for she dropped her silly gloves and she stooped and fished about, looking exactly as I felt I looked when my aunt made me sing to people. Her music might be grown-up but she wasn't. And nobody ever was nearer to plain crying.

"Miss Potts, go dots," sang somebody, changing the game back to a taunt.

Oh, I felt sorry for Miss Potts! I felt sorry for her in the way children do for one of themselves when they see through adult cunning. It was in the vehemence of triumph she had been included among us and now she had to face us. I felt that blindness one gets behind the eyes after a shock or an accident like falling down or cutting your finger – something instantaneous which is there to protect you, but which bewilders you too and makes you wonder how it happened.

Instead of running past us she stood there staring. The tears started to crawl out of her eyes.

"She's going to cry-ee!"

The faces swayed forward.

"I'm not crying! My nose is going to bleed!"

She twisted her shoulders – she was gone; part of her face that I had seen was a fierce red and white, one suffused eye glaring over the handkerchief.

"Ha, ha, ha!" we laughed. "Ha, ha, ha. Hush, hush."

Another one was called.

Remembering that afternoon, and the way she used to walk whenever I saw her, always between two women as though the world were a slender path endlessly enclosed – I wonder more than ever whether she was secretive, found things dull, hid from everybody the laughing foot on the bough and the hand that shook the birch leaves into the movement of climbing smoke. But my Miss Potts Collection is after all so slight! There is no guessing. And probably there was nothing, nothing at all interesting, one way or the other. Six years passed. B.B.S.H. had been gone a long time and Miss Townsbridge with her bursts of shopping and her boredom was teaching me technique which I couldn't translate into action. Searching back, I cannot find a trace or a murmur of her remaining.

Yet she did that once come back. When I read the letter which was going to be burned on my bonfire. She came, as she has come to-night, abruptly, not with a speech, but with a certain astounding brevity, like a ghost story in a newspaper.

The letter fell off the wheelbarrow out of a heap of papers, music and magazines I was trundling through the snowball bushes. I picked it up and read it: it was signed by Amy Holman. It seemed I could actually hear the voice of the writing and see it spoken out of Beata Beatrix's frail profile. She had been rather a friend of my aunt's; after they had gone away she had written a few times.

"My sister is rather worried about Constance."

(Constance – Constance? Oh, Miss Potts.)

"My sister is rather worried about Constance. She and my mother have taken her away to Weymouth where my sister hopes to settle if they can find a small flat, and if the air does Constance good. But so far they are having nasty wet weather. And Constance is so devoted to her music that there is no holding her back."

That letter was the very last I ever heard, the final mention in my life of any one of them. I have never heard that Miss Potts *died,* nor for that matter that she lived. She has not become a celebrity. But I wonder, did they settle? Did they ever find anything to hold *them* back? I can imagine them living in that small flat for the rest of their lives. Sometimes I see her one way, sometimes another. Now she is growing unobtrusively older between them: walking along the esplanade in that kind of seaside rain which seems to oil the roofs and the waves, glancing occasionally aside uneasily and rapidly at the swishing, dishevelled beach, the whorls of clinging, shining shells .... And then another time I am sure she gave up music and took to lipstick and dancing and marriage with the rich proprietor of a garage, storing her fiddle on the top of a wardrobe and allowing the women a pension of moderate affection only. Nothing lonely, slow or wistful after all .... In fact, it's quite probable that I have been close to her without recognizing her: have passed her in some park, sitting in the square shadow of a statue, reading, watching the birds and sometimes vaguely lifting the direction of her face towards the band under the cupola, to whose rosy music she feels so placidly and distantly related.

Yes, I wonder.

But it is so late that even the moths have ceased to butt at the candles and with folded wings have settled in little chequered lumps on the curtain, like limpets on a dark green rock.

I'll go to bed. Wind, tree, darkness and Miss Potts are all inscrutable.

A Modest Adornment

ULL'S eyes are boys' sweets," said Miss Allensmoore and popped one in her mouth.

She and Miss Plant had lived together for many years in a cottage just outside a small village. It was difficult to guess whether they liked each other; but they didn't seem to quarrel. They didn't seem to be poor and they didn't seem to be rich: they had plenty of food apparently but no clothes, except what they always wore; and they were squalid, eccentric and original. And rather old.

Miss Allensmoore was a fat black cauldron of a woman frequently leaning on an umbrella. She had a pair of little hobbling feet which turned up at the ends and which were usually bare. Miss Plant had great silky green eyes and soft silver hair with yellowish patches in it the colour of tobacco stain. She was very, very pretty with strawberry pink in her thin face, but in her enormous eyes which were truly half blind, there was a curious sort of threat. But she was the meekest of martyrs. She was an odd rambling creature, always dressed in a shawl and a mackintosh, and she used to pass a lot of pleasant time writing letters to the farmer who owned the cottage asking him to send a man to trim the hedge. They were rather peculiar letters. He kept a few to smile at. "You are such a shy man," wrote Nora Plant, "that I don't like to stop you, although I meet you so often in the lane."

Miss Allensmoore was an atrocious but, alas, perpetual cook. Coming down the garden path to the door which was generally open, their few visitors always heard furious frying or the grumpy sound of some pudding in the pot, bouncing and grunting like a goblin locked in a cupboard. Miss Allensmoore also wrote letters which she sent by the baker and always expected to have answered in the same way. She played the oboe. She played beautifully, and she kept a great many dirty black cats.

Miss Plant only kept silence. A sort of blind silence which was liable to be broken at any moment by her falling over something or knocking something else down. It wasn't a quiet silence: and it hadn't the length or the loyalty needed for music. When Miss Allensmoore played in her presence, Miss Plant would sit looking desultory, like

116

a person who is taking part in a hopeless conversation.

The cottage smelled of soot and stale shawls and burnt kettles.

And now it was January and Miss Plant was dying of cardiac disease. And Miss Allensmoore was standing in the garden on a paste of brown leaves, eating bull's-eyes.

It was very cold. On the banks of the steep fields the broken snow was lying like pieces of china. A wind was going round the currant bushes.

"Cold, cold," muttered Miss Allensmoore looking down at the snowdrops. It would be nice to pick them and have them indoors, she thought. But on the other hand, if she left them how well they would do for the funeral!

"I won't. It can't be long now," she said. She breathed a long silent phrase and moved away her hand.

Miss Plant was, in fact, almost through death. At half past three in the afternoon two days later, the district nurse quietly pulled down her cuff. Miss Plant had parted with her dazed, emaciated body.

Miss Allensmoore was again in the garden, picking some washing off the thorns. Suddenly she heard the nurse calling, so she hastened indoors and met her coming out of the cupboard where they kept the stairs.

"It's over," said the young nurse uneasily.

Miss Allensmoore looked confident and unchanged.

"Oh, don't be upset," she said. "What time did she die?"

"Twenty-nine minutes past three exactly," said the nurse more powerfully. "Can you give me a bit of help? That bed's so heavy."

"Certainly," said Miss Allensmoore affably, "it *is* a solid bed. Just let me hang these things up before I put them down somewhere and forget them. There's no reunion so hard to bring about as a pair of stockings which has separated."

It was dark in the narrow rooms. They lit candles and went upstairs. Castors screeched as the bed was moved out from the wall: a flock of birds flew low over the roof with a dragging sound like a carpet being drawn over a floor. The dust could be felt on the teeth. Presently Miss Allensmoore came out fumbling with her candle and dropping grease on her toes. An unfinished smile tinged her face for a moment before she licked it away with the point of her tongue. It was a fat, proud, eternal face, and the little smile gave it a strange brevity. She was thinking Miss Plant would never send things flying again, reaching for others.

But the nurse having finished, stepped back from the candlelight and gazed at the face above the tallowy folds of the sheet. Beneath were the vivid hands, hands in new green knitted gloves, bunched on the breast almost as if they had been a knot of leaves. A woman from the village who used to come to see Miss Plant had made the gloves for her. And she had asked the nurse if she would do her best, please, to see that she was buried in them.

The nurse again went to the bedside and quietly looked. There was a kind of daylight on the face which was the colour of the flesh in that pale, plastered light. Poor Miss Plant didn't look wonderfully young, or beautiful as the dead are said to look: she just looked simple and very, very tired. The nurse sighed as she picked up her case.

She went downstairs. Miss Allensmoore squatted on the fender holding a cup and saucer under her chin. She had lit two lamps which were flaring and she was frying chips on an oil-stove. She got up; her naked feet, dark as toads, trod the hundreds of burnt matches which covered the floor.

"All over now. Funeral Friday," she announced.

"My God, she's a hard old nut!" the nurse thought. She said: "I'll let the doctor know. And would you like me to call on Billy Prosser as I'm passing?"

"You mean Mr Misery. I simply can't think of him as *Billy Prosser*," said Miss Allensmoore. "Oh, yes, please, if you would. I'd sooner not go myself."

The nurse smiled. The village was a great place for dubbing and nick-naming. People called Miss Allensmoore "Sooner". It stood for Sooner Not Do Anything.

"If you'd be so good," muttered she, eating chips. They were long and warped and gaunt as talons, Miss Allensmoore's chips were. She threshed them in her gums and spat them at the cats that caused an idiotic darkness by gambolling before the lamps. Wands of flame flew up the glasses and then shrivelled, while the dirty ceiling swayed with clumsy shadows. And the sagging black cobwebs.

The nurse got ready to go. She sidled away saying: "Not nervous, are you?"

"Nervous? Nervous of what?" demanded Miss Allensmoore, and

she added, "I've known Miss Plant for a great number of years," as if that were a perfect explanation for everything.

The nurse went, nodding mildly. Somehow she seemed frightened, Miss Allensmoore thought. In fact she was only relieved, for how dreadful it would be for anybody to have to sit with the old slut in that awful cottage! Every time she walked in the tables seemed more and more crammed with washing up, with crumbs and tea leaves and the hilly horizons of many obstructive meals. And then, the pailsful of refuse, the tusky cabbage stalks, the prowling smell ...!

So she was gone. And Miss Allensmoore turned the key on her. Ha! She was alone. Now she would gently, gently put out her hand and take up the oboe. Presently she would play. How beautifully she could play! Between the pieces sighs of joy broke from her and loud words that left holes in her breath.

"Ah – ah – my beautiful – when you sing like that ...." And again she would cry: "My beloved ...." Ah, oh – it was the loveliest thing in life, music – the only wise, the only sagacious thing. And afterwards she would play again, until the fire was out and the cats all slept, and something, rain or insects or mice, crinkled in the shapely pauses.

Silence. With her instrument ready, Miss Allensmoore turned to face it. It was to her what the mysterious stone is to its carver who will presently unfurl from it the form which he observes inherent in it. As stone is to the sculptor only a gauze upon the idol of his mind, silence was transparent to Miss Allensmoore. The musicians' dawn she called it. And now she was face to face with the biggest silence she had ever known and all the time the nurse was gathering up this and that she was longing to breathe across it the first dangerous phrase.

With ecstatic anguish she loved the melodious shapes of her breath; she noticed how other people breathed: to her it seemed terrible that most of them used this art only for scrambling about the world and gossiping. Out of breath! She only wished they were! They weren't fit to use the supple air. Or if they were, she reflected sometimes, it was a pity she was obliged to mix such a common medium with her music. For when she played she knew gravity and posture: she felt the formal peace of her heavy body as it centred the encircling grace of Palestrina, Handel, Gluck ....

Palestrina to-night ....

"Art is science," said Miss Allensmoore, "there is no sloppy art. There are no sloppy stars."

She talked to Ada Allensmoore every night. It was no use talking to Nora Plant, anyway, even if she happened to be alive, and she often talked about the stars because for some reason she had decided they were "scientific and accurate". In the hours of her playing the universe went round her in satellites of sound, and that irrelevant ingredient, her identity, lapsed into an instinct so rapt and so concise that it amounted to genius. She yielded. She yielded to her breathing, to her transformation. Apart from the Voice, hers, she said, was the most physical form of music. So she gave way, but not lusciously. Always decorously, utterly and unselfconsciously.

Sometime in the night, sitting in her hard chair, her feet crossed, she *noticed* Miss Plant was dead – and then she wondered if one felt dying as one felt music. A giving up, and a giving back, thought Miss Allensmoore. Because she knew the feeling of music was quite different from the listening to it. Of course. Just as different as any two arts could be.

So she laid down the oboe, and she went with a secret intensity to look at Miss Plant who lay hardened to the sudden light in the bed-filled little room.

"Just like a statue of herself," thought Miss Allensmoore, who had been pondering on stone and sculptors. A statue with hands of vernal green. These, however, she didn't observe. She wanted to ask her a question, and she even prepared a breath for it as for a note, but somehow no question was spoken. Miss Plant's silence had been no more than a continual state of never being spoken to. It was now her turn to be superior and uncommunicative.

Miss Allensmoore gazed down upon her friend somewhat severely, as if she were going to lecture her for lying there. Not that she ever had. Miss Plant had been absolutely free. It was just the way Miss Allensmoore looked for a moment. She had, in spite of her chubbiness, strict features, and if momentarily a definite expression replaced her usual abstract glance, it was a disciplinary one.

"But it's nothing after all," said Miss Allensmoore, her eyes leaving the wistful dead face. And going to the window which the nurse had shut, she opened it, letting in more darkness than her candle could go round. It was nothing. The nurse had shut the window as she had shut Miss Plant's strange eyes. If they opened now, would darkness come out of them? Ridiculous idea, said Miss Allensmoore leaning out. How a little light does revive one! You feel drowsy and helpless and then someone lights a lamp and then! You're full of energy again.

She saw the lamp from the room underneath shining out on the earth below her. Cabbages had been grown there. There were their gnarled stumps curled like cows' horns. Suddenly she remembered her mother and the way she used to cross the cut stalk with her knife so that in the spring fresh leaves frilled out. Bubbling with green, the garden all round them. And the cuckoo flying over. The sound of summer too in a window which seemed to be its instrument. Rustling rain, and her father's singing.

Beyond the yellow light it was as dark as if one's eyes were shut, and as silent as if a bell had just stopped ringing. Every death brought a little more stillness into the world. But what she couldn't command was the feeling that the darkness was Miss Plant's eyes not seeing –

The village was only a dozen or so cottages all at corners with one another, each one askew, and each one butting into a neighbour's sheds or gardens. The people, primitive, yet not unworldly, entertained themselves with conversation over the hedges while they hung the washing, set rat-traps, or planted their seeds.

Everything was talked over. Yet there was caution and a native secrecy. A person not of their kind might live among them for at least five years before noticing that the sexton in the churchyard gossiped like a sparrow to people in the lane, and even the ringers nodded news under the bells.

And Miss Allensmoore and Billy Prosser the carpenter and undertaker weren't the only people who had nicknames. There was Squatty Gallipot, the fat little shopkeeper, and there was George Ryder, the postman, a tall crooked-headed man whose height and low opinion of himself made him known beyond even his wide and hilly round as Mr Little-So-Big. The people had, however, a sense of situation and the wryness of circumstances, which at times was apter than the truth. To one man surnamed Beer they had erected a memorial stone inscribed: Tippler of This Parish, which their vicar had caused to be erased, without, however, their permitting it to be forgotten.

The morning after Miss Plant's death a neighbour, calling to borrow something, found Mrs Little-So-Big with a burst washer and a roaring tap. It was getting light. People were cracking morning wood, carrying pigswill and paddling out to feed the poultry. Mr Little-So-Big sat in the least wet patch of the already sodden back kitchen, a candle near his feet on the floor, lacing his boots to go and run for help; while the two women with hands reaching out towards the noise, eyed with disdain the bullets of water bouncing madly from the sink all over everything.

"What're we to do?" screamed Mrs Little-So-Big.

"Tie a scooped out potato over ur," yelled the neighbour. "Miss Plant's passed away."

"Yes, I do know she 'as for I saw nurse go to Misery's. Oh, 'urry you an' get yer boots knotted and go and fetch somebody. No, Nance, I yen't doing anything fancy for meself. Let it run till it do choke itself. Do you s'pose Mrs Webb do know? I bin to see if I could make her out but them weren't up."

"Oh, her's sure to know."

The candlelight swaying in the dank draught of the jet made the nimble lips and eyelids of the women twitch. And a cockerel crouching on the copper among a lot of sacks and boxes leapt dustily and rapped upon the whitening window. The daylight which was creeping upon them seemed to cling about their faces and hair, like a fleecy hood. They wrung their hands busily.

At last Mr Little-So-Big, tying an audible knot, jumped up, looked grievously at them, put on his hat, and then took it off again to go through the door.

"Him ought to live in a steeple," said his wife. "One thing though, the wind do keep 'is 'air short. Oh, come in, Mrs Webb."

"Why, what's up yere?"

An elderly thin woman, in a grizzled overcoat was stooping to put a milk tin on the doorstone. "Why don't you turn it off at the main?" she asked in a shy, rather invalidish voice, which went with her complexion and the sort of pedigree hat she wore.

"Come in – come inside. I've bin three times up the gy-arden to see if you was up. So Miss Plant's dead?" gabbled Mrs Little-So-Big.

"No!"

"Why, 'aven't you 'eard? It's as true as Satan's false. Yes. Nurse 'ave bin to Mr Misery's already."

Mrs Webb had sat down suddenly on a plain old chair, leaning on the table and arranging her hands finger by finger before her. A nervous colour came into her long cheeks, her eyes filled with tears. Childless, an orphan, a widow, she had been attached to Miss Plant. She had the pallid devoted face of those who naturally develop best in the shade of others. She wore their clothes – clothes which had "atmosphere" and a vague kind of dignity. Round her neck today she had a little fence of starched net, with posts of bone and a cameo brooch; she was as neat and clean in the early mornings, they said, as if she sat up all night watching that no dust fell on her. But for all her differences (and different she was beside their splashed broadly-shadowed bodies) she was as much one of them as were her speech and her brown sensible hands.

"Yes," said the neighbour. "Her's as dead as Sooner baint. Ain't it a pity 'twasn't the other one?"

Mrs Webb said nothing. She had a sensitive imagination for which common talk was inadequate, and her timid grief was real.

"Maybe Miss Allensmoore 'ool be sorry now," suggested Mrs. Little-So-Big. "If you do neglect to do things they do often turn on you at the end. Look at this tap! A was a-dripping all yesterd'y."

"When did Miss Plant pass away?" Mrs Webb asked.

"Sometime yesterd'y afternoon I'm told. Ah, poor soul! She's gone. I seen Nurse leaving."

Mrs Webb sat up, saying defiantly: "Well, I be glad for 'er sake: it were time. Her sufferings was bad."

"Ay, strangled by her own breath," declared the neighbour. "And 'twasn't only that ..." they cried, "what a life!"

"Such things. I wouldn't 'ave such things done," Mrs Little-So-Big said. "*I'm* not afraid to speak. 'Ow do you think that old baggage spent the night – the first night after Miss Plant died, mind you! Why, a-playing on them bagpipes till three in the morning. I do kna-ow because our Arthur 'eard 'er when 'e went up past after an early yowe 'e 'ad twinning. Ah."

There was a silence. They rested like people close to a weir breathing the cold, wild smell of running water. Mrs Webb thought of trees turning ashen, and the drifting, groping winds of yellow leaves. Like most people, she imagined it harder to die after the turn of the days. Miss Plant would never again hear bees in the orchards, the voices of skylarks, the shy singing of waters in the valleys. However, she had no proof Miss Plant had *ever* heard them ....

"Them's educated things though, them musical instruments as Miss Allensmoore do play," the neighbour was saying, "spite of sounding like our owld cat a'spaggin' the Vicar's. Some folks do say her's a cleverer woman than us working class do realize."

"What of it! 'Er be an old turnip for all that and can't 'ave no heart for anything 'uman," retorted Mrs Little-So-Big, "no education can't make up for that, nor change it. Clever! 'Er's no more clever than a dog as has bin brought up to yet [eat] bread and butter and chocolate and fish paste. It's a dog for all that, any road, yen't it? I say this: you do kna-ow, Mrs Webb, after what you told us. Is it educated to sit on top of a great fire a-frying yerself, and let a body die upstairs without so much as a match? Come on now, Mrs Webb, be it?"

"Pah, education! If that's it I'll wear me eye in a sling," the neighbour said very angrily.

Mrs Webb didn't answer. Nervously she danced her fingers on the table. Mrs Little-So-Big sneezed and wrung her nose in her apron. The cock again scuffled and gave a dusty crow. He struggled for the light and the bright shadow on the water in the butt outside the window. And there suddenly was nothing in place of the cataract. The jet ceased, the tap coughed.

"George 'as turned it off at the main! Now what am I to fill the copper with? Oh, whatever do us women marry for? If I'd another chance I wouldn't pick George out o' a field o' turnips."

"I want me breakfast," said Mr Little-So-Big, walking in.

"'Aven't you brought somebody with you? Oh, you 'aven't. Well then, you can go and look for yer breakfast somewhere else. 'Ow am I going to fill the kettle?" his wife demanded.

"There's a bucketful outside," said Mr Little-So-Big faintly, "I pumped it."

"Oh, tha did? George, where was Miss Plant's part? Where did she come from?"

"I dunno. I never yeard anything about 'er except that daft walk to London she done once, years ago. 'Twasn't from yere she done it, mind. Ah. 'Oo do kna-ow if she done it all?"

"Oh yes, she went to London," said Mrs Webb, "yes, that's true. She told me herself."

"She did?" The two women looked at her sharply. She had been several times to sit with Miss Plant while she was ill. It was possible she had the secret. There was, they knew, always a secret when anybody died. Especially a woman like Miss Plant, who had never known people. But Mrs Webb's face was empty. They saw that and went on mutually on a more monotonous level.

"Ah. Yes. Time and agen – yes, time and agen, I 'ave said there weren't anything *to* her. No, as you mid say, there weren't nothing *to* 'er. But that jaunt to London, that's true –"

"As I do kna-ow. Our Arthur, 'e asked 'er once. She said, 'Ah, but that was long ago!' So 'e said, 'What you done it for, Miss Plant?' 'Love and scenery,' she said. That was what she said, love and scenery."

"Eh? Did she now? Did 'er s'y that? Poor thing, 'er 'asn't 'ad a lot."

"Tchah – women!" Mr Little-So-Big puffed, and he wrung the cockerel's neck in a decided but rather inattentive manner.

"All right, all right, George. It yen't me as you're strangling," reproved his wife. "Give yer mind to it, do. 'Tain't as if the bird'll 'elp yer. Ah, if she said that there must a' been a man."

"I've always thought so," said Mrs Webb sadly.

"Huh! It must a' bin Adam then, 'twas so long ago," the brisk neighbour countered, her eyes spell-bound and her deep pink, old-fashioned workbag of a face gathered tightly round her mouth. "Miss Plant must a' bin forty or fifty a score years ago, I'll be bound. Not," she calculated, "not as any a host of women don't go queer in middle life, as we do kna-ow."

"Ay."

"Ah."

"Oh, they do." As they sighed, bracingly, the clock struck. The neighbour stepped startlingly out of a pool, and Mrs Little-So-Big seizing a house flannel said she mid as well mop up.

"I must do up me fire and make me a seven o'clock pudding," said Mrs Webb, rising. And they separated candidly.

A seven o'clock pudding was a recipe for a mixture of currants, apples, suet and flour. It was called that because it was supposed to take all the time from seven o'clock until noon to cook. But it was long after eight when Mrs Webb sat down in her own kitchen to take off her hat after she had carefully rolled up the blind. Her dog, which had a mouth like red meat, yawned and came and lay down on her feet. Mrs Webb patted him and then she sat with a sedate gravity on her face worrying a little over what she had told people at different times. She *had* been angry – yes there was no doubt. But she had no wish to set anybody against Miss Allensmoore. It wasn't as if Miss Plant had ever *said* anything. Only the eagerness with which she had exclaimed "Gloves – I should *love* them. My hands get so cold –" Only that. And yes – but it wasn't much – hadn't she said, "I don't like music, and I don't like cats"? She certainly had, for Mrs Webb perfectly remembered it.

That cold bedroom, Mrs Webb breathed. And Miss Plant with only a faded old-rose velveteen coat round her shoulders! While downstairs Miss Allensmoore had a fantastic great fire, trained up sticks like some gorgeous climbing flower, right up the chimney. Hadn't she seen her sitting there with her bare legs and her sleeves pushed up, with her fat, soft flesh that looked as if it had been mixed with yeast, all naked, and flushing? Selfish and cruel, that's what she was, and didn't she deserve to be disliked? At any rate, it didn't matter surely? Unless – unless it would have grieved Miss Plant?

Mrs Webb was uneasy. Not that Miss Allensmoore seemed the one to care or even to notice. Nance and Ellen had been comic, but it wasn't funny really, what they meant. Hostile feelings in the village could be ugly. And ugliest when it was no more than a look .... One look, from everybody.

She had unconsciously gathered up a tiny ball of wool – green, the remnant left over from those sad bright gloves, and she rolled it round and round in her palms until it was moist and had a clinging sticky feeling. Tears came into her hazel eyes. Miss Plant had had such lovely eyes! When the lids were quivering, flickering their crescents of lashes against gaunt cheek and brows, they had reminded her of butterflies in summer. It was in summer Miss Plant had walked to London, she'd said. When she told her that Mrs Webb had seen her in a flourish of dust, dragging past the brambles with their thick pink and white blossom, along some highway hedgerow. And then perhaps stooping to wash her face and hands in a roadside stream with a lovely little fish-shape of clear pebbles underneath the water ....

In this way, and in others, she had often "seen" Miss Plant. She had always interested her imagination. Sensitive, tender, romantic Mrs Webb, pictured her going those hundred and thirty-seven miles to meet the unheard-of man she adored. Walking because she was afraid to go faster with the fragile words she carried. Looking slowly and quietly about her with her shy, cool, light brown hair stirring, at the earth's monopoly of green ....

"Love and scenery," said Mrs Webb, feeling for the flour. "Love and scenery."

It was strange how certain she had always been of Miss Plant's slow errand long ago, even though she had never before heard her own admittance. It was strange how she guessed at a dominant feeling taken there, a passion which had kept her there, in spirit ever since.

When she had asked Miss Plant why she had gone the answer had been she had forgotten. Mrs Webb wished she hadn't heard that. If she had sounded bitter and suffering it would have been all right, but she hadn't – she looked and spoke as if she *had* forgotten and was indifferent at it. She was, of course, very near death, though.

London! That was a superstitious long way. Once the women of the countryside had collected themselves and taken a trip there in a char-à-banc. They had seen St Paul's and the Zoo, and at the end, the Tower. "Just a broken-down castle like any other round yere," had been Mrs Little-So-Big's comment. No one remembered anything very distinctly. The hoardings, the banks of faces, the number of people in a Ladies, a shower, after which one of them had sat down on a seat in the park and dried her shoes with a paper bag – those had been their individual memories, for they weren't old-fashioned enough to be at all aghast, and found London, as a matter of fact, far more like their own cities than they could have guessed.

But Mrs Webb again was different. She remembered looking at some people sitting on the steps of St Paul's and wondering if by chance Miss Plant had once sat there to rest and listen to the misty whirr of the world. And at the Tower she thought she had never seen, anywhere, brighter April grass. And (this was queerest of all) when they told her some great man had walked across it to have his head cut off, she had seen not a figure out of a story, but poor Miss Plant, in her old brown burberry, the worsted shawl drawn over her stained white hair, wandering over to the tragic corner as she wandered up and down the hedge the farmer wouldn't cut. She *saw* her. She seemed to quaver across the air, across the sunshine, weaving herself, as it were, *behind* the April light.

Coming home, Mrs Webb remembered she had taken off her hat and gone to sleep and dreamed Miss Plant was in the next seat, asleep too and leaning on her. Odd, she thought, to dream that someone else was asleep! Odder still that the time should come when she was telling the dream to Miss Plant. Oh dear, she wished she had gone to see the poor woman long before! But she hadn't liked to: it seemed rather presumptuous, for they weren't "ordinary" folk, and besides Miss Allensmoore was formidable, and, she had been told, unfriendly. But Mrs Little-So-Big was right: what you neglected turned on you at the end. It made her weep now, to think how solitary Miss Plant must have been. There was something – yes there was – in the way she had jumped at the offer of the gloves, in the tone in which she said she didn't like music – that made Mrs Webb consider whether she wasn't more like one of themselves really? Only she had got marooned with Miss Allensmoore, who didn't encourage people to be neighbourly and who would, now she was left alone, probably end up as one of those queer women who are found dead one day, dressed in newspaper, after they have shut themselves up for years.

"With seven days' milk sour on the doorstep," Mrs Webb exclaimed. The picture was dreadful and she felt quite sorry for Miss Allensmoore, even while remembering the weeks, when alert with indignation, she had waited only for the chance word to speak her mind. But Miss Allensmoore had utterly defeated her by her silence and her acceptance of things. She sat, or she walked about prodding the garden, and that was all. She had a way of standing in the lane just outside the gate with one hand just lifted as if to seize even a robin's twist of song, and catch it, as one squeezes a gnat. She was listening, anyone could see. She listened to every sound as if it were news. And she leant forward meanwhile in the attitude of one who is prepared to grab anything that comes close enough. At Mrs Webb she even smiled one day when the wind was coming out of the garden, swinging the gate like a white curtain in a window. The smile was even more remote than her speechless indifference to the visitor.

When the pudding was on boiling, peacefully knocking at the saucepan lid in a subdued and proper manner totally opposite to the peremptory frenzies of Miss Allensmoore's fierce creations, Mrs Webb went and peeped through the window into her orchard. The south-west breeze was blowing, the bare boughs all but knotted against the pane, were full of the village notes of blackbirds and thrushes, and her troop of hooligan young hogs was galloping crazily over the grass under the trees. The weather was yielding, the snow would be melting off the hills, and there would be water over the road for Miss Plant's funeral without a doubt.

It was in that orchard, walking up and down, she had knitted most of the gloves, while keeping an eye on a hen who had a mind to lay in other folk's hedges. For several afternoons after having a wash and doing up her grate, she had walked and twinkled her needles until it was time to go indoors again to get her nephew's cooked tea ready. She had knotted the last stitch there, close to the old perry pear and then she had brought them indoors to sew on their backs, at the table, by lamplight, the sprightly woolly flowers that were to bloom in the grave.

Miss Plant must have been *used* to cold hands, Mrs Webb told herself, in tears again, so that the orchard looked all blurred and warped through the shrunk glass. And the fact that she was apparently determined to be *buried* in Mrs Webb's gift showed that it was not so much for themselves she wanted them as for what they represented. Friendship. Company, Sympathy. Although she had cried joyously when Mrs Webb promised to make them. "They'll be pretty too ...."

Mrs Webb thought they were pretty. Not that she had ever seen Miss Plant wearing them, for she grew worse very suddenly as it happened, and after they were finished and taken to the door she had never seen Miss Plant again. She had given them to the nurse and the nurse had brought back the message: "Thank you. They're a great comfort. She says she'll never take them off. She wants to be buried in them, she says ...."

"Is she – dying then?"

The nurse nodded: "She may rally but I don't think it's likely now."

So Mrs Webb had gone away to wait for the event which was in spite of her foreknowledge such a shock to her. Often and often she thought of Miss Plant lying there under the old dark army blanket which gave her long body the look of a rough image dabbled out of earth. She had known Miss Plant was dying – oh yes. Hadn't she told herself there was a look no one could ever mistake particularly when the face of the sick person was seen in profile? Remembering this and the hair like glass or ice, and the strange fluttering eyes, the shape of which was an intensity in itself, Mrs Webb felt how easy it would be to see Miss Plant's ghost.

Those eyes! They focussed the tiny room, furnished it; and Miss Plant herself became in some strange way only the brink of them. As she grew weaker, their characteristic passionate stare seemed to withdraw further and further. Rather than being fixed on distant visions, they appeared to be retreating from everything they gazed on. She would lie and look at the small, low window at the foot of the bed where the wind flopped in the shred of coarse white lace. Close to her hand would be a saucerful of peeled orange left by the nurse, her silver spectacles and the book of Common Prayer. Scales off the white-washed rafters fell in among her hair – thin brittle flakes which Mrs Webb would comb out, and pick from the bed-clothes. Then one day when she was doing nothing at all and thought Miss Plant was asleep she had suddenly been asked if she would read the Litany. That was the time she remembered best. She had gone very red and hasty as she said, Oh dear, to tell the truth she wasn't a very grand reader.

"Not even with my glasses on. And without them, well, I can't read a bull's head from a duck's foot as I say. I expect I haven't been as well educated as you. We all do say you must be very clever to live with a woman like Miss Allensmoore."

"Why?" Miss Plant asked, as if she were astonished.

"Well, I mean she – Miss Allensmoore as do play such educated music! Not that I like it if you can understand me. It's above me. A good hymn now – some of us like that. That's about all. Yes, you must be very clever indeed and I'm sorry I can't read to you. But if it's the Litany you want I don't need to. Shall I repeat it to you?"

Miss Plant looked wondering for a moment. Then she closed her eyes and the two women began to mutter the sorrowful rhythmic words. But in the middle Miss Plant suddenly opened her eyes again and in them was a cunning, confidential look – something sleek and furtive and yet rather defiant.

"I don't like music," she said shortly: "And I don't like cats," she added. "I wonder if anybody *ever* thinks of me?" she speculated faintly.

Mrs Webb looked down, sorting her fingers as if they were skeins and making a row of them on her knee. "I dreamt about you once," she said. "It was the night we were coming home from our tour in London. I dreamt you were asleep next to me in the bus."

"Music's too good for me," said Miss Plant bitterly, "and too queer. Did you know I walked to London once?"

"I have heard you did. Whatever did you do that for, Miss Plant?"

"I've forgotten," said Miss Plant. "I've forgotten everything about it except that it was one summer, and I used to walk along in the dusk because it was cooler. I saw owls. They were like moths," she sighed. "There were bats too and I was always afraid they'd get in my hair. Tell me, Mrs Webb, do I talk in my sleep?"

Mrs Webb shook her head. "I don't know. I 'aven't heard you. Why?"

"I feel as if I do. I hear myself. I can't change it though –"

"You're free to talk in your sleep if you want to," Mrs Webb nodded hotly.

"I saw an old woman," Miss Plant mumbled; "it was once when I'd lost the road and I went round to the back of a big house to ask the way. I thought I ought to go to the back for that, but I was so frightened always of dogs! I'm very independent, really, you know and I didn't like asking. I saw such a little old woman, pumping. She had on a skull cap. Yes. A big blue apron with pockets and a skull cap. I couldn't make her understand at all. She kept saying, 'The mistress is round the garden, feeding the chickens if you'll just step that way.' No, not step, stroll, was what she said. I've often thought she might have been me. How funny to remember that. I'm sure there were only the two of them living there and they both ate their meals in the kitchen together. And it was such a big house! All the beautiful rooms must have been shut up. Lovely furniture and curtains I'm sure. Eh, don't you think so?"

"Very likely," said Mrs Webb compassionately. "Maybe you dreamt it. I know I remember what I dream much better than anything else."

Mysterious and rambling, Miss Plant shed no intentional secret but lay there talking and letting the irrational light of her sick memory fall here and there on what must have been a coherent life once. And filled with pity, Mrs Webb tried to arrange her in the bed, to make her eat the eggs she carried to the cottage, warm from the nest, to please and soothe her. Never once did Miss Allensmoore come upstairs. If she had it would have been she who would have been the stranger, Mrs Webb thought. And she calculated how she would get up and where she would stand when Miss Allensmoore came to the bed. Glimpses she had of her, as she went out, sitting on the fender in the kitchen, nursing her foot. Inscrutable glimpses. That was all. Except the smell of burnt toast, and the sound of the sick woman sighing over herself upstairs.

Yes, it was quite warm for January, said Mrs Webb, going to look out of her door to see if anyone were about. There would be water over the road, surely. She leant far out, right over her door-stone. She heard the slow shuddering calls of the ewes with early lambs, and a wind which was swift sunlight touched the land as with a white flame. And wasn't that Mr Misery coming up the hill on his motor-bicycle? Yes. He fled past, popping, the silver sidecar flashing a sunspot in her eyes. She listened for the engine to stop, and it did, at Miss Allensmoore's.

Sunlight eddied round the cottage. Through wiry curtain and dusty glass it shone and settled. Under the thinnest shifting film of shadow, it bubbled and stirred like a spring in the wall at the head of Miss Plant's bed. Presently Mr Misery's stooping head and shoulders obliterated it.

Downstairs, Miss Allensmoore lolled, waiting, turning her head with a turgid movement on its thick neck as she looked for the undertaker to appear. She had planned the arrangements. No relations, no expense. A walking funeral. But the weather worried Mr Misery. Did she know floods were already out in the lower meadows, he inquired? Gumboots, snapped Miss Allensmoore, and if there were any mourners, which besides herself there wouldn't be, they could paddle. Personally – here she looked preoccupied and Mr Misery glanced about him.

"What do you do with yourself all day?" he asked.

"Call the cattle home," she said lazily. She smiled in her dormant way and added, poking her foot at a cat: "No doubt you're used to domestic hurly-burlies. Spring cleaning and all that. Now I detest all that sweeping and dusting and polishing. Scrubbing occasionally or washing a floor over I don't mind. In fact it's a sort of pleasure to me."

"You don't give yourself a treat very often, then," Mr Misery observed: "'ard on yourself, aren't you?"

"Witty, aren't you?" she retorted: "it's your calling, I suppose."

After she had got rid of *him* she went out and picked the snowdrops. She took them upstairs, putting them in a cup on a small table that looked as if it were made of wet hay. She sat down with a drowsy sigh, blinking as she watched a sunbeam dazzling itself in the mean little mirror. Soon all would be quietly over ....

She gave Miss Plant's feet quite an affectionate pat.

A few days later, in her shaggy black, with her healthy wide open gaze which seemed to refuse to mourn, Miss Allensmoore followed the coffin of her friend alone as far as the village. The bearers *were* in gumboots, and, listening to them going champ, champ, champ, along the lane, she smiled to herself.

"A lot of melancholy indiarubber elephants," she thought, delighted.

But when they came to the village where glass, stone, and slates were giving back a greyish reflection of the flat afternoon light, there was quite a crowd waiting. Quietly, and rather drolly, as if someone else had made up her mind for her, Mrs Webb came forward carrying a wreath of moss and aconites which she had made the night before. Mr and Mrs Little-So-Big and one or two more who were standing by, also wandered up and began vacantly to follow until gradually a funeral shaped itself under the serious and wand-like gestures of Mr Misery, over whose tall black hat and deft flexions, Miss Allensmoore's ironic eye perpetually tripped in spite of her straightest efforts.

"What can they all be looking so peculiar about? Surely it's what's called a 'happy release'," she reflected, twirling the identical snowdrops, laughing a little in her bottom chin as she saw aside, other figures trying to catch up. There was a child, alone, who seemed happy, who seemed to think that such a procession must mean a celebration, and who began most respectfully to dance, while all the rest walked silently, with a touch of fame, with transparent gaze and opened lips, as in a story, down to the edge of the thin water where its blue and brownness flowed over the lane.

There they paused a moment as long as a leaf might take to sidle to earth from the top of a tall tree, before the bearers' loaded feet stepped into the flood.

"Oh, will they be drownded?" the child quavered, in her high drawling voice.

As clearly as if the coffin had been glass, Mrs Webb saw the green hands curled in Miss Plant's breast .... she scrounged up her skirts. The water was in truth hardly deeper than the heel of her shoe, but psychologically she seemed to require emphasis.

Miss Allensmoore stopped. What revelation possessed her she didn't, for a moment, fathom; it was something *warranted*, something far too assured in Mrs. Webb's action which convulsed her into perceiving, for the first time, the people who surrounded her.

She stopped. She would *not* share this absurd funeral with that woman or anybody else.

"Can't go any further," said Miss Allensmoore. "Here, will you take these?" she addressed Mrs Webb directly, with a most uncharacteristic courtesy. And she looked past her at the coffin now being slowly borne up the hill, with a terrible expression on her face, like the obstinacy of death. In that second her sight became myriad. She saw Miss Plant, who had somehow at the last moment contrived to amass an undreamed hostility against her. She saw the stupid, avid stares, the dancing child moving only her hands and her eyelids, in her mimicry of joy, the church steeple poking through a hill like a giant darning needle, and five white and golden hens pricking proudly over a swell of winter wheat .... She saw the onyx clouds, the beautiful wind that came so suddenly that it was carved like lightning in the silver water fields ....

Mrs Webb didn't turn, so the snowdrops fell on the water and gaily nudging one another, rippled into the ditch.

"Well!" cried Miss Allensmoore furiously. Trumpets of rage and grief sounded for her. She went so pale that many of the small crowd thought she would faint. But not she, not Miss Allensmoore. There, in the middle of them she stayed, staring with paralysed eyes until the coffin and its few followers were round the bend. Then she moved, and prodding and pushing the road behind her with her umbrella, she climbed to a point from which she could see them creeping to the churchyard across the ribbed fields.

The church gate was open making a gap in the wide stone wall that was flung like a noose round the top of a hill. And the coffin was being borne forwards like the huge fated black stone that was to fill up the space. On and on they crept ....

"That woman –" Miss Allensmoore said to Miss Plant. "That woman! You *talked* to her. Coming up day after day, lying and spying. Both of you up there *talking*. And who *knows?*" cried she passionately, "who's to judge? What *could* I do? What use is a wise friend to a fool? People. I hate them! I'd sooner shut meself in and tar my windows than ever endure the sight of one of 'em ever again."

As she stood on the hill, watching Nora Plant's body being taken to the earth, it was useless telling herself she was going back to silence, useless to say the uproar was over and there would be no more crashes, no more fidgetings, no more nurses and neighbours coming. For the foundation on which she had suffered these things to be, was gone, and nothing was significant any more, and perhaps never would be again. Miss Plant had, she believed, destroyed that profound, if secretly weary, fidelity which had bound them, and in so doing had revealed the astonishing reality of her own quaint affection. She could not speak: her outcry was mental only. There, leaning on her umbrella, she stood, speechless, as when, with her oboe, she turned towards silence with the first low summons to the hordes of sound, as when, all those years ago Miss Plant had come to London just to say to her, "I can no longer bear to live away from you."

The Ruin

ESSY stood perfectly still under the sycamore trees, looking with wide, reflecting eyes at the stream. And the breeze furling her skirt, suddenly died away, or as she thought, folded round her insteps as if it had been some light, caressing material which she had carefully loosened and let fall before stepping entranced into the sparkling outburst of water on her left, or the beautiful easy world of the Sun on her right:

"Oh, oh, Gabriel, isn't it lovely? Oh dearie, look, do look. *What* water. Did you ever see such clearness? What makes it so clear? All those golden and green and blue pebbles overlapping! And the trouty-brown ones. You can see every one. It's like scales."

Her husband lifted his head abruptly from where he was kneeling on the opposite bank, hanging over, his hands hidden in the pallid primroses.

"It's not a river, it's a fish disguised as a river," he called: "and what enormous white primroses. They make me think of a cool dairy and winter butter. It's the shade that smells of water ...."

"Cool, cool shade, the colour of brown hair," Jessy thought.

Gabriel, on his knees, moved, and laughed, as the green earth seemed to melt its cold shock of life against his warm, sunburnt flesh:

"By gum, this grass is as cold as a dog's nose," he shouted with the breathlessness of a bather: "Beautiful – beautiful to feel," he added, staring across at her with his long hazel eyes which, except in moments like this, still looked fevered with the dryness of that overseas station where, he had told her, the shadows were like cracks in walls that were bursting with heat. Walking hand in hand all afternoon, or else narrowly apart for the pleasure of calling each other, they had got off the bus miles away. Together again, together again, each said to self. They were together. Their worlds had fused; or rather for him the world which with her he saw and comprehended, and which, except for starveling glimpses he had forgone, had come back from behind the false, hateful, manufactured appearance of things more vivid, more significant than ever. For Gabriel, Jessy thought, there had been nothing, except a few rare, irrepressible aspects of nature in the human sum, to depend on. And Gabriel was no more interested in human beings than herself. Beauty was beauty: but he would rather see it in mountains than in the faces and souls of men.

So there had only been the sea, and in the letters which they bandied, that delight which she nursed for him and for herself, suspended, yet animate and mortal, and inevitably of course, more falsely related than experienced. Those hundreds of hard letters which had taken so long even to scribble, which supposing she had ever wanted to, she couldn't have helped writing to him, groaning as she was under the pressure of a solitary vision!

For there was no one else. No one except Gabriel, whose eyes and whose mind were focussed exactly, as it were, over or behind her own.

"Of us two," she meditated, "it's he who has the strongest power to interpret. Though as *I'm* the writer, no-one knows it except myself. Oh, my imagination needs him dreadfully." Even now, so close to him, looking across at him as he rose and strode away, she wondered how she could ever have expressed on paper this delicious sensuality when all the flowering readiness of the earth, the grace of all she touched and saw, seemed to loiter and sway in the mirror of her living being. Yes, from the smallest, flat oak, yellow with encurling leaf, distended with dark tracery, like branched and glimmering gothic, to the distant shine of the mountains themselves.

But now, Jessy knew, there was no need to capture. He saw. They were together perfectly. So that even in turning, as she did, along her own path, and forgetting him she had a sort of three-cornered sight of him out of an eye and a half, slipping away in the mottle of leaf and sunshine, as neat and quiet as an animal which no purpose fussed.

His walk, Jessy was proudly sure, was like no other man's: as most men could not, he combined almost a poet's detachment with his own fervour and yet moved smoothly, scarcely shaking the mosaic of green leaves in which the landscape finally lost itself on the far bank of the beck.

Gabriel neither kicked, nor stumped, nor hurried. Jessy, sighing with pleasure, moved on, her alert eyes noticing the lichens, the bloom of cherry petals fallen on the turf, the broken-glass water tossing over its bleached bed.

She picked up a silky pebble. It struck the stream with the note of a mandolin, and out of the circle of drops shot the dark-brown tongue shape of a fish. The breeze, reaching over her shoulder, blew out her custard-yellow scarf, with its chiffony smell of the town, its dead perfume of the shop window; while like bubbles, the light green branches swelled and rose ....

"Gabriel!"

And far away, from the anonymous oblivion: "Jessy!"

"Oh Jessy, a bullfinch. Look ...."

"Where?"

"There ...."

In the same excitement he had cried out a thousand times – at the hawthorn in bud, at oak apples, the lake reflected in the misty mirror of the heat. Everything was a cry to him.

"No, it's a chaffinch. I think a bullfinch's breast is much more brilliant and darker. It's more *rose*. And doesn't it have a black cap?"

"Does it? Ah, how *very* quiet he is. I say, isn't he tame?" Gabriel smiled, observing the sleek, silver-fawn of the belly from underneath, the madder of the breast, and the eye which flashed at each slight twitching of the head. "He's arch. He knows he's out of reach of everything except our admiration! But, now I can see why that chap thought he'd seen a robin."

"What?" she asked bewildered, before she remembered how in one letter he had told her he had been arguing with a sailor who had sworn to seeing a robin in Malta. "Oh," she said, vaguely, and for a moment in her eyes was a weary expression. And the chaffinch flew away as Gabriel jumped the beck and took her hand and asked her if she were tired. No, she wasn't *tired*, she answered astonished.

"But wouldn't you like to sit down, darling?"

"Why, no! Let's go on," she cried, turning on him eyes so remote and reminiscent that she had almost to bring herself to see him. And when she had assembled him from the bright, basking hordes of spring, it was strange how nearly a figure of a dream he appeared, with a quality of being once seen and eternally pondered on – as if, in fact, he were not there, but only his memory. This was what her gaze was saying as it fell on him. He seemed not unaware, and for this or some other reason he dropped her hand

and looked away, as if he would not venture into the region of her eyes.

"Gabriel," she said.

"What?"

She wanted to say, "You feel everything I feel, don't you? Just the same as ever."

"Nothing," she said: "Poor Gabriel."

"Why 'poor', love?" he smiled.

"Oh, you know."

They walked on, silently, the sunlight falling on them like a meditation. The beck grew narrower, dryer, the pasture poorer, the rocks and boulders paler. Rivulets of stone flowed through the land. The sky was all one dust of blue, and like a monomania came the strange, shimmering, lonely warbling from somewhere far off in the rushes.

"People might not exist," he said, softly, solemnly. And then he chuckled:

"My ducky walks about like a naturalist," he said as she pecked along, nose down in her whiff of chiffon scarf. "You are silly," she said. Thank God he is silly, she thought.

"Silly? You're always saying I'm silly. Why am I? Anyway, I can make toast."

He could. He could do a great deal more. He could do anything, and he didn't mind anything. No need to keep in your absurdities when you were with him. He disliked facts, Jessy knew, except those which were fantastic. It was as though he had chosen to illuminate his brain with candles rather than the high-powered efficiency of electricity. Even a night-light he would prefer to that terrible clown-white pseudo day. And Jessy had a flash in which she saw a crouching Gabriel, with a candle in a bottle, groping over cavern walls after picnic-makers' poems, while above his head, in a dark landscape, cobwebbed with high tension cables, a race of unlaughing men read the mammoth bones of swift civilizations.

And Gabriel turning and seeing her touch her hair, almost winced at the way the gesture brought back the way she would come into the bedroom just after they were married, and sit down at the mirror and give her head just a nervous sort of push, and then walk out to tea, or somewhere. He saw her, a thin woman with shreds of arms which she waved at him: a person who was irritable, and talkative and secret, and who never cried ....

"Witchcraft and ghosts," she laughed aside. She remembered her brother's astonished disapproval after an evening when Gabriel had sat on his bed and talked about nothing but vampires. Of course, Thomas said, it was all right, and Gabriel was a good fellow – it was just being Welsh and all that. As a matter of fact, it was Thomas who had drawn the queer little map in Gabriel's pocket, which looked like an egg and a fly-whisk, and which was to help them find the ruin they were seeking in this countryside, new to them both ....

Change? No one so changeable *could* change. Oh, those lovely, blue, blue pebbles! And the great purple tent of a mountain pitched over the fells!

"Why," she heard herself say: "but .... But Gabriel – we .... Where are we? Listen. I've just noticed something. How queer! Gabriel – the river's running the wrong way. Look. I *wondered* what it was. Don't you see?

"Is it?" said he. "It can't be." He did not glance back.

"But it *is*," said Jessy, "unless it's another river. And we can't get out across the footbridge because I stopped there yesterday on the way to the village. There's a waterfall just below the bridge and the water runs *towards* the road. It's .... wonderful. Gabriel! I want to know why." She stood, turning her face this way and that:

"The water's coming against us," he muttered, and she stood there moving her hands, as if she were unwinding a spell.

"Come on, darling": and at last she came on, her hand curled round his finger, their feet making a sound on the whin and heath like horses grazing. But she spoke no more. "He'll see," she thought, "by and by." Across the brooks of rock, by a yellow and brown path through the gorse, ambled a group of cows and calves, slowly driven by a hobbling woman in a cone cap, with a fleshless branch in her hand, and three liquid-leaping greyhounds, like a frieze running by her feet.

"Must be milking time," said Gabriel. Then all at once he began pulling her, and pointing:

"There it is! That must be it. No – half a minute – I'll have look at the map – yes. That's it. Hunter's How."

They ran. It was green. It had small, green meadows and stone walls. The blunted garden was full of currant and gooseberry bushes, and grass, and trees, and the smell of desertion. But it wasn't rank. Wind had kept it clean and bare.

The cottage had pale grey walls, and its scabby, silvery roof was in thick, scaly chunks. A squat door inside the porch was locked by an enormous padlock of some modern metal which looked like zinc, new and stainless. Ashes and sycamores, twisted and dwarfed, topped the chimney. From them fell morsels, shards of buds, crumbs of flowers, a faint slow-falling rainbow, impalpable almost as a perfume, dusting the oblong blue stone which was laid like a footmat before the porch.

Gabriel, swinging silently on the balls of his toes looked without comment, his eyes running over it, describing it to him, while he kept a silence like a wise child's. Here it was at last, the two hundred mile away ruin which they had hoped they might patch and prop together for a home. Perhaps later on, when they were better off, rebuild. Fifty green and brown acres of fell and water land with it. Jessy thought, if I ever have to live here it'll be what I'd wish. A lovely, lovely place. But we don't even know if it's for sale.

In an angry gesture she lifted her thin arms, clenched her fists, as if she were stretching a concertina, and wailed:

"Fancy, *fancy* letting it go like this! How wicked!"

"You'd need a car. And there's no road pass. They built it like a fort," said Gabriel: "Ducky, think of the winter. Think of the wind and the snow! Why ...."

"I couldn't see it without thinking of them," she said.

Gabriel was looking at the trees. Already the dust of their flowers was on his bright black hair. "They're a mime," he declared.

"They are," she answered, thinking how Thomas might have precautioned her, but how differently he would have put it. And she slowly circled, shivering a little, noticing the absurd, distorted size of that door chain and its lump of lock. Really it seemed almost as if they'd handcuffed it, she decided.

They walked round close to the walls, trying their eyes against the horny glass of the small, low-placed windows. The nettles and docks mingled their smell with the sweet, hot scent of the currant leaves which, unfluttering, hung round the pale, dripping clusters of greenish white fruit. Butterflies jigged above the grass and trails of fuzzy grey wool, hung mistily from the rotten stump of a branch.

"They keep it to store things. I can see a bicycle. There's a copper, Gabriel – look. And there's a fire-place with a bread oven. Oh dear, the rafters have fallen in here. I was thinking of mammoth's bones just now."

"Yes, they are," peeped Gabriel, "hmm – I think it's a stone stair. I love a stone stairway, but those flags look damp to me. I say, surely nobody *lives* here? I can see up the stairs and there's a bed. Hasn't any bedding, though. It looks like a sort of loft ... oh, a drying-up cloth – and a blue jug – there, on that hook – see? Someone *does* come here then."

"Let me see. Oh, I do wish we could get in. It seems a long way to come to be shut out."

"Oh well," sighed Gabriel, backing, "my word, the place does show the shape of the weather! Trees – everything as flat as it can make itself, even the chimney. It can't be once in a year you'd get a day as still as this up here. Well, I think I'll go round the buildings. I say, don't you feel somehow that's chaining the cottage in the place? Looks sort of taken prisoner, don't you think?"

And pointing to the padlock, without waiting for an answer, he walked away, booming, "By jove, what a crop of currants there's going to be. And the gooseberries ..." his voice went round a corner.

"That's just what I *was* thinking exactly," Jessy breathed in a small, aloud singsong. And she went quietly to sit down on the doorstone in the drowsy sunshine, murmuring, "Don't be long."

The greenness about her seemed to act upon her like closed eyelids: the grass, the doorway, the stone threshold, became, as it were, a picture in her mind. Many pictures. She felt herself in childhood. Only children felt the sun as she for this one afternoon was feeling it. As if she were a means to light and spirituality, and life and joy, and not an obstacle; the real sun, the sun that children see. Had Gabriel noticed them, she wondered, that little group she had watched through the bus window? A few girls, in long, poorish cotton dresses, following one who wore a cardboard gilt crown, their May queen. Their lighted faces. Their carelessness and certainty, as the bus went by, never even turning their heads from their loitering march, lifting and swinging their thin, bare arms, as they laughed and smiled at their own secret path through the concrete town. Had he seen? And could he have been moved as she had been by the reflection of their world? She thought it was then she had begun to open her eyes to life and sight.

She looked at the low, powerful roof, at the trees which made a shadow like a hole near the chimney end. The form of everything here suggested storm so vividly that the lack of it conveyed a loneliness which was outstanding in a way that no mere human desertion could ever be. The absence of an element made the lifelessness unnoticeable. Nothing human could fill the vacancy which brooded, waiting for shape and shapes to return. Children would play, would bide, romp, process indifferently and go away. But herself – and Gabriel? They had no children, and never would have any. But she no sooner made the effort to visualize their life here together, than she seemed to land, without any beginnings at a point somewhere near its end, where she was old and familiar with it all. A sense of prophetic past, as in myriad dreams, came over her without warning, so that it seemed she had already lived here many, many years. Smiling, she saw herself step out of the porch, an old woman carrying an earthenware bowl, its brown lip pressed into her breast, looking down on the stone where one afternoon, long ago, she had sat dreaming. Down on her knees, kneeling on her apron, went this Jessy, to pick the currants, breathing the spicy sweetness of the ruffled leaves, brushing the bits off her damp fingers ... from the byre, behind the wall came a cow's lowing, the hiss of a cleaning broom – the smell of baked cow dung, milk, and straw.

Gabriel called and she answered. She heard hasped doors rasping as he pulled them open, and his tread tramping the dry yard. Glancing along the eaves, she saw the row of grey rough-cast swallows' nests: "One year, I took an egg ...." The nests were quiet as a row of bee-hives in winter, and the pebble she threw fell silently into the grass. She would like to live here and savour life: taste the honey of the fell, see the swallows come back, build on a room where she could play her violin and Gabriel could write – a room in which she could forget every other she had ever hated. Suddenly, as she had seen in her own old age, she saw the threshold spotted with whitewash, the door open, and on a ladder, Gabriel in bleached blue overalls, dipping a thick creamy brush in the suspended bucket. Then all faded away except his image in the dusty blue, marvellously distinct, in the centre of her mind, in the centre of a picture of nowhere, a young man with bright hair, and an unbroken mouth, having no relationship to herself, mysterious, youthful, unconnected.

Gabriel stood before her, holding something out: "Look, what a beautiful thing."

It was a sheep's skull, horned, a gentle mask of bone, exquisitely subtle to touch.

"We'll take it with us," she said, stroking its smoothness, holding it against her. "It's some poor ewe which died lambing alone, I expect."

"Probably," he said. "It's lovelier than the loveliest carving I've ever seen, though. What curves! We'll hang it up." Jessy jumped up: "Let's go round the cottage again. Oh, Gabriel, do you like it? Do you think we could build on? There's not much room now, is there? I've been sitting there and seeing everything at once, all mixed." She suddenly realized he was talking:

"The buildings are in better repair than the cottage," he was saying. "I think they're used. Let's go now. My eyes feel twisted, I've peeked through so many cracks."

"It's a lovely place," said Jessy as they turned away: "I'm sure I'd love it, Gabriel. Wouldn't you?"

"Ah, but the ogre's away, remember," said Gabriel.

"Oh, the wind. I'd forgotten that. Yes ...."

"You'd be the first to hate it."

It was true: Gabriel would endure. The one who would grumble would be herself. She would grow irritable, would swear, shout, go into a frenzy. She confessed it.

"Besides," he was going on, "the inside looks very small and green. It would need a new roof, new floors. A lot would have to be done before one could live in it."

Aware of missing what he was telling her, she assured herself it didn't matter: in another moment he would surely say something which would, even if they never went there, give her the essence of the place forever.

"I wonder," said he, putting his hands to his brows, and gazing under them back at the cottage: "yes, it does – face the wrong way. If we *did* think of going there – one day – we should have to make new windows."

"But –" cried Jessy.

"How peculiar," she thought, "to hear him talking like this when I've lived there so long already!"

And she stared at him as if he were some new, wide countryside which she had never seen before. If it came to that, she wondered, with a shock, what had *he* seen? What mute country, what ruin, what river, oh, what world? The children, the piper in his fluted tartan, playing 'The Little Red Lark' to the bus queue? She dared not ask. And the Gabriel in the washed blue, with the bucket and the ladder, who was he? He seemed to smile, and bending from the rungs to laugh, nobody you know! She began to run through the buttercups, swinging the skull by a forefinger hooked through the eye socket. There, there at the corner of the field was the foot-bridge, the waterfall, and beyond, the lane, just as she remembered it.

"Now we shall see," she called. A car had been driven through the gate and lying on the grass were several people, smoking, with baskets, towels, and books thrown round. A brindled pug began to bark. There was a confusion of staring, whistling ....

"There," said she, standing still in the middle of the plank. "It *is* flowing towards the road. You were wrong, Gabriel."

"Go on, Jessy," said Gabriel, "I can't move. Wrong? What d'you mean? It flows exactly as I thought it would. Of course. What are you talking about?"

"It doesn't! I mean it does – you said –"

But Gabriel stalked through the people, got over the stile and only stopped in the lane to break some greenish blossom out of the hedge.

"You said it couldn't run that way!"

"I never did. Rubbish. Now listen. We were walking with the current, weren't we? Well, we are still. Now do you see?"

"We were walking *against* the stream," she said hotly.

"Certainly ...." She couldn't remember. She turned her hot, dazed face towards the river. Then she swung round and saw that Gabriel had the most extraordinarily distorted expression, at once sour and humorous, like a laugh turned inside out. He had branches of flowers in his arms, and he looked at her over them, over his shoulder, as a man looks at a woman who is being tiresome.

"Good heavens, how I bore him!" she thought, stupefied. "Gabriel," she gasped, "you know you said ..."

He didn't care. He wasn't interested. It didn't matter. But she was right, she told herself. It was most queer, and he either couldn't see it or didn't want to find out why it was. Now he was saying, don't be silly. Contour, he was saying. Configuration. Anyhow, it didn't matter. But he was explaining, teaching, homilizing like any one else. If he had had one he would have spread out an Ordnance Survey Map for Walking. Like Thomas.

Jessy glanced backwards in the direction of their wandering, at the stream, the unknown country. Good-bye, strange hills. Oh, stupid, stupid, dull life.

"I wish I could get away. I wish I could get away and be alone again," she thought. Anger darkened all around. Something had happened to them, indistinctly, slowly, terrifyingly, it had begun *there*. She looked at the ground and noticed that in the middle of the lane there grew a strip of thin, green grass, and that some of the flints had moss round them. Gabriel's arms were brimming with the bloom. She saw the edge of his lower lip against the glistening, pale mass, with its weary fragrance that reminded her of the air imprisoned in the loggias of certain expensive hotels. She saw in his depressed face, angry hollows, and the lashes, which, lifting from his dark brown cheeks, sped the glance away from her – from anything near her. And also she saw the silence in those eyes was not anything to be tempted or challenged, but was the incorruptible silence of the mind. Had her flashes of communication ever reached it, she asked herself. Sickened! She wondered whether this moment was just a moment, or a mimicry of always; and breaking, in a quick, wild way at a spray, she looked over the top of the hedge towards the ruin where she had rehearsed the wrong life, the wrong possibility .... The ruin which was, though so slightly hidden, out of their lives, as she guessed turning her eyes on Gabriel, for ever.

The Old and the Young

Their hands are deep in the hedgerows,
their faces are solemn with sun;
A moment ago I was with them,
A moment ago I was one.

The shrill of my childhood's language
beats round their heads like birds:
they have taken my country from me,
they have beckoned my singing words.

And left for mine only a murmur
within me, monotonous, sad
like a clock that is gently ticking
Time that I never had.

Part I

TILLY

T was afternoon in very early summer. The world was vigorous, flowery: the wind had a push in it.

Tilly Luce sat by her window, snipping the pearl buttons off a castaway shirt. A pair of small scissors was twisted on her silvery old hand, almost as if they were jewellery. She dropped each button carefully into an old tea canister on her knee, snipping slowly, for as she always explained to everybody, she never wasted anything.

"I throw nothing away, and so I need nothing," she used to say. And because Tilly's needs were frugal and her means sparse it worked very well. Her goings and comings were worn threadbare from habit, but at eighty-nine she had never experienced monotony.

The canister on her knee, the clock and the fire with its hob were the only ornaments in her parlour except a pin-cushion stuck with a star pattern of old-fashioned blue-bead-headed pins. (A neighbour found one of those pins in a tiny glass jar behind the window

147

shutter after Tilly's death and kept it for years.)

There was a delicate scent in the room of sunny woodwork and old black silk. It was the beginning of June, the season when the corn is heard hissing down the hedges and the Whitsun bosses are turning from palest lime-green to pure white.

Sometimes Tilly would stop unpicking stitches to look out of the window: when she did she saw the shadow of her chimney smoke blowing across the lane, pouring into the garden opposite through the iron edging that was like croquet hoops. Sometimes it almost seemed to slip under the crack of the door, and then again it would seem to be soaked up by the dusty ground, like the water the neighbours turned out of somersaulting pails.

At half past three Tilly took off her glasses, wiped them and wrapped them in a white handkerchief. She put on her walking clothes and got herself ready to go to the shop. This was an afternoon of nearly thirty years ago: nobody dresses like Tilly nowadays – there would not be anywhere they could buy their bonnets, beads and braid, their mantles shiny black as wet coal, or the soft-as-soot wool indoor shawl they wore to work in.

When she went to the shop she had to walk a long way down the footpath under the wall of the big house garden, beside the calm, wide main road through her village. She gathered up her skirts in her left hand, and paused with the other, as if she were going to shake hands with someone or perhaps point at a fine flower in one of the gardens. When she looked upward and saw a white gull floating above the river, the vacant hand lifted itself in vague motion and streams of black sunlight flowed down her mantle with the movement.

All sorts of slowness were on the road that day: at the bottom of the village, beyond Mrs Spring's shop, and The White Lion, a flock of sheep was contracting towards the Bridge; and at the top, outside the cornfactor's high door, a sleeping horse with a trolley wagon behind, had gone slack in its harness, and suddenly woke up, shaking the loose bit in its jaws. Very slowly a sack fell into the road and burst, and slowly too (more slowly than ever now) an unseen man laughed "Ho, ho, ho," till the lazy language of his laughter went all up and down the village, under the trees, and in the corners where the early roses were beginning to shake off dark red and dark gold bloom.

Ho, ho, ho: that was all. Tilly turned round. What for did any one want to laugh like that on a nice quiet day? – like a fist banging on a door, for all the world. *She* wanted to look. There were days in the autumn and winter when she felt blind; but on such a one as this, when she sat close to the light, smelling the wallflowers in her garden patch, the sight of her youth seemed to come back to her.

Tilly lived mostly on oatmeal and tea. She bought a pound of each at Mrs Spring's, scooping them across the slippery counter, and paying for them with money which she took out of a pocket in her sateen skirts. She and Mrs Spring did not say anything. They exchanged an elderly smile. Mrs Spring knitted with bright pink wool: the packets were ready cornered and tied and she only nodded at them and then pushed the coins in a little side drawer with a slur of her fat elbow. She was a woman who had moles on her face, two, prickly ones, like thistles and she also had eyebrows like hedges and sawn-off prickly hair. In the end she was obliged to unwind her fingers because her customer wanted two penn'orth of white peppermints. Half she would eat and with the other half she would wait for the children coming out of school, standing watching up the road with her hand clutching the big wooden post at the end of her lane. For Tilly adored children. Whenever a baby was taken to its christening she was sure to meet it on the way.

"And what name have you chosen?" she would ask.

The answer would be "Beryl" or "Desmond" or some such. Tilly felt a remote emotion for Elizabeth, Fanny, Thomas, but with her jerky old smile – "A pretty name," she always said politely. And then according to the usage of her time, she would slip a shilling under the baby's clothes. Nobody knew that for a Matilda she would have given half-a-crown. Matilda was her own name.

When Mrs Payne from Ell Hall drove her dappled cob Kitty into Salus she used to leave her three young nieces in the trap while she went into the cornfactor's. Augusta, Arabella and Esther. Tilly was especially fond of them. She used to see them nearly every day when she fetched her milk from Mrs Payne's – wild things they were too. Arabella was always nervous. Tilly would stand and stroke Kitty's moleskin nose.

"Is she all right, Tilly? Are you quite quite *sure* she can't get away?" cried Arabella.

"Don't you worry, my dear. Fast as a church to a hedge, she is," Tilly would reassure her. I was Arabella. How would Tilly have felt if she had known I was always to remember her standing there – was one day to look at her little house and ask with a shock, "When did she die? Where's she buried? Where's everybody? And what has happened to us?" The village has changed. Nobody there has ever heard of Tilly and Mr and Mrs Spring. The bridge has been widened for war traffic, and ruined, the eighteenth-century sundial has been carted away and left in a corner, a tomb without a grave. But Tilly's house is the same as it was that afternoon when she returned from the shop and said, "Nearly time to fetch the milk," the afternoon she danced for us .... Tilly's house! it stood back under the trees, on what was little more than an alleyway of white dust and grass – a tiny frail white box with a trellis porch, surrounded by that slender kind of iron fence which looks like wicker-work painted green. The tiniest place! with its mat of lawn before the door, its one chimney, wispy with clematis and jessamine, its slack, pale roses – roses like the crumples of tissue paper one tosses out of a trunk. The paint on the shutters was a shade of emerald-green mixed with white: and that faint colour, old and thin, still shreds on shutters and porch. No – nothing is different, nothing added. So small the roof, the chimney, the little front that all the flowers and trees really looked out of scale, and Tilly's house wears its bouquets of roses as a child might wear a buttonhole of cabbages. Nothing seems missing: from the elms in the background comes the rumbling of pigeons, and the little houses on either side of the alley, with their wire hen-runs and gardens full of scarlet beans, are still as quiet. I don't know why, but that single old corner of W— always seems to be my idea of New England. Something delicate and undefinable in the clean-swept lane, the brass knockers, the rambler-covered fences? Or is it the flowering trees, hanging so gracefully over their own shadows, or the old grey posts and rail which prevents all but foot traffic? I don't know, but whenever I read of "frame houses", vines, the swept yards of quiet New England villages, the association arises at once, and I see that docile place with its angles of sunshine and Tilly, leaning on her stick with one hand on the wooden bar.

When did she die, and in which of our hayfield churchyards are her bones hidden? Again I don't know. Probably it happened when

I was away from home on one of those miserable excursions into life which always ended (urgently) in a stampede for my own country. But if not I might not have heard. Such very old people die as unobtrusively and *invisibly* as earwigs and wasps and black-beetles at the end of summer.

Tilly wore no false teeth. In her upper jaw, in the front she had a pair of long delicate incisors which gave her face something the look of a wether ewe. As she stood by her gatepost, feeling the back of her bonnet, she nibbled gently at her lower lip. Her eyes were blue, three-cornered and charming. She was absent: memory, and not sight filled them; she stood blank and calm, her long forefinger gently pressing against her stick; she had forgotten the beginning of the afternoon but remembered suddenly when she was a little, little girl becoming conscious all at once of a thing like a huge black hood looming in a corner and her mother standing her on a corner of something high, to say "Father, Father" to her.

"Father" had been a blacksmith once, but he had left them all, and gone away to a war astride his own horse. "Mum" fed the pigs in the forge. Tilly couldn't remember the bellows and the light with its spangles and stars, but only the buckets and the hogs and "Father, Father".

She had been a strange little girl with a wilful delicacy of her own. They were poor people: there were seven other brothers and sisters; and when Tilly was eight she was sent to live with her grandmother who was a Welshwoman. Alone with the sulky, sigh-ing old cottage invalid, the child never forgot her sufferings. In the dead of night she would repeat them to herself as if they were a fairy story – the early mornings when the earth looked as if it were being seen through a very dim or ancient eye, the cold, her aching feet and cold hands as she chopped wood in the back kitchen. Every day she had to boil a huge black kettle and take up a cup of tea to her grandmother in bed. Rolled in flannel and patchwork, she would always wake up in Welsh, with a wail of words whose cadence was of the direst. But Tilly could not understand any more than she could understand the sound of the trees when they were loaded with weather. Only in her mind the sound stayed forever.

Until she was sixteen she looked at a world without her own image, for until about that age she had never seen herself in a glass. By that time she had learned to manage without: she knew she was

small and extraordinarily real to herself, by touch, as theirselves are
to the sightless: in the seven times in her life when she had worn a
new dress she had simply gazed down at the waist and the hem to
see if it fitted; and dressing was to her a precise alphabet of gestures, from the chin to the small, shiny, black-laced feet.

She had gone a long way back, standing by the post in the
blithery, blowy sunlight. Her hand when she took it away had a
piece of hard space in it the shape of the wood, and she looked, as
she came to, as one who is going into a dream.

"It was a cold road," she said. And she saw the wheels of a yellow
gig revolving. "She did look like one o' them women in the play-
cards," she said, and she was remembering her miserly guardian
sitting sideways in her hearth, watching dismally the twine of the
smoke up a chimney that was filled with tabby light, like dawn. The
things that Tilly's eyes rested on that moment – her own front door,
with its glass eye-hole, the path, the bees that swayed and swung
like pendulums against the petals – had no possible interpretation.
They were as the objects of reality one meets when one has just
opened one's eyes after sleep – vacant symbols, strangers waiting
for a meaning. Bed-post, clock, dark blue, bright window, world
without a use ....

Part II

THE LIGHTNING TREE

Esther had been watching Esau, the red cat: all day, to her
amazement had he slept, head curled into his legs, among the walnut
twigs on the wall, taking no heed of the bucket swinging, the pumping, the hob-nail cavorting, the shouting that was going on below
him. Queer Esau! Everywhere he went he seemed to find a hole the
shape of himself to sleep in. Now she and Augusta and Arabella
had come out to play with Maureen and Pudge under the lightning
tree. This was an immense admonitory dead ash, naked of bark, its
buds of years ago ossified on its limbs, which the children liked to
think had been struck. For the idea of some unseen freak of disaster in that place made it, in their minds, perfect for themselves.
Heads leaning back, dangling almost from their skinny spines, they

would look up at its delta of branches from which no bird ever plunged, in which the wind made only the slightest of rigid tremolos. The skinned wood of very pale and beautiful colours shone and glimmered hoarily but intensely, like those glimmering patches of hills among the moving misty mornings, which seem the very *inside* of the weather. So emphasized, the lightning tree towered, its roots, the colour of wash-leather, still convulsing the turf. Yet tall as it was, in its zig-zagging clutch at the air, it seemed not so much rising out of the ground as sinking back into it. And all the time the children wondered at it, and cast it, in their imaginations, as a sort of being who made a place especially for them. And all the time the other breathing trees between it and the river threw birds at one another and were stirred like sand, and were painted and told by the wind.

"It'll die."

"It won't."

"Look, it *is* dead."

"It isn't. It's asleep. Uncle says it has long di-gestive sleeps. I'm going to dig it some worms. That's why I brought the trowel. The other leg'll get better. Anyway, it's a bird's wings that count – not its legs. There, he'll fly lovely, won't you? I'm looking after him, so I've got to do it for him."

From a little cardboard box Esther took a fledgling greenfinch with one foot tied to a matchstick splint. Carefully she held it up and cleaned its bottom, with a grass. The bird looked at her kindly, with quiet interest in its large bloomy eyes, and then it opened a mouth of the most wonderful, profound crimson colour, like a great triangular jewel. Esther pulled some crumbs out of her pocket and fitted them into the cavity. The fledgling danced cheerily and clapped its tufts of wings. Then it shut its eyes. She put it back in its nest of dried grass and stood up uncertainly waving her trowel. She was a thin little girl of seven and three-quarters with scattered drab hair. Her grown-up cousin Josephine called her Orphan Annie. Fastened into her suit of boy's blue overalls, she might have been a mermaid buttoned into her tail.

"A nice *oily* worm," she said anxiously.

Pudge was frying hunks of fat bacon. He had a little stick fire

153

going between bricks under a tree, flaming thinly among the tremulous buttercups. A yellow-and-red horse blanket was flung over some poles, and his gay equipment of a flowery teapot, a frying pan, a new bright tin saucepan, a dinner bell and a hubbled china toad called Fred was thrown around. Fred was said to like being out-of-doors.

"That's done," Pudge flung down the hot frying pan: "Ow. Now I've got to chop some more sticks;"

He did it with a broken spade.

"Is that *your* axe, Pudge?"

"Yes. It is. I found it in the stream."

The stick bounced in halves.

"Here, I'll do it," cried Augusta. "Let me! Now where's the other half?"

"No, you can't. No, it's mine. I like doing it. It's my axe," said Pudge, pushing: "Here, go away. This axe is sharp. It chops stones. It'd cut off somebody's head. I was chopping stones with it this afternoon, wasn't I, Maureen?"

But Maureen only sat smiling mournfully and poking at the grass: "They've drowned all the kitties. It's cruel. I think it's cruel. They might've saved one."

Her eyes, seen sideways, seemed to hover with a sensitive quivering flight in suspension, over the grass. Marks like bruises on her downcast cheeks showed where the tears had dried in the sun, yet they were full of a marvellous clear light. Tilly's eyes had light in them too, but it was that of horizons, entangled with the web of earth. Yes, in Tilly's eyes were horizons: in the children's was pure, glittering, untouched space. Surrounded as they played by the bright grass, the trees, their own boundless gestures, no one could be blind to them as creatures of supreme significance, rightness, and primitive harmony. There was something floating in the action of their hands, in their wild jigging hair and dirty dabbled feet.

Pudge was shaking the teapot: "There's a ladybird in this teapot. I'm trying to shake it out of the spout."

"Let's run races," Augusta said: "Come on, Pudge."

With all her mind she dreamed of the race when she would beat Pudge at tearing down the hill to the hedge at the bottom. She looked at him and her heart seemed to sparkle with excitement, as if she had done it. She was the oldest child there but Pudge was bigger. Always Augusta wanted to win everything – to ride galloping, to be a stableboy, a jockey, a judge at the jumping. She read horsey stories.

"All right, but my toe hurts," said Pudge. And he dropped the teapot and began to toil up the hill which was all short yellow grass that squeaked and slipped with dryness under his sandals. Soon they could be heard wrangling over the start.

"Twee-twee," said Arabella to the fledgling. Speculatively she put some grass in the frying pan and held it over the flames till it burnt. Then as the smoke soaked into the bright wind she stared away.

"Let's fry Fred," suggested Maureen sadly: "Oh, I do wonder what'd happen if we did."

The wind had gone a hundred yards away. They couldn't see it but they could hear it humming in the trees. Arabella looked up at the lightning tree. It seemed like a fountain, and yet it was so dead and dour. It shone. For an instant nothing moved. The tree seemed to be right in a ray of stillness: to stand there in the middle of the day. It seemed sad as a fossil, as a stone torso which has lost its moment of life and has to be eternal. She looked at her hand and suddenly her hand was a memory.

"We shook hands in the night!" she said. "We did really. Esther and me ...."

A cock was crowing. She saw the bedroom where they slept side by side, white with the dust of dawn, full of sleep. Out of its warm place in her hair she had put her hand, feeble with drowsiness, and there was Esther's! They had shaken hands. And then they had gone to sleep again without a word. Would Esther remember? And Arabella's eyes opened to take in the immense, still look which she felt driving into her head – the look which when it was like a dream over her face used to make Uncle ask what she was thinking about. What light was it she had seen curled on the leaves outside the window – starlight or the dawn coming? Suddenly she ran off to look for Esther. She found her standing under an alder. Carefully, her eyelids lowered, Arabella waded in her sister's footmarks through the broad green shadow. The two sisters loved each other profoundly in spite of there being three wide years between them and no likeness. It was as though before they had been born they had been twins in eternity.

Esther was listening to a lark. There was recognition in the twitch of her lip although she continued to look up into the sky under her hand.

"*I've* found a wild strawberry," she said, showing.

"Oo – it's nearly black! It's over-ripe," Arabella gasped.

"Yes. It is. *Twice ripe*," said Esther with awe. And then they listened to the lark in silence. Two cuckoos were calling at each other, throwing their notes across and across like Esther and Arabella playing with two balls. Their responses seemed to pass each other in mid-air.

They stood on their toes. On top of the hill where the house and buildings and trees were, the blue sky hung down to the fringe of grass –

"Shall we go to the shop? What're you listening to?"

"I'm not listening, I'm looking," said Esther. "That lark's coming down. Do you think we could find his nest?"

Arabella shook her head. She knew that only plough boys found larks' nests because Uncle had told her so. Still they had found several lapwings' and a meadow pipit's. Esther had found them. Esther found all the nests. She used to go off alone and come back hours later, dumb, full of stares and stubbornness with burrs and brambles in her frocks, sucking her scratches. As they watched, below the sky burst out the lark with his whirl of song breaking in bits. Then he hovered, and then straight he sank into the wheatfield scarcely fifty yards away, without a sound. The great green field took him as a single flower takes a bee. And brushing over the hedge, the silence came nearer – a yard nearer.

"There," said Esther: "the shop? We haven't any money," she muttered.

"We can say 'Father will pay'."

"Oh yes."

> "Father will Pay
> Some Day,"

they sang.

Esther carried her fledgling. Arabella strutted along singing 'John Peel' and sometimes blowing on her knuckles. She walked wishing she had black hair down to the ground and that she could play the violin so violently and romantically that everybody in the world wanted to hear her. Not a big fiddle like Josephine's but the little darling doll of a violin in the shop window in Salus. She stopped dead in the middle of the path when she thought of Josephine playing, and as one bird will follow another across the sky, her hand lifted to fly with that voice singing alone in the music. And then – how awful it was – Josephine – Something would happen – she would be walking about the lawn in all the bright green plumage of the garden, playing, playing, the mouth, the eyes, the fingers and the heavenly strings all singing – and what – what was it? She would stop – her legs would straddle and stiffen and out of the violin came the screams of a parrot in a rage. To the child it was terrible – as if the deck of the lawn tilted over a big wave and the leaves reeled – those parrot notes ... till away away collected again on Josephine's smooth swaying body the voice aspired once more. And when she was standing quite still, in her white dress in the shadow, quietly moving her arm, so big, so white she was like sunlight put down in an unexpected place, *then* the tune would fall, would drop half a tone as if the horizon had darkened, as if the sun had been lowered like a lamp – and Arabella knew it was Beethoven.

Half-way across the field "Katy Hopkins" they lay down. Wasn't it funny, Arabella said, she didn't want to do anything this afternoon. Esther, lying on her stomach, said:

"I can hear six winds."

All along the grass was a moonshine of dandelion balls. Soon the wind would blow them all away and they would all be one o'clocks.

"Has my hair grown, Esther?"

"No."

It was true: the end of her brown plait was no nearer her waist. It was a shame. She sighed. In the brown pasture where the clay hoof holes were like cracked saucers they saw Mr Spring coming along with a wrinkled smile on his face. Mr Spring collected the money in church and dug graves and mowed the grass. When he came to them and held out the funny little tinsel bag, he always smiled and they knew it was nearly over, and they could begin to unroll their white cotton gloves and feel if their big Sunday hairbows were still on.

"And where are you going, Mr Spring?" they asked.

"Why, it's a nice d'y, I thought I'd take a walk."

Mr Spring's white hair came out from under his cap like steam from under the lid of a kettle. He wore a white shirt and a waist-coat which was made at the back, Esther thought, of the same stuff as a feather bed. His face was as pink as it could be without having any red in it, his eyes were rare blue, and the boots on his feet were not the respectable church boots with the rubber soles but his digging hobnails. This was Mr Spring when he was free. On Sundays he had a master. Arabella and Esther were not decided as to whether it was God or the Vicar.

"We're going nowhere," said Arabella.

"Nowhere? I wish you'd show me the way, little girls," said Mr Spring.

"Oh, but we *were* going to your shop. Only we haven't any money," Arabella explained: "Is Mrs Spring there?"

"She be. Oh yes, the Missus be there, I s'pect. Safe and sound," declared Mr Spring, and with a rather surprised expression, as if his clothes were tighter than he'd expected, he felt in a middle pocket, saying out of the side of his face: "No money? No pennies? Dear, dear, dearie dear! Have you looked high, low and level? You *have*? Well, here. Don't tell the Missus now, will you. Eh?"

"No, no. Pink cigarettes," they screamed, taking the gift with no false pride and quite unconscious of the absurdity of spending Mr Spring's pennies in his own shop: "Pink cigarettes. Are there any?"

"Oh ay. Ah well, they're very nice, they are. Mind you don't tell, though. Promise," the old man said, moving away.

"Promise," said Esther.

The old sexton stood looking after them, still with the same huddled little smile, the meaning of which no child would be able to understand. Flies began to whirl over his head. He noticed how hard everything was: the big gaunt thistles glittered like tin, and the dried horse manure lay shapeless and burst and trodden out on the path, showing the seeds of grain and glistening needles of chaff. A woman was dying in W—: he wondered if it would rain before he had to dig her grave.

Esther and Arabella crossed the road in the village an hour after Tilly had gone home.

The village smelled of dust and clipped holly hedges and there was a quietness in it as if people had gone away. The shop was this side of the bridge: inside, behind the broad black counter with the brass scales, the big glass jars and the flies, sat Mrs Spring with her eyes fixed on the half-glass door, the bell, and the fan of coloured newspapers.

"Well, it's 'ot tod'y, yen't it?" Mrs Spring said. "What do you want, my dears?"

Esther and Arabella pushed Mr Spring's pennies across in a row, their eyes on Mrs Spring's prickly face. For it, too, was one of their haunts. They bought the cigarettes – four little packets done up like faggots, with red blobs on the end for fire, and two sugar mice, in a paper bag, please, for these had to last until bed-time.

Mrs Spring hadn't only been knitting, minding the shop and watching the road, but also making some green gooseberry jam, she said. She went into her back room and came back with a little basin full of pink froth.

"Taste," she said.

Arabella ate some on her finger and said, "Nice. Thank you, Mrs Spring."

But Esther ran away. "It was just like pink spit," she said, when they were safely over the road. "And Mrs Spring has *weeds* on her face."

"I know."

They both felt it would be worse if they had liked her.

Over the river there floated a mauve and white gull. "There's a storm at sea," they agreed. Then they walked on "smoking". The wind went a step ahead of them, lifting the latches of the leaves, swinging in its many doorways. When they came to the lightning tree there was nobody to be seen and Pudge's fire was nearly out. They stopped to put sticks on it.

"I'm sure there was something I wanted to tell you," said Arabella.

Esther looked in at her open mouth: "Go on then."

"I can't, I've forgotten."

Before they had got as far as the gate, Wally the farm boy came rushing by on Midge, from turning out the cows. Midge was a vicious liver chestnut with a white eye, quick as a comet – "But she dishes," said Augusta.

Wally leant out of the flurry, his features all slanted back in his face, his mouth was the shape of an halloo and his chin and cheeks looked almost mouldy with the bluish bristles.

"Comin' up be'ind?" he shouted to Esther.

In a second she had gone, and Midge's feet were shovelling up the dust and turf by the gate. It clanged on them and Arabella could hear the loose stones spinning from the pony's shoes as they went up the track.

Part III

TILLY DANCES

She went up the sandy path alone, past the snowballs and laurels, through the two low wooden wickets, over the stone slab under which a tiny sandy spring sometimes flowed, and then slowly through the tall dark bushes and the yews where the ground was dead with pale brown holly leaves. Voices and laughter were coming from behind that high door in the wall. She could hear the separator and smell the woodshed. The sparrows were making short flights like clockwork, crisscrossing the shadow, and outside the door which-was-never-opened, in the end of the house, stood a barrow-load of plants with Josephine's fork under them.

Suddenly there came a louder laugh. Arabella pushed open the door into the courtyard. It was Wally's sister Florrie's laugh; and the great walnut tree over the woodshed gave a shake as if those terrible peals had bumped into the leaves.

They were all there. Inside the back door Wally was turning the separator. Its loud humming was making them all talk loudly. Josephine, in her gardening breeches, was snatching a comb out of Esther's hair. Kate, the servant, arms folded in their tight, creased, black sleeves, was leaning against the wall. Tilly, leaning forward on her stick, was sitting on the pump trough, looking at Florrie Harford.

And Florrie – young, contemptuous Florrie, black eyes narrowed, mouth wide open, cherry hat dancing on her head – was jigging about on her patent leather toes. Her blue satin blouse! Her red cheeks! The Dutch-doll hair which looked as if the brush had slipped and painted a streak on her cheek!

"Well," screamed Florrie, kicking, "I says it must be s'long now for a bit. Good night, all, I says." She threw up the hat and caught it. Kate screamed with laughter. She winked. There was a smell of milk and parched, dirty boots. Arabella knew Josephine had only just come on this scene of idleness and laughter: it was in her face.

"Mrs Probert's baby's come and it's a girl, Miss," Kate was saying.

"Oh. A girl at last. How many's that?"

"Eleven," Florrie capered.

"Ay, well now p'raps they'll down tools," said Tilly. She looked up at the great heaped roofs and the smoke that came up out of the middle of them, and the sparrows on the guttering.

"Get away, sproggers. Shoo shoo," she said. But she looked at Florrie and Kate.

Josephine turned in at the door, sharply: "Get on, Wally. We shall never be done. Tea's awfully late already. Well, Tilly, here's yours – a pint and a bit of skim. No, you needn't do *that*. Don't be silly – put it away. Aren't you going to have a game with the children?"

It seemed almost an obligation on poor Tilly that she should chase Arabella and Esther into corners. They hated it. Afterwards, Josephine, a big dark woman with fierce eyes and a tall iron nose like the pointer of a sundial, always said: "Fancy! such an old woman! Isn't it *wonderful?*"

Josephine managed the enormous, sleepy old house with all its china pantries, dairies, stone passages, and quarries of cellars with only Kate's help. She did the garden, balancing great beds of even flowers on the tilted lawn. It was only on week-end afternoons she played her violin, drawing from it those long hard breaths and cries which got lost in trees and seemed to wander about the air looking for a hermitage.

Tilly slowly got up. She held out her black skirts with both hands so that she looked like part of a silk umbrella. And then, instead of the usual game of tig, she began to dance! She had never done that before.

She danced on tiny forgotten steps, with little skips and trills of the feet. Arabella could see the tiny doorway just as high as her bonnet through which she curtsied and retreated over and over again, in an elvish minuet; the soles of her worn strap shoes dragging on the flags, for music, the perfume of the dance was not there for this small black ballerina. Her face grew happy. Perhaps after all Josephine understood her better than the children? Absorbed in her dignity, she looked only at her feet, but Arabella, entranced, watched her face. Shoulders hunched, the child leant hard against the house until it seemed the old stones were sinking in and softly overlapping her bones. She was making the first promise to her grown-up self; she was giving herself her word not to forget. "I'll remember this," she was whispering. "I'll *always* remember this."

But now the minute steps altered. Tilly changed her direction, and seemed to form herself into ranks of dancers. There was a host of merriment in her bobbing skirts, for now she was moving with greater vitality, in what must have been a faded country dance.

"Oh Jo, oh Jo, do play," Esther screamed. "Oh do let me get your fiddle!" cried Arabella. And Josephine nodded – "Yes, run." Quick. She was turning the china knob. The drawing-room was blinded with green: the petals of the Whitsun bosses had fallen on the piano keys – there were the lustres, the Dresden figures, pearly in the shadow. And there, in its blue case, like a mussel in its shell, lay Josephine's big mongrel violin, the G-string snapped.

She was frightened.

"Oh! Josephine, I didn't do it."

But Josephine only glanced at her faintly, dazzled and muttering, "No, it was the sun."

She was almost as she was in the garden, in her white dress, part of something you remembered even while she was really there, Arabella thought. And suddenly, while she was still unready, her eyes on her cousin's face, the bow pounced .... On that first rough, part of a note, kicked it seemed from the toe of Tilly's shoe, something happened to them all. Long, long afterwards she thought, "Everything became one." They were songs Josephine was playing, songs with a dance in them, old songs. Like a giant needle the bow darned in and out, quick, flashing its white hair. Sometimes the violin sounded like a simple voice singing while the hands work, but mostly it was a boy whistling ... Josephine's wrist turned in the air – she was playing in the middle of the bow ... they were penetrating moments ...

"As beautiful Kitty one morning was tripping –"

"Kate, Kate!"

"... With a bucket of milk to the Fair of Colraine ..."

"Kate, Kate, where *are* you? The toast!"

Kate screamed she had forgotten! There was Aunt Fran behind the window, knocking on the glass with her knuckles. Her face was cross. Josephine's bow cut the song in half and stopped it. Tilly, breathing smally, stood still: her feet had gone into her skirts and disappeared just as if a pair of scissors had cut off her toes.

Tea was late. Hands washed, mouth rubbed, Arabella slid into her chair beside Aunt Fran. Aunt Fran's mouth was sulking. Her fat white hands with the lace edges and the wrinkled veins shook with anger over the china. Only when the cups were poured out did she bend and look round and down at Arabella and whisper:

"You can pour the cream in."

"Oh, Aunt Fran, *may* I?"

The feeling of shame had gone. She could look around at the faces, and the stately pattern of the spread food, dark red jam, yellow butter, white and brown cake – Josephine was talking to Uncle.

"After tea we'll go up into the granary," she planned. She looked at Esther – oh, she had never asked her if she remembered the night!

"Esther," she said, "after tea shall we go up in the granary?"

But Esther sort of jerked. She wasn't eating. With a piece of cake in her fingers she glanced at everybody first, and then as if they bored her and she didn't care for one of them she began to speak to her plate.

"You know what Tilly was saying, about Mrs Probert's baby," said Esther carelessly – "Josephine – what *are* their tools?"

All Through the Night

HELENA and Augustus came out of the pictures and found they had missed the bus. After a wonderful rummaging staring day after spending two shillings each on sandwiches, apples, and chestnuts, they had gone into the cinema. Augustus slept on Helena's shoulder, but she had sat seeing each thought illustrated in the music that rolled out from behind the quarrelling shadows. Finally Helena slept too, and when they came out the bus was gone.

It was nearly eleven. They had only their return tickets and two apples left, and home was twelve miles away.

They walked round the entirely empty square, Helena holding her brother by the hand. He swore and scutted his feet: "Damn," he said, "damn, damn. Now what shall we do?"

Augustus was nine. Helena was fourteen, a short black-haired girl with thick eyebrows. Augustus was small too, but strong. In his blue eyes was a high light – a kind of silvery glare, beautiful and astonishing.

Helen said nothing. She was frowning. Augustus began to forget they had missed the bus. He held his sister's fingers and looked up between the roofs. In the trees whose leaves had fallen outside the railings he saw cockatoos and butterflies with folded wings, clinging asleep to the branches.

"It's no good," said Helena at last: "We shall have to walk. Do you think you can do it?"

"Yes – oh yes. I'm ever so rested – are you, H? Shall we walk all night?"

"I dare say. Good thing we've got the torch."

"And the apples. Do they turn these lights out?"

"Yes."

"Oh, hooray. Then it will be the middle of the night," Augustus cried, dancing wildly.

"We'd better start. Here, don't let go of my hand in case the lights go out," said Helena.

"But I can find you if you shine the torch. It's easier if I have my arms, H. They row me along."

They left the square and turned down the long street which became their country road. Blinds with white lettering were down over the shop windows. They passed the station, hearing the wind somewhere in trees and walls, then silence, footfalls, and a train coming or going. The sound it made was like chains, but through that a perfect expressionless steel pulse beat, untouched by any lonely quiver. The people walking by them were bent, and isolated by the hour. They seemed to materialize out of the stone background, surging and receding without language. The cathedral clock pounded. The lights went out. Augustus felt for a second that his heart had gone out too. "Oh!"

"Here I am, said H, shining the torch. She stopped: "Now, A, we've got to get used to it." She turned it off. "Can you see me?"

"When I'm further off I can, but not when I feel you."

"Well then, follow me. You can hear my shoes. Listen – if anybody offers us a lift we don't want one. Remember?"

"No. If a car stops we'll hide," chuckled Augustus. "They all look wicked. Full of ruffians," he added cheerfully.

The shops got smaller and smaller and the doorways became tunnelled alleys. Streaks of light showed in the top storeys. From all along the street sounded the rumble and squeak of old sash windows being pulled down, and the mouselike chinking of keys turning. There was a smell of gas, sprouts, and damp paper bags.

No cars passed them. They were at the bridge. On the other side lay the vast, cold flat fields, the shut fairground, and the gipsy camp with its cauldrons of fire and bearded blackness. Helena stood still, her hand on the parapet. "We've walked a mile," she thought. Augustus went on, but she called: "Don't walk so fast, you'll soon be tired if you gallop like that. Stop a minute – I want to look down."

She shone the torch. She could see the air like a cloud, but hollow and writhing, with a mirage of yellow water.

Augustus nudged up close. "Oh, it's like an eye. Isn't it like an eye, H? Make it move."

But Helena only stared intently: "Why? How can it look so far down without any sides?" she muttered dreamily.

They walked on. And now they could smell the hedges and leaves rotting in the water. The wandering figures of trees walked away from them loaded with wind. "At night it's all smell, isn't it?"

said Augustus. Helena went striding along, not at all afraid of the distance and the dark. Augustus began to sing: "When the moon gets up, Mother gets up, to look for us, to look for us." He stopped: "No, it's rude. Why isn't there a moon, Sis?"

"Oh A, how do I know? Come on," Helena scolded. She was exquisitely happy walking along at midnight. Would Mother and Father be in bed or would they sit in the study? Would they go down to the gate? No. She did not want to think about home. Home was awful. Suddenly she saw the brass bowl into which a few particularly nasty elderly women had dropped their not quite fresh calling cards. They had not long been in the old Rectory, but already she was terrified that whenever she went out she would have to meet and talk to one of these strange people.

Suddenly Augustus came up to her and slipped his hand under her arm. Helena squeezed it with her elbow, looking over his head. She was noticing the stars – a pale red one to the left in the horizon, and the Milky Way flowing westwards in its continuous ebb. But it was very dark. The starlight did not reach down to earth; only round the trees a faint light was thrown forward by their deeper tone.

"Oh, I do like not being seen," sighed she.

"But doesn't it smell cold? Do you know why I put my hand there? It's because I think there's an ear-i-wig in my pocket and he is going to pinch my little finger. The stars just go out, don't they? Isn't it funny we can't see the clouds?"

When they had walked five miles Augustus began to sway and stumble. Helena sensed that the hand under her arm was asleep. She decided to rest in a barn. There was one by the roadside further on. That was the hardest part of the walk, for Augustus was sagging on her. Finally she took him on her back and stumbled up the stone steps. It was an empty hay loft, but in the corner was a drift of dust and ropes and sacks. Holding her brother up with one arm she moved the torchlight over the bare boards. She started. At her feet was a a square black opening, and blinking up at her a hen's eye.

"I know," she said. "Lie down over there, A, and go to sleep. I'll tie you to this post with your belt."

"Why?" yawned Augustus.

"So you shan't fall through here."

She passed the belt of his raincoat round the post. And then, feeling drowsy herself, she did the same with her own.

Augustus went to sleep at once with a deep sigh. Helena lay down, but the snuff of feathers from the pungent hen roost below, and the cold sour poultry tang, kept her awake. The dusty boards made her sneeze. She sat up. Complete stillness came with a flash. The air swelled inwards against her forehead as she sat with her chin on her knees, clasping her ankles.

"Stars, it's Helena," she whispered. "I'm Helena – Helena."

Augustus's breathing seemed to be going further and further off. Her own respiration was so slight that beside her Augustus seemed to breathe for her. She was roused by his turning over. As he curled up again his knee jabbed her side and she knew that the brain in her waking body had left it for a dream. Then they became one, her eyes closed. She slept. She woke laughing, not knowing anything. Her senses were vividly awake, and they told her that she had seen and heard something. It was real. The moon had risen, the doorway was light, and down in the road something was shuffling. She heard the hens moving their feet on the perch.

"A, wake up. Wake up! There's somebody coming," she whispered.

"I heard," Augustus whispered back. "A dog came in. He came and looked at us and now he's gone. There's a man with him. He called him."

And then the man ran up the steps and into the loft. "Now then, what are you doing?" he cried. "Come out." His clothes were darned with moonlight. He struck a match. Helena could not speak. The man pushed the small light at her. It burned in his hollow hand, as in a lantern.

"Young lady, what're you doing here? Who are you? Where do you come from?" the little man jabbered.

His face was turnip colour and his tiny three-cornered grey eyes blinked their dusty lashes. It was a small, delicate, elderly face, not one to fear. It was when he touched her Helena shrank. His hand on her cheek felt cold and smooth as eggshell.

She tried to explain. "We lost our bus. We only came in here to rest." The second match betrayed his agitation – he was quivering and shaking all over. A square patch of hair, like fur, on his upper lip, seemed as if it would jump of its own accord into her lap.

"We live at Borlace – at the Old Rectory," remarked Augustus. "We shall have to walk twelve miles! All night."

"Father a passon, is he?"

"No," said Helena.

"Can't leave you here, can't leave you here," said the little man wildly. He muttered something; then, "Where's that damned box?" he stuttered, and began shuffling under the eaves: "Looking for some candles – light's failed, light's failed. What are we to do?"

"Helena, let's go," Augustus whispered.

"Here it is, here it is. Now then, young people, don't be frightened. There's nothing wrong in what you've done. I see you're a young lady. You come with me. I'll give you a drink."

Confusedly they followed him to the door and down the steps. The moonlight laid a violet tinge on their faces. The little man's jaw shook so that it broke all his words in pieces. Under his arm he carried not a box but a square tin. Across the yard from a doorway there stared a bare oblong of electric light. It seemed to fall forward with a weight upon the shadow.

"Come on again. What a game!" gasped the little man, plunging towards it.

"Goodbye," said Augustus. "We've got to go home."

"Oh no!" said the broken voice. Helena went after it as though hypnotized: "No, no –" and the shifting inchoate figure solidified before the glare. "C-c-come *in*."

And still Helena went forward. "I'll drive you home, I'll drive you home," the constant voice spluttered. "Wait a moment – wait just there."

The little man flew forward through a doorway. He shut the door. The silent light poured itself out all round the children as if from the walls, the ceiling, and the floor. They saw the threads of hay on their clothes, the cracks in the flagstones, the bulging coats bagging from a sham mahogany stand.

"They're all dusty – they haven't been worn for years," Augustus said in a shy, low voice.

They were standing in a hall passage, bare of everything but one piece of furniture and the naked bulb, from which streamed light. But there was one other thing in that over-intense, silent place. There was a smell. It was dreadful, and as they stood they seemed to feel it fixing them, as the light fixed them, in its solid whitey-yellow block until they could not break their way out by even a full breath. Augustus's dazzling eyes hung on Helena's, but she would not help him. They listened. Helena never knew how it happened that all her leadership deserted her and became her brother's. She felt gradually his hand in hers tugging at her: "Run, run," he was whispering frantically, "H, come, do come." And they ran, without stopping, until their hearts were falling out of their chests. They ran a mile. The distance was like a wall at their backs. But they weren't followed.

At last they stopped. Helena instantly doubled up, clasping her knees. "A, oh A!" she gasped and sobbed.

"Something had happened!" Augustus said.

"Yes, yes – oh, what do you mean?" Augustus sat down on the bank intent on getting the apples out of his pocket. He was pretending not to be frightened, but suddenly he remembered the smell. "I was nearly sick," he said. "That's why I had to get out."

"What was it?"

"I don't know. But H – there was – did you notice – there was –"

"Horrible place, horrible light," said Helena.

"Yes, and *nobody breathing*." Augustus began to polish the apples on his sleeve: "I dare say he meant to be kind, poor little man," he said off-handedly. "Here's *your* apple. Look how it shines in the moonlight."

"I'm sure he didn't. I think he meant to murder us," Helena thought, but she saw Augustus's forehead sleeked with sweat. "Oh, poor darling A, how brave he's been. It's four o'clock," she said, looking at her watch.

They ate their apples, walking on and on, tasting the coolness, the exquisite freshness of the faintly peppery green skins. When they tossed the cores away into the ditch a bird cried out. They had slept several hours and they were not tired, but they walked close together, in the middle of the road where the moonlight glittered as on scales of frost, and neither of them noticed that Augustus had lost his belt. The apples left their lips cold, touched to silence. Thus they walked on hand in hand, without speaking. They went through trees. Unseen in shadow, the road felt less hard to their feet, aching from its even callous surface. In the middle of the wood they heard a patch of wind. The trees over them were quiet, shedding their leaves. When they came out into the light again Augustus found one in the fastening of his coat: "How funny I didn't feel it!" he cried. "Don't I feel things in the dark?"

"I do," Helena thought. She remembered the feeling of the man's hand: that single cold contact seemed to blot her whole body with touches that made its flesh surge. She thrust her hand deeper into her pocket. Augustus began to skip.

"Why don't we talk, H?"

"Because there's nothing to talk about."

"I've got something – I've always got lots. Shall I tell you a story? I say, H, shall we tell Mother?"

"No!" said Helena.

"Just tell her we've walked all night? Let's run down this hill."

They ran, their steps volleying from side to side of the narrow valley. At the bottom the fallen chestnut leaves pasted on to the road and pressed out flat, glittered with a weird iridescence under blackish pearl branch light.

"Never, never," Helena said. "Never," screamed Augustus, and the scream went north and south as he tossed his word: "Oh sis, I've made a wind rustle in the bank!"

But the dried hemlock flowers went on rustling on the tops of their hollow stalks after the two had gone by. A hare crossed the road behind them, sitting for a moment quite still between the two banks like a bundle fallen out of some vehicle. Then it sprang over the car tracks where the raised edges of mud glittered like rods, and down into a tinkling drain course.

Augustus trudged on at his sister's heels. He knew that she had forgotten him, but his child's mind did not for an instant lose sight of *her*, although when he was out of her thoughts he felt a freer person. He had seen the hare. If his hand had been in hers he would have told her. Walking behind her, he only listened, holding his breath to hear the faint breezy sound of the trees and the fields. Then before he knew he had thought it, he spoke. "Helena," he said, "what were they doing in that house?"

His voice surprised himself. It was like his mother's when she cut her finger in the lawn mower and saw her own blood on the grass.

Helena turned round quickly. "Don't talk about it," she scolded.

Augustus burst into tears to his vaster and vaster astonishment. "But what *were* they?" he heard himself sobbing.

Helena would not reply. She walked faster and faster. At first

Augustus could not stride out for sobbing, and then he could not sob for striding. He looked up and saw the moon dripping through the tears in his eyes. It was like looking through a rainy window pane when the storms blur the pane so fast that no drops can be seen. He rubbed his eyelids and the heavens dried. In the very bottom corner of his dragged-down pocket, like the last humbug in a three-cornered sweety bag, he had a conker. He took it into his palm and shut his hand on it and warmed it, rolling its smoothness under his fingers. It comforted him. Whatever had nearly happened to them, the conker had been there safe through it all; it was going back home where it had set out from. Perhaps if he put it in the garden it would grow into a tree and he could climb it one day and think about its horrible adventure when a conker.

Augustus chuckled.

At last they were at the turning to the vicarage and the Old Rectory.

There the tyre-tracks swept round a curve, away from the leafy, stormy hill-lane that had a rusty iron smell of cottages and pigscots. The hill went up abruptly above the roofs, and the slates shining looked like sealskin. At the top over the stile a lonely ash tree was shaking its black branches, making a crinkling sound in the open silent light of the field. The children listened to the minute cries of plovers floating up and down on the waves of their flight, to the ash tree's rustling, and the tang, tang of a wash-tub hung up on a cottage wall. Suddenly a plover wailed loudly over their heads, leaving a whimper in the air.

"Come on, A, we're nearly home," shouted Helena, and resting her hand on the low stile she vaulted over. As she touched the wood she felt herself feeling her way into her dark room by the bedrail and falling – falling on to the bed. How wonderful, how wonderful! If only she were there! Next instant the drowsiness had gone, and she stood looking up into the sky while Augustus climbed over. "Come on," she repeated gently, and took his hand. It was cold, but it came rather twitteringly to life. As soon as she touched him, Augustus began to tell her about the hare. The only way to silence him was *not* to touch him. Then he would throw back his tousled head, and kick his foot and brood ....

"Didn't you see it, H? Didn't you?" he was saying.

"No," said she, singing her Mozart minuet: "Tee da da da. Da-

da-da – da da da da," she sang, walking along the little glazed path that bumped over the furrows whose shadows split and wrinkled the earth as if it were the bark of a tree.

"I did, and I heard it go all down the hill," said Augustus, sending messages of comfort along his veins to the conker nestling in his fingers. "It's all over now, old chap," he said silently in his father's voice, that he heard speaking in himself. The dentist was called Mr Salt, and his path was a tiled one between high dark green hedges. Mr Salt ... a chestnut tree .... Augustus yawned and wondered why some leaves were so small and others as big as great yellow hands.

"I shan't go to bed. I shall go to the kitchen and make myself some tea, and write it all down," Helena was thinking. As soon as she thought of writing she felt a strange heavy feeling of responsibility in her breast. She saw herself stepping on the chair to reach to the top of the dresser for the ink bottle, looking down meanwhile on the table where the steaming white cup stood on its shadow ....

Augustus was running. Helena ran too, and caught him up. He had his arm round the gate post. "We're home – home!" he shouted, as if they had been playing a game in the garden.

"We've done it!" said Helena. She dropped her voice as she looked at the lawn and the bushes. "Doesn't it look queer, A?"

It *did* look queer, all white, silent, staring. Not a shadow moved on the grass, not an ivy leaf. Augustus was hushed: "Yes, it's never looked like this before, even out of the window."

"No, never. Look at the moon."

"It's the wrong way round."

It seemed to be. Its slender curves yearned to the south without a wrinkle of cloud to break its solitary place in the air. Helena stood breathing softly, with the light in her eyes. "It's the other end," she whispered, "the other end of the night, and the sky."

But she couldn't explain. It was something that had never happened to her before – something whole which took time and which could never be seen in glimpses "out of the window" as Augustus said. She had grown and not unconsciously. "How funny!" she muttered. "How funny I've never been awake for a whole day and a night before!"

"The door's locked, sis," said Augustus, turning round on the step. The brass letterbox had swallowed his arm. "Home's going to eat me," he giggled: "Shall I shout? Or climb up and get in at the lavatory window?"

"Nonsense!" said Helena. "We must find the key. They must have put it somewhere."

Augustus was laughing, shuffling the geranium leaves, kicking the doorscraper: "They've locked us out, they've locked us out."

"Yes," said Helena grimly. What parents, what amazing parents they had! Anything might have happened – *anything* – and they had locked the door and gone to sleep!

"Here it is!"

Augustus had found it under the heaviest flower pot. He had seen the damp dark circle on the concrete that the pot had left when it had been moved.

As soon as they were in the hall each child was alone with itself. The mysterious relationship was over. Helena took the lamp away to the kitchen; it was turned so low that the glass was only a faint gold-rimmed bubble floating steadily away down the passage. Augustus stretched his neck to look. It was gone – he sighed and ran up the stairs, subduing his footfalls to the dim dusk of the landing where the thin air was stirred by their mother's open door.

He ran across the room: "Mummy, Mummy!" Mummy was asleep, the bedclothes masked and crowded round her dark head. "Mummy, Mummy, we've walked all night," he cried, hurling himself on the bed.

The mother sat up sighing, covering her eyes with her hand. Her breast was bare – she had no buttons on her nightdress. The warmth of her twilight skin made the night's adventures unreal to the boy.

"Oh, go to sleep!" exclaimed the mother passionately.

"But we've walked all night! We have, we have."

But he was clinging to her, and he was falling asleep, his separate being ebbing, tip-toeing away.

Mrs Pike's Eldorado

UDDENLY, in the street an elderly heavy man with a blowsy nose, dressed in a dreadfully best blue suit, stood before Mrs Tourney, stopping her way. She had been walking along slowly, sniffing because there was a sort of screaming in the air, all through the town, and being a little deaf she imagined she might with an effort smell what it was.

This man said he was going to be married.

"But I don't know you," said she.

"But you know Mrs Pike. It's her I'm marrying."

"Goodness gracious! Alice – my sister Alice!" gasped Mrs Tourney. "Well!"

"Yes. I'm in a good job. Regular. On the railway," he gabbled, leaning slightly forward as she leant slightly back. And he went on with swelling confidence: "You see I earn quite a tidy bit per week. And I don't want to keep it all to meself neither. So why shouldn't we be comfortable?"

Mrs Tourney could think of nothing to say but, "As I say, why not?"

"So ..." said he. And he went on talking very fast, changing a brown paper carrier from one hand to the other and confusing Mrs Tourney's sense of the public thoroughfare with some strange semi-sacred words. Heaven, he was saying. On weekdays Mrs Tourney called it Paradise. He seemed to be pointing to it with the brown paper carrier: it looked as if he meant the Shirehall. She looked at him.

"I don't often 'ave a day in town," she remarked firmly: "I be afraid o' getting rheumatism. Last time I come I caught it. And I'd bespoken me cooked dinner right up at the other end o' the tarned old place, and would you believe it, I never touched it. Never got there. And my word! getting on that bus! Well, if you'd a seen me you'd a bin heart sorry for me ...."

"Just like Alice," he interrupted.

"Alice! What nonsense. She never 'ad anything up to it. Not but what she's 'ad an 'ard life," said Mrs Tourney, doing up the top button of her coat as if she felt rheumatism blowing round the corner: "And she's a good 'eart, you. It's *in* her. Always had, as I say. But I be a twelve-month younger than 'er, so you've no call to give me your qualifications. Only I'll tell you this. Don't you be so fortunate. Yes, she *as* 'ad a life. I'll say that."

"I'll look after her," he vowed and nodded: "I'm going to let meself go over Alice. She's nigh on sixty your sister is and never 'ad no 'ome for years. I'll make her happy and look after 'er like she was in heaven. I haven't got nothing else to do."

"Then I do reckon she's lucky at last," said Mrs Tourney, and they separated as abruptly as they had conversed, she standing on the corner just long enough after he had gone, to utter, "Good gracious what a thing."

She peered about. Her hand, groping about in space, pointed and appeared to press a bell button somewhere in the middle of a young girl with an umbrella.

"'Ave you the gumption to kindly tell me what the fate this awful noise is?" she inquired.

"It's the factory," the young lady said crossly.

Oh, so that's it. Making bombs and things like as not," Mrs Tourney surmised. And she walked on down the street holding tightly to her shopping bag which contained two kippers for William Tourney and one for herself, some scarlet thread, a new hair net and her bus shoes into which she always changed for a ride of more than five miles.

The news had upset her. Her heart felt as if it were a purse full of coppers. Alice going to be married! Well, might as well have a cup of tea – there was a nice café near the bus stop.

She marched herself in and sat down at a wicker table, first removing the artificial flowers which annoyed her because they reminded her of Alice's children's curl papers. She had some of the fastidiousness of "the toffs", this alert middle-aged woman with the pale brown eyes. A piece of holly was pinned to her coat collar. Her speech, like her home-grown teeth, could bite but not tear. The man who was going to marry Alice had gone away laughing, pleased with her face.

Alice's children were all grown up now. Some were married. "Why she's a daughter a widow!" Mrs Tourney thought. "Some women are born widows. I'd a thought Alice was one. When *we* was little uns, 'ow grave-like she was! Trouble couldn't 'elp coming on one that was so like it. 'Ow long is it since I seen her? Two years

– no – yes. Two years come next Saturday fortnight. No, Friday. No Saturday. I'm telling meself a lie. It was Saturday because I were cleaning the fowl house –"

Yes. Two years since she had seen Alice to the bus. Alice in black, broad and infirm on her feet, had lumbered up the step. She settled herself near the window and then she had turned and smiled, and lifted her scoured hand holding its grey cotton glove .... As she put down the teapot Mrs Tourney found she was shaking. Why did her sister's face come back to her so? It might have been in front of her that moment.

Alice was a poor woman. What was it that man had said? He would give her "good measure". Well that was funny, she didn't know she'd heard it until just then. Good measure: there was just that in the look of Alice now she came to call it to mind. She saw her sister's dark eyes, with pain in them. She was going back to a miner son-in-law's home. How hard she had worked all her life! And it was no fun living with relations. And now, look, she'd met a steady respectable fellow as was going to put his whole life to making heaven for her. But that wasn't married life. Couldn't be with Alice anyway.

"No," said Mrs. Tourney absently, "it don't fit. It just don't."

It was as though she were warning herself.

She stood up and paid and then she went out into the hard December air that was chopped into little prickling splinters by the cold strange city winds. The screaming factory was silent now. Standing waiting she heard a typewriter begin tapping like a wood-pecker in the back of the café she had left. The cold crossed spires were very dark.

Soon afterwards Edward Tanyard and Alice Pike were married. Her children were in the church, resentful, weeping. Mrs Tourney did think that unfair. They wanted walloping she muttered to William. It was odd for her to see Alice in a brown costume. She always *had* worn black – a long black coat that cracked open to show still blacker folds inside. Indeed the closer to Alice's body the clothes got the more determinedly darker, if possible, they grew. But there she was now wearing her gold cross and chain, and look-ing at them all, high, low and level.

Tanyard, in the same blue suit, winked at her. She sat in a pew on the right side of the aisle, having refused to stand behind Alice because her back wouldn't allow it.

When the wedding was over Tanyard insisted on kissing her and calling her Maria. She was embarrassed and puzzled by him. He seemed to her pathetic. He gave her the sprig of mistletoe he was wearing in his lapel. He seemed to like her. He called William Tourney "old cock". "The old cock won't crow," he said when they were going. William gave him a brief look and turned away: "I do want to get back to me work," he said. On the way to the station he didn't want to talk.

"Now then, Maria, come on you. Us must get back to milking," he called sharply behind. You could have hung a meat hook on her lower lip all the way home. They walked the three miles from the station grimly, and Mrs Tourney threw the piece of mistletoe over a hedge. She was thinking of Tanyard's childish eyes and his bent head as he laughed with her. Poor Mrs Tourney couldn't but think there was something ominous in idle good humour. But William did so plonk his feet down. Why must he plonk each foot like that? And was it right to love work so dearly? Yet he was a kindly man with just sufficient meanness in his nature to give it alertness. And he had a wonderful face, full of the arts and crafts of his nature, every wooden fold and feature with just the irregularity of good hand work. His crisp blue eyes, his short workable old body which had come to the second wind of life's agility that sometimes enters the old, his wiry smile, all these made people who looked at him suddenly think of a God who made him as a testy but pleasant creator, somebody home-bred in fact, very much resembling William himself.

You went down a green lane all lined with grass and trees to the Tourney's little farm. There was a yard and a cowhouse on one side of the cottage. Rushes grew by a stream near the gate, and every flower of the winds'. The fruit trees were so many and grew so close to the walls that in summer each window from the inside was a small square picture of leaves. In winter, when William stumped in from the cows with his flash he could see every bough and twig hung up like a spider's web that sagged from the stars. Their cat Harold used to crouch by the bootscraper looking like a stone. Its life belonged nowhere: it was a sort of haunting. William would talk to it, feed it, encourage it: "You don't want ter tremble so. No you don't. And you don't want to roam away," Maria heard him saying in the cowhouse. He had gone at once to the cows, plodding round the manure heap which was steaming thinly upward into the primrose green twilight. He set each boot on one of the semicircles of large stones that were half-buried, half-floating on the squelchy straw. Mrs Tourney heard him as she unlocked the door and stepped inside the glass porch which smelled tepidly of plants and the sun's warmth. "Gw'ine to freeze," she heard him say.

It wasn't until their late tea was over she and her husband fell into conversation.

"Your sister Alice," Mr Tourney uttered, smoking: "She's gone and done it. What for do a woman like that want ter go and get married agen? I shouldn't wonder if she 'aven't made a mistake. After all, you, there be plenty o' work in the family without taking a pair o' 'ands such as she 'ave over to another chap's."

"Reely, Will! My sister Alice bain't no beast of burden," retorted Mrs Tourney, bristling, "she can do as she pleases."

"Oh, ah. Course she can."

A pause.

"That Tanyard!" Mr Tourney said.

"Why what's the matter with 'im? Nice chap perhaps. Says he do want to give Alice a rest. Just a minute, you – don't move. I seen a beetle," and she tiptoed round the table with the lamp.

"Rest!" William laughed: "She wean't get no such. 'E's a mean bugger too. Tried for ter borror money off someone I do know as wasn't far off ter-d'y. And grabbed all the beddin' afore it ever got inter 'is fust wife's sister's sale. Ah. Rob Jesus of 'is shoe strings them Tanyards would."

"Will! Wherever did you 'ear that?"

"Never mind. I did."

"Then why 'aven't I? I do always year everything *you* do year."

"Why do you? 'Ow?" William was interested.

"Because you do talk so much," said she.

"All right, missus. We wean't neether of us year no more. We'll see instead."

Maria, wrapping herself in her arms, sat down on the horsehair sofa to think. It did seem queer to have Alice so much in mouth and mind after all these years of distance. Of course there had been another Alice – a young one, but she Mrs Tourney always thought about as if she were dead. It was hard, impossible to remember her as joined on to the wise, elderly Mrs Pike.

Higher up the stream, years and years agone had stood the cottage where Maria and all her sisters and brothers had been born. Six of them. Nothing was left there now except a tall pronged old pear tree, not even a few unturfed stones, for these William had carted to Button's Cott, their home, to help build a sty. The chimney, Maria fancied, lay heaped under the green hump over which the footpath leapt, and the pump, she was certain, had been where now was a large nettle patch.

All her life she had heard the same stream: she and the young ones had messed their feet in it, and a ditch near it, catching tadpoles, snatching rushes and cresses, and wetting their boots till Mum had sent Alice after them with a switch. How they'd laughed! And then all at once Mrs Tourney seemed to see Alice in a long-forgotten pale red muslin dress come down the bank one summer's afternoon, not alone but with that Dyson's son, the drover lad, who was killed. She could just see the peculiar colour of that dress with its soft yellow dots – see the very material – a fine stiff muslin such as couldn't even be seen nowadays. And she heard young Dyson say as plain as plain could be: "The piglets is all dead, Alice," and Alice started laughing, and slapped at him, and they went on across the fence and out of sight. "What's that, Maria?" William growled, for she had been muttering, "Strawberry colour."

She wondered if you could make a dream out of something which had really happened, for as she opened her eyes there was her husband turning down the lamp and saying loudly: "Come on now, missus, or the'st never be up in the morning."

It seemed to her she had been out of the house.

She thought she had the same dream in the night. And when it was getting light enough to see next morning, something led her down to the bank of the stream. She felt the dent of her own weight on the frosted mud all among the shrunken rushes where they stood up like brown besoms in the white cat ice. Mrs Tourney stooped right down to the stream and felt the sharp scalloped edge of it ....

This was in January. In March she had her bronchitis again. She had to stay in bed. William fretted, hating to be indoors. She could hear him grumbling in the pantry: "I do want ter get on wi' the work." He told her he had a plank down in the yard over the muck. He was wheeling the manure heap away on to the garden. The wheelbarrow rolling, the plank springing and William's solid tread broke the silence of the dusk.

One evening she asked for some clean sheets, and while he was crumpling the dirty ones into a box in the corner, she said to him:

"Will, I don't trust things: I do hope as how my sister Alice be all right."

"Why the'st had a card from 'er on yer birthday, didn't tha, and that yent nobbut two months gone? What fools women be!"

"Two months wus Monday," said Maria.

"Well then, 'ow could anything 'ave 'appened? You be always on about Alice now-a-d'ys. What's the matter?"

"Gracious goodness, *I* don't know. I don't know everything as goes on. But it do seem queer. As if I was waiting," sighed she. It was true: every thought seemed to lead to Alice or to the past. When she bought her brown shoes for Sunday what must she do but remember how Alice had had a pair that were too light: "And what do you think she did with 'em, Will?" she said: "She went off and *tarred* 'em. They wore splendid too, only she never could come near a fire, you know."

"I shouldn't do that," William said gravely.

It was an exciting year. Although they heard nothing of the Tanyards, the Tourneys made their own news fast enough: it was a wet season, and after the small rick had cowered for weeks under a cloth they decided they must try to thatch it themselves instead of waiting their turn. In doing it William somehow fell and broke two ribs and an ankle. His wife couldn't endure to think of him in hospital; besides she needed his daily advice, so there he lay upstairs, and "three days before the doctor would let her take off his prickly shirt," she moaned to a neighbour. They didn't think he could live, but he did, and lost, from pain, the brackets of laughter round his mouth. They never showed again: his face grew smooth and empty, and he himself became strangely sensitive. He used to watch the sparrows on the wall, the sheep on the upland pasture on the other side of the brook and count the lame ones.

"There's another of 'em hobbling ter-d'y, Maria. I don't like ter see it. I don't like ter see the creatures in p'ine. Bain't right."

He noticed too how the mass of the flock rolled this way or that on their high flat pasture, for all the world like marbles on a table.

Poor Maria. Her arms ached from carrying: her bones growled with rheumatism and overstrain, and when she looked at her husband's face her heart felt as if it were hanging in chains. She did the milking, she fed and looked after the cows, pigs and poultry. She picked the damsons and the early apples by herself as well as nursing her husband and cooking. She continued to speculate about Alice, but now she began to think differently about her, with envy and weary bitterness. She felt as lonely as overworked people usually do.

"She might've come and lent me an 'and," she used to mutter: "She's forgetting what it is to work morning, noon and night, with that fellow to wait on 'er."

But William mended. He began to milk and then to tidy up the garden a bit. Then as no harm came of it he started the hedge-cropping. It was restful and pleasant to hear his hook taking off the brambles. He talked serenely of pulling up the raspberries in favour of black currants. But a curious thing was that he never again would kill anything: Maria had to wring the fowls' necks, and the pig killing they postponed.

One November morning after a hard frost or two had quietened the stir of the air, Maria suddenly felt that rest had come. She couldn't explain it to herself but simply knew that some punctual event had arrived at its destination on earth. She knew it as soon as she saw the sunrise, and then she went outside.

"It's winter," she said. She stood rubbing the back of her neck, her flat hair falling, her eyes as bare as the sky. The morning was all still, spare branches, and cawing rooks: the soft pastel bloom of frost was stealing away from the grass, and here and there a yellow leaf twinkled like broken glass. High in the twigs of the naked trees, some late apples gave their bitter red tint to the scene.

She looked downwards along the field to the five barred gate. Some red dead leaves blew over the grass like a fox crossing the path. It was still again.

Then she saw Alice.

"Good land, Alice!" screamed Mrs Tourney. She couldn't move. For Mrs Pike that had been was coming up that open field as if she were reeling along a tight corridor. Maria put her hands over her mouth, terrified, unable to run and meet her.

In a few moments she was near, and then she was leaning up against an apple tree, bowed and panting. "It yent death nor accident, sister," Mrs Tanyard gasped out with a hollow look: "No, I won't go inside for a moment. I come on the workman's train and I just felt I'd 'sphyxiate all the way. Just let me sit down on this owld stool and then I'll be all right. Oh *Maria!*"

Maria rushed into the cottage and poured fresh water on the breakfast tea for she saw there was no time to spare. She snatched a couple of aspirins, wrapped her sister's knees in a coat of William's and watched her sip the weak scalding tea. As Alice sipped her bottom lip trembled, and she muttered:

"My marriage yent all we'd a hoped, Maria. No, it's very bad. I've 'ad to leave 'im."

She sobbed.

"I've 'ad to, I've 'ad to. And I won't never go back. I've been too miserable. Work!"

This was dreadful. Maria was very quiet. She looked at the landscape as if it were a task she had finished, holding the saucer out in front of her like a candlestick.

Mrs Tanyard clutched the empty cup under her chin. Her feet, stretched out in front of her and lying flaccid from the ankles and turned over on the edges, were in men's boots: her hat was wrestling with her hair. Her eyes were a darker brown than her sister's, her skin was swarthier. But they resembled each other, only there was a gap in the likeness, a space, as it were, that was filled by the dead brother's face. She was Maria seen by twilight. Both had the same seeking expression. "Oh, dear, oh dear, come into the house now, do," said Mrs Tourney at last, and she pulled Alice to her feet. The lamp was still burning on the scullery table, and there were crumbs and a white cloth dog-eared back from a saucepan of scraps and a paraffin can. The fire was unlit and full of mist-coloured ash. "You'll excuse the paraphernalia, Alice. It didn't use to be so bad. I don't know what's come over me lately," said poor Maria miserably. "William 'ave bin very ill, it's bin that bad and what with one thing and another – 'tarnation it all 'ow we've got through I can't tell thee."

"Oh Maria, I was 'eart sorry I couldn't come, indeed I was," cried Mrs Tanyard.

"Well, well, sister. Sit down yere and tell me all about it."

"I can't understand it, I can't. I couldn't tell you – I don't think I could tell anybody. It's strange, it be that queer. Yent as if 'e was a *bad* man. No 'e yent – Seems 'e's too good. It's summat you can't understand, Maria, but when it comes to keeping another woman it was off to go with me. 'Er's there now. Come last night with a suitcase and a wireless and one o' them spotted fur coats on. Sat down in Ted's chair and says, 'I'll wait.' I didn't say nothing. It was *below* me though 'er come right into the wash-house and watched me sortin' the potatoes. When Ted come 'ome, I says, 'What's this?' 'I be bound ter keep 'er,' 'e said. 'Then,' I said, 'you bain't bound to keep *me*.' And I never said no more, never asked no questions, but sat up in me chair till four o'clock this morning, and then I did just say to Ted, 'I'm going now,' and then I come away. That's the finish of it, I said."

Mrs Tourney opened her mouth: "The wicked bounder!" she said furiously.

"No, Maria. You'll not believe me but I be sure it yent that. No it yent, think 'ow tha will. 'E'll give away any mortal thing – 'e'll do anything for anybody, that fool will. And I've bin fond of 'im. But if that's the way 'e's going to comfort me old years! Comfort! I've bin patient, I yent said nothing for a year, but Maria there's 'is daughter May there too, living on us, and never so much as set the bucket under the pump for me. It was work, work, work all d'y long, job after job – ah, I could always find a job. Gracious goodness, if on'y I could *understand*. Kept 'er 'e did – bain't no end to the folks as'll turn to Ted and e'll 'elp 'em – washing, washing and cooking and mending all d'y in 'igh boots with my legs, 'cos when the floods come and the bridge went down, the water was all over the floors. It seems as if he can't 'elp promising everybody everything ...."

Mrs Tourney looked two ways, as if she were about to cross a street. She looked at the clock and she looked at the door and then she bent forward:

"If that's the case, Alice ...."

Alice glanced up. The sisters looked at each other quietly, their eyes full of tears.

"If that's the case, then 'ow'd it be if you stopped yere? A bit anyway. I don't know 'ow it is Alice, but we was born yere and lately I can't stop thinking about us all when we was young. Do you remember 'ow you tarred your shoes? Do you remember Dyson's lad, as used to drive the cattle years agone?"

"'E died," Alice answered in a strange lulled voice and she stared at her sister softly, as if she saw herself; softly, patiently, as a person resigned to her own familiar reflection, Maria looked back.

"They're all dead," she said calmly: "I see 'em at night when I can't sleep. You mayn't believe me – I yent never told anyone else but I do see 'em in the dark. Only their heads a'lookin' at me. I do. It's true, Alice." Then she began moving about and shifting plates to the sink. Alice thought her more bent and older than last year. Her walk was brittle and her feet made a dead noise on the floor.

Alice had stopped speaking. She stared out of the window. She pulled off her hat. After a moment she turned to her sister and said:

"You ought to rest, you. You bin doing too much. You musn't go to begin seeing things. That's very bad, Maria."

"Oh, I bain't ill," said Maria.

"These folks as you – see," said Alice; "do um speak to you, ever, be chance? Eh?"

Maria shook her head: "They do come to comfort me."

Alice got up.

"I can't sit yere all day. You must let me 'elp you."

Yet she seemed as if she couldn't stop looking through the window. She lifted her arm in a dull gesture and then she uttered what was possibly the only passionate reference to her life she ever made. "It's terrible. It's terrible. I was a-looking at the sun rising in the train. Maria! don't tha feel .... it be just as if summat was stolen from you everyd'y? We don't never get the day as we do see rising. No, never. We do see it over there with the sun rising and then summat else do seem to slip in, like, and that un be what we do get."

Maria nodded: "Yes, yes, Alice. It's true." She wondered, though not in words, whether happiness was too small a thing to contain her sister's nature.

Alice had sat down on the sofa. She was weeping again. Maria touched her gently: "Now, now. You do want to go to bed. You go to bed, Alice. Tha'll feel different after."

"No, no," Alice sobbed, "I couldn't go to sleep not if I was to try all d'y. Seems as if there yent no d'iark (dark) left to me. Oh, why did un treat me so?" she moaned.

She pulled herself up. "Lord!" said she sharply, "don't you listen to me. I be better moving about. 'Ow can I 'elp *you*, Maria?

"Hush," murmured her sister. She had heard William's footstep. She went to the back door. He was there sweeping his boots with the besom. He had been hedge-cropping up at the top field and was all over a silver pattern of melting rime. Drops hung along the caves of his brows.

He gave a wizen jerk towards the inner door, pointing: "Visitors? Oo be um, missus?"

"Nobody. Be quiet, you. It's Alice," she whispered. She bent forward to his face and at the same moment her eyes seemed to retreat. She looked extraordinarily like William.

"Trouble?" William hissed. She nodded.

"Told tha so," he said: "left 'im?"

"Yes, 'er 'ave – and – "

"Best thing 'er ever did. Come straight to tha, eh? Good job. Do tha think 'er'll stay? Splendid 'ands that woman 'ave. We can do with 'em. 'Im and 'is 'owld cock'! Aye me lad, the owld cock ool crow last."

He spat.

"Will ..." she said. He was tearing the burrs and goosegrass berries from his clothes. What he didn't tell her was the terror he'd felt when he'd seen the chimney wasn't smoking. He hadn't seen Alice coming over the fields: as it happened no human eye on the pair of hills had done so. And suddenly he'd looked down. There was no bloody sense in him these days, he thought, but since he'd been ill he got funking what would happen to them one day. When the chimney didn't smoke. Old age is fearful, even with improvements.

"Will ..."

"All right, missus. I do only mean she's as welcome as a week's wages. There!"

He laughed. His blue eyes stared into her own. "She yent to work," Maria muttered, stooping, hovering to his face.

"Course she bain't. Let 'er rest, I say."

But nothing could alter the secret, instinctive look which passed between them.

The Sea

AST night, from the train which smoothly crawled round each scallop of shore he had watched the waves. The soldier threw away his paper and let down the window. That wild, bitter, lonely smell! The soldier seemed to sweep it into his breast ... in the twilight between the glimmering rocks and the grisly seashine, figures stooped and probed.

He heaved a great sigh. The breath of a bigger man seemed to fill his slight body like an idea. Now to find the sea, to take from it one small token, one salt keepsake for his nephew of six years.

Softly he shut the bedroom door. Softly, carefully slotting a sly catch, he fastened himself outside "Board Residence". It was cold. With the small hyphenated steps of a nervous creature, he hurried through the streets asking the way to the sea.

The people he asked looked at him as if they had forgotten something.

"Oh," they said, "you'd be meaning the harbour?"

They always said "harbour". They seemed to avoid the other word.

In the end he said, "Yes". They were quiet people with voices soft as rain water, shopping in hat shops and fish shops and chemists and grocery stores. The fish on the slabs had a raw, abysmal smell and on many blackboards were scrawled in chalk the words, "Trawler Owner". He paused curiously, hanging over the fish pinks, the pearly blacks, the opaque greenish fins, delighting in the odd dots and thrush-like, snake-like markings. He noticed that the vegetables had a feeble appearance as if there was a quality in the air which drizzled decay on the green leaves.

Suddenly a man in an apron ran out into the street slapping his wet, red hands on which the fish scales showed like little white blisters. It was the soldier.

"Can *you* tell me the way to the sea?" he begged.

But the soldier, without a moment's recognition, too directed him to the harbour, seizing as he did so a great sickle-shaped fish and rushing back with it into a den of skeletons.

Harried thus to the harbour, he went there and sat down on a sort of wall. He soon saw there was no sea. Only truck lines, coke dust,

a commercial foulness. And he had no hat; and it was so cold that
he shrank shapelessly inside his clothes. If it had not been for his shoes
and tight leather gloves giving him an outline of toes and fingers he
would have felt unbounded. His mind blew helplessly away.

He saw the lane before his brother's little house with its tricky
firelight vaulting into the dusk. He even saw the broken straws
hanging from the trees as motionless as if each one had on its end
a tiny drop of lead. The roadman's broom leant against the bank.
Charles was astride the wall. The fair head with its crystal hair was
above the dusk, against the clear sky. The voice was treble as a star.

"What do you think you'll bring me from the sea, Uncle?"

"Well, I shall have to find something, shan't I?"

"Oh, yes, you will. What d'you *think* you'll find?"

"A shell?"

"Got a shell."

"A pebble ring, a pickled buckle, a merman's moustache then."

He laughed rudely at the empty harbour. It was boatless, floored
with tins, with slime, with dunce-shouldered, stupid-shaped boulders. How about a nice rusty tin, he said, filled with drain-brine,
the colour of iodine? A salt-licked stone, his mind said. Oh, damn
the mind. How false – *false* – and as a sprawling rain began he
started from his seat on the wall into the shelter of some glass-
doored, lettered shanty which pared off a corner of the wind. And
then he found that by leaning forward and manoeuvring his nose
he could discover, between two stunted towers, the sea.

It was a long way off. Grey, hollow, straight, dark at the rim,
underlined in two dashes, as it were. Those dashes were ships.
There was a remote mathematical look about the vision, as if it had
been created by instruments and could only be worked by them.
The two little towers were like candles on the end of stone promon-
tories – the harbour lights, of course. The clouds and the ships were
going in the same direction.

So there was the sea. It reminded him of a human eye – the sort
of grey eye which has an austere dark circle around the pupil. This
eye, or part of an eye seemed to look at him. It was severe, vast,
blank. He glanced away, sea-shy, into the harbour with its iron-
ringed sides, like a stable. Sea-wagons, he thought, came in the past
meekly loaded to those rings. Why was the sea all past?

He began to walk up and down, up and down. The cold was a

kind of desperation. But he had to wait here or at the bus stop, a great open-ended shelter where all the wind in the town collected, as he knew, for he had passed it. A piper was playing to the queues – piping the mist into the streets and the sadness and the swing of a Highland regiment, gapped with ghosts. It was better here, even with the truck lines, the gritty black ground and the backs of houses. He could hear the wind in the chimney pots and the rotating cowls. He could pretend to imagine that the shack was not an inspector's office or some such official goblin's den, but a place where one could hire a pilot, who sat perhaps reading a paper on a wooden bench in front of a red-hot stove.

He shut his eyes, groping in all the old joyous clap-trap of the nautical life – wooden legs, ships-in-bottles, maps.

"A-roving, a-roving," he hummed. Then back came, as in a mirror, stilly, the lane, the house, the fair boy on the wall. The trees were yellow and black – the goldenrod –

"What've you *brought* me?"

"An old story."

Hadn't Melville written, all stories lead to the sea as all paths ultimately to water?

He looked at his watch. It was time to go. He must be there at least half an hour before his bus left, his landlady told him, if he wanted to get on.

So he walked away. All at once he gave up. Bristling with cold he went rapidly up a rickety, tattered street full of steps and black windows, to the bus station. A great Dutch barn of a place where the patched starved old buses waited alongside the crowds, the whole scene painted (or rather obscured) gun-grey. Cries, mutters, feet, made not noise but a shuffling silence around the people. A distinct-shaped wind, a muscle of air, embraced them all, and blew every loose thing about them sideways.

He struggled to his place in the iron passageway. He had been standing there for about five minutes when a loud voice behind him made him turn.

"Hum. Well, he needn't have done it here. Surely the laddie could have gone away somewhere private?"

The voice was very strong and somehow bare. It belonged, he saw, surprised, to a very old woman. Beside her, hushing her, was a younger one, wet, laughing, with the rain red on her face.

He looked down hastily. Then he grinned over a pale, pawky little boy, who was in tears.

"Lord, what a grandmother you'd make," he said.

"Well, I'm not. I'm not married." And then she murmured something inaudible. He couldn't help looking at her. She had a long, pale, sealed face, very pale blue eyes and the peculiarity of possessing only one lip – the bottom one. It supported a single tooth. The voice which came from this singular mouth was lonely and strange.

"That's a beautiful little dog," she remarked, looking at a white spaniel which, he saw with astonishment, was sitting close to his feet: "I like dogs. Spaniels are the most faithful of all. He'll never leave you. What do you call him?"

"It's not mine," he said: "it must have followed me from the sea."

"Eh?" she said: "Eh, the sea? I'm the daughter of a sea captain."

"Oh."

"It was a barque," she continued. In all his life he had never heard a voice like this one.

"There were no pensions then," she concluded: "they never came back."

She paused as if to give him time to catch up but he could only blink. Her odd speech, though so loud was at times clouded. It was a duet for one voice, and it seemed to convey to him physical impressions only, so that he knew he would never forget what this old lady looked like down to the utmost detail.

"Yes, a bonny doggie. A bonny, bonny doggie." She suddenly started again: "My father's was one like that. A spaniel – Old Jessy. What do you call those men who take a ship out of harbour? The – the – ?"

"The pilot?"

"The pilot said if they had only waited for the next tide!"

The turquoise ear-rings. He was sure nobody could ever remove them unless they cut off her ears. In the collar of her black false-fur coat she was wearing a Barnardo's flag, shaped like a pansy. He found himself storing up the flag as if it were a retort likely to come in useful during an argument with his memory, time hence.

"They were lost?" he said.

"They never came back again, not one of 'em. Oh yes, lost ...."

She mumbled. He wondered if she concealed patches of forgetfulness thus. She was a mortal eighty at least, he judged.

"... Some believed it was in the Bay. They sailed from this town. Never seen again. Ah dear. I was a little girl then but I remember it. Them going ...."

Because he had just come from the place where it had happened he seemed to remember it too. But what *exactly* was a barque? As a boy he had been moved by sailing ships, and had looked up their technical differences in nautical books. Bits came back to him sometimes. Square-rigged, clipper-rigged – once he had woken himself out of delirium with pneumonia bawling, "About ship! For God's sake, put her about –" not so long ago. A brig had two masts, but a barque? All he could picture was a little ship like a shoe, heel down in the water, sails just loosened, freshening to the wind. He could hear the rustle of her movements and the footsteps of farewellers turning away. Out they had glided between the two light-towers, out into the grey eye of the sea which had never looked them back.

"Have you always lived here then?" he asked.

She shifted her breath: "Yes. I was an orphan once, though I had a mother," she smiled.

He tried not to scrutinize. She did not seem a townswoman, yet neither had she the air of the woman who thinks the wind blows to dry her washing.

"Silly it was – it amuses me, but one of us had to go into a Home. There were no pensions then," she explained. He wondered if she were conscious of this phrase which she repeated so often. She always said it without emphasis, on the retreat, as it were, and in the background of her voice.

He jumped. A two-decker bus, lean and toppling, made, it seemed, of the lids of dessicated cake tins, jarred alongside.

"Mine?"

"Where are you going?"

He told her.

"Next one. *That*," the old lady said, "would never take your road. My mother was a dressmaker."

She held up her thimble finger, and it nodded to her: "She worked hard. She never sent us to bed without something in our stomachs, and her own too. But I sometimes think if they had only waited for the next tide, how different things might have been. Perhaps not ... I mean sooner or later – in those days. How I hated that place! Do you know, I had to get up at six o'clock and scour the pots? I was only nine years old. We used to like visitors. We had cake then ... turn round! Get ready for it. This is your bus ...."

"Good-bye," he said.

"Good-bye. Good luck. Your lovely dog ... reminded me of Jessy. She lived to be twenty-one. She was my father's dog ...."

She was blundered over, hidden, to focus once more through the window of the bus, frantic, pointing. He shook his head:

"Not mine," he yelled.

The wrenching of a corner, a boggling over cobbles and they were climbing the roofed hill. He felt an obscurity, a sense of jumbled coherence as if he had been trying to read a book here and there, for a long time –

"And no numbers on the pages," he thought. Now where was he? "What have you brought me from the sea?" "The sea, Charles." "There were no pensions then."

They drove on. A looser, warmer light seemed to fall around the faces near him. There seemed less bleakness. The moors relaxed about them. Suddenly, seeing a cloudful of gulls, he cried: "Stop! I want to get out."

"What for?" they wanted to know: "Not ill, are you? It's twelve miles and the next bus is next week."

"No, I'm not ill. I want to look at the sea. And I'll walk and I dare say I'll get there before the next bus."

"Can't give you your money back," they said, as he got down. He shook the bus off as if it had been a consolation. It drew away, and he turned towards the sea, standing quite still and passive but with a feeling that his nerves formed exactly five feet seven inches of the magnificent pathway to it. All the vague self-conscious words, all the frivolous, superfluous terms of his mind were forgotten. He saw in it three fixed horizons, mounting the clouds in steps of grey. And now to him, the air was like a flower.

Notes

The Wicked Woman
This story stands apart from the others in the collection, for it is the only one written before the Second World War. Margiad Evans wrote it in October 1933, at the Lough Pool Inn, Sellack, a few miles away from her family's home, Lavender Cottage, in Bridstow. She had spent the summer trying unsuccessfully to write her novel, *Turf or Stone* (1934), and eventually decided to stay at the Lough Pool Inn for seven weeks so that she could work without interruptions. While she was settling in to a routine she wrote at least two short stories, one of which was 'The Wicked Woman'. She sent it off immediately to *Life and Letters* and it was published that winter (vol. 9 (1933-4), 468-73).

The Lough Pool Inn may well have been the model for the "Harp", the public house in the story. In her journal for this period Margiad Evans notes that the story was based on "things I heard", perhaps gossip she had heard from the landlord, Mr Preece, and his wife.

p.19. *washy.* Weak, watery.

p.20. *scraffy.* Not found in the *OED* or *English Dialect Dictionary.* Perhaps a variant of "scruffy": shabby, untidy.

p.21. *yorks.* A strap or piece of twine tied around the trouser leg just below the knee.

p.22 *stone jars of hot water.* Stoneware, a kind of greyish pottery, was used to make hot-water-bottles to warm beds.

Thomas Griffiths and Parson Cope
This is one of the first stories which Margiad Evans wrote while she was living in Llangarron in the 1940s. According to her journal (Margiad Evans MS 35), she started writing it on 26 August 1943. It was probably based on an anecdote she had heard from her neighbours, for she told Gwyn Jones, editor of *The Welsh Review*, that the story was "literally true – I was told it" (Gwyn Jones Papers 74/130, postmark 30 March 1944). She had to fit her writing around work in the house and garden: "Today I have fed the gray bees, picked blackberries, made jelly and begun to write 'Thomas

Griffiths and Parson Cope'." As usual, the characters and setting were clearly pictured in her mind before she began to set the tale down in writing, but at times these strong visual impressions became almost overwhelming: "I see far too much in my stories. I see that garden gate in the wall and the way Thomas's spade thrust into the earth, all night" (Margiad Evans MS 35, 26 August 1943).

Perhaps she felt that these images interfered with the process of turning the tale she had heard into a literary form. Certainly she remained dissatisfied with the result, for in the same letter to Gwyn Jones she refers to the story as "poor old Parson Cope". A few months later she used stronger terms when noting in her journal that this story had been accepted for publication in an anthology: "a dreadful piece – Parson Cope – [is] with *Penguin Parade*, which I regret" (Margiad Evans MS 36, 21 June 1944). She had sent the story to Rosamund Lehmann, the editor of *Orion*, who had passed it on to Denys Kilham Roberts, the editor of the series *Penguin Parade*, an annual collection of short stories. Margiad Evans put the story out of her mind at this point and had quite a shock when the proofs turned up in December (Gwyn Jones Papers 74/134). She decided that she must rewrite the ending: "Oh what a mess it is! I must try to sum it up in one last paragraph but of course it's hopeless" (Margiad Evans MS 504, 9 December 1944). The story, with its new ending, was published in *Penguin Parade*, 11 (1945), 73-85.

When Gwyn Jones saw it in print he told her he was glad she had altered it: "the first draft you sent me ... had a bitten-off end". He reported too that no less a critic than Edwin Muir had reviewed this number of *Penguin Parade* in *The Listener* and singled out Margiad's story as the best in the volume, calling it "a little masterpiece of wit, poetry and fantasy" (Margiad Evans MSS 717,723, 14 & 21 September 1945). "Parson Cope has beaten them all!", she wrote gleefully to her husband. "Ha ha, good old parson. And he's not so good as 'People of his Pasture'..." (Margiad Evans MS 718, 15 September 1945).

p. 24. *spouting.* Roof-guttering.

p. 25. *the copper.* A large, cauldron-like vessel used for heating large quantities of water for baths or for washing clothes. It was usually installed in the back-kitchen or wash-house, set upon a stone or brick-built base in which a fire was made to heat the water in the copper.

p. 25 *spurted the potatoes.* Sprouted the potatoes. At the end of the winter potatoes are laid out in trays in the light to encourage them to sprout from their eyes; when they are ready for planting they are disbudded, leaving only the two strongest shoots. Traditionally they would be planted out on Good Friday. As it appears to be only early spring in the story, presumably Thomas Griffiths had in mind setting out his potatoes to start sprouting.

p. 25. *a fallow d'y.* Probably a dull day: "fallow" is a pale brown or reddish-yellow colour.

p. 26. *mole-tump.* Molehill. A tump is a hillock or mound.

p. 28. *shandrydan.* A rickety, old-fashioned vehicle.

p. 28. *glimey.* More usually "gleimy": sticky or slimy.

p. 29. *I must riv out they stones.* To "riv" or "reeve" is to sift; originally it applied to sifting grain that had been winnowed.

p. 30. *Salus.* Ross-on-Wye. This is the name Margiad Evans uses for Ross in all her published writings.

p. 30. *finish that digging while it's set.* Thomas Griffiths is probably referring to the weather: "while it's settled".

p. 31. *the whip wriggled in the leather horn.* The horn was the cylindrical container at the front of a cart or carriage which held the whip upright when not in use.

p. 31. *breechins.* The breeching is a leather strap passed round the back of a horse between the shafts, which enables the horse to push backwards to manoeuvre the cart or other vehicle.

p. 32. *'ow do I 'ave 'e on.* "How I do tease him".

p. 33. *paunched.* Gutted and cleaned.

p. 33. *a famishing candle.* A feeble candle, about to go out, probably reaching its end.

The Old Woman and the Wind

Potacre, the cottage where Margiad Evans lived from 1941 to 1947, stood at the top of the hill above Llangarron church. It was exposed to the weather and she was only too familiar with the constant noise and tug of the wind. In her journal she noted that "in this cottage when the wind dances and shakes all round you feel that the tiled floor will puff up any minute. There doesn't seem to be a straight line or a still wall anywhere" (Margiad Evans MS 35, 26 August

1943). Like Mrs Ashstone in the story, she had to go down to the village to do her shopping, or catch the bus to Ross, and then drag herself and the heavy shopping bags back up the hill. The story was completed on 20 March 1944 and was published the following June in *Life and Letters To-Day*, 41 (April-June 1944), 163-73.

p. 36. *Garway Hill*. About six miles north-west of Llangarron and a familiar landmark to Margiad Evans.

p. 36. *slurred turf*. Perhaps with its tussocks smudged with mud, or flattened down by the wind.

p. 39. *mouse-pill*. A piece of mouse-dropping.

p. 39. *a strange sallow smell*. "Sallow" is a sickly yellow or pale brown colour. The use of a colour to describe a smell is characteristic of Margiad Evans, who often describes something perceived by one of the five senses in terms of another.

p. 41. *rick-cloth*. A tarpaulin or similar cloth tied over the top of a hayrick to keep the rain off.

p. 43. *bettle*. A beetle.

Into Kings

Margiad Evans was working on this story during the autumn of 1944. Her journal entry for 5 October records a crucial step in the process of composition, when she saw the whole story very vividly in her mind's eye: "the most *intense* realization of 'Into Kings' coming up the hill. In the old couple's room, the great gilt glass come down in the world. It has pillars, a golden wreath; and there is a magnifying shaving mirror lying on the table, reflected in its reflection. The child, five, a boy. Suddenly his shy eyes see the wreath, enlarged and blurred in the shaving-glass – a queer slanting crown. A crown! His eyes kindle, oh widen! with the ecstasy of the sight – the gold, the pure gold, as a child sees gold, for the first time, not valuable, but legendary. The king and the queen, their child like himself, yet not like himself – sometimes a girl, sometimes a boy, And the intensely sweet, small white roses, the iron railings, the donkey – those are the kingdom. It must be short, but full and quiet" (Margiad Evans MS 36). Writing to her husband a month later, she told him she was writing "a short story about a little boy and some old people", which is probably a reference to 'Into Kings'. She had just spent a few days in London visiting a friend and had hoped to finish the story while she was there "but some-how I couldn't" – perhaps because she needed to be in the right setting herself (Margiad Evans MS 485, 11-12 November 1944). She finished it on November 25, and told her husband she would send it to *New Writing*, but if she did so, it was not accepted (Margiad Evans MS 494).

It was at this time that she began to consider offering a collection of her stories to Basil Blackwell, who had already published four of her books: "When 'Into Kings' is published and I've three stories (recent) to show I'll sound Mr B" (Margiad Evans MS 513, 18-19).

p. 44. *peewit.* The lapwing, *Vanellus vanellus.*
p. 49. *the little black tub.* A tub is a kind of covered horse-drawn carriage.

People of his Pasture

Margiad Evans started working on this story in 1944. As usual, she had to let the story form in her mind before she could set it down in writing. It was spring and the countryside offered too many dis-tractions. "I ought to be starting 'We are the people of his pasture'", she wrote in her journal, "but the hills contradict me and the pale green wheat that begins to lighten the rough darkness of the ploughed land" (Margiad Evans MS 36, 3 April 1944). Throughout April and May she struggled with it, fearing that it was slipping from her grasp, but at last on June 2 she recorded triumphantly "'The People' is appearing, casting itself". She set it aside for several months, picked it up again in March 1945 and finally completed it in April. She sent it to Reginald Moore, who accepted it for *The Windmill*, paying her eight guineas. (Margiad Evans MSS 558, 601, 656, 711, April-September 1945). Rereading it when it was published in *The Windmill*, 1 (1946), 120-7, Margiad Evans thought it "a grim story ... Almost a horror if one stops to think" (Margiad Evans MS 814, 29 January 1946).

The title is taken from Psalm 95, verse 7, in the Authorised Version of the Bible: "For he is our God; and we are the people of his pasture, and the sheep of his hand." The idea of the faithful as the sheep of God's pasture is common in the Bible; see also Psalms 79.13, 100.3 and Ezekiel 34.31, for example. Although Margiad Evans was not conventionally religious and certainly not a Christian, she knew the Bible well and was particularly fond of the Psalms.

p. 51. *plants of God's hand.* Wild flowers or weeds.

p. 51. *a child was playing by herself quite happily* .... This passage seems to have been inspired by an incident Margiad Evans witnessed, perhaps during a visit to Cheltenham with her friend Margaret Scudamore. She recorded it in her journal with an account of that visit: "the little girl Angela, playing in the back garden. Her plaits fair, tied with white tape, her blonde glasses. She runs to the foot of the playworn tree and begins to turn cartwheels. 'One-two-three-four' she counts rapidly for each effort. Then as if realizing that she'll come to the end of the known numbers before she reaches the garden seat, she stops, smiles beautifully, and beginning once more shouts One (Cartwheel), Two, Cartwheel – at the end she dusts her hands and gives me a smile full of unfathomable meaning" (Margiad Evans MS 36, 24 June 1945). She was in the middle of writing 'People of his Pasture' at the time and returned to work on it the very next day.

p. 52. *the span bridge.* Presumably a bridge with a single arch or span.

p. 55. *garget.* As the story indicates, this is an inflammation of the udder in sheep. It also affects cows.

p. 56. *mizzling.* Drizzling, fine rain. Here it refers to the child's cheek wet with small tears.

p. 58. *... hair, watered sleek by the wind into two thin weeds.* Hair as water-weeds is a common image in Margiad Evans's writing, for example in *Country Dance* (1932), when Ann Goodman, picking watercress in the brook, sees her reflection in the water: "There is my face staring back at me out of the brown water among the weeds, almost like a person drowned" (p. 17), and in the poem 'Resurrection': "For when in my resurgent hands / I take the mirror weedy with brown hair" (*Poems from Obscurity* (1947), 15).

The Boy Who Called for a Light

In a letter written 23-4 November 1944 Margiad Evans told her husband how a little boy called Desmond Poyner had knocked at her door and begged her to lend him a light to go home by. "I resisted him until standing at the gate I heard his frightened footsteps going down the lane and then I called him back and lent him the torch. He's naughty but not nasty, and I made him swear to bring it back tomorrow. He'd been playing down at the garage "an' Stanley's gone on home without me", he said in a trembling catching voice. Poor little brat slopping through those evil haunts of mud in this wet foggy moonlight. I was a brute not to give him a bite and sup and I suppose not to go with him – a nervous child" (Margiad Evans MS 491). A few days later, while Margiad Evans was again writing to her husband, he called again, this time asking to borrow the torch. She had already told her friend, Margaret Scudamore, about the first incident: "Horrid little boy, always at somebody's door, Margaret says, wanting to borrow things like bicycles and ponies" (Margiad Evans MS 496, 28 November 1944). She began working on the story straightaway (Margiad Evans MS 36, 25 November 1944), but the final version was not finished until the following March (Margiad Evans MS 554, 8 March 1945). Within a matter of days she wrote to tell her husband that she had had an offer to publish it: "Well, I got rid of that wretched little Derry Painter pretty quickly. This morning Reginald Moore bags him neatly for some collection or other and asks for another." Moore paid her ten guineas for it when it appeared in *Selected Writing*, 4 (1946), 35-48 (Margiad Evans MSS 564, 584, 16-17 March and 5 April 1945).

p. 61. *nesh*. Mild, gentle.
p. 62. *burr*. A bur, the rough, prickly seed-vessel of plants such as burdock or goosegrass.
p. 62. *cloam*. Clay or earthenware.
p. 63. *Father was an Insurance man*. Margiad Evans probably had in mind her own father, Godfrey James Whistler, who had worked for the Sun Life Assurance Society until his resignation for health reasons in September 1918, when Margiad was nine years old.
p. 65. *Bain't you afraid of the visions?* The character of the stammering Mr Gregory was inspired by Mr Harry Amos of Langstone, Llangarron, whom she described to her husband as "a bit of flesh and blood Herefordshire tradition" (Margiad Evans MS 494, 26 November 1944). Two days after Desmond Poyner had called at Potacre and asked

Margiad Evans for a light, she visited the Amoses and had a meal with them. "The talk was all on ghosts. Mr Amos sees them. Come to think of it, he is just the kind of man who would .... The little man was pathetic and poetic. He calls them 'the visions'. The visions he sees round the farm, walking and going into the buildings .... I was hot with interest. 'It's n-n-nothing. They won't hurt you. They don't see you – they just go by you like anybody else in the road', he said. 'B-b-but you needn't be frightened', he said twenty times" (ibid.). Mr Amos's family was very dismissive of his stories.

p. 65. *He said the Cobblers' Point, the bridge I had to cross on my way home, was haunted.* This detail is again drawn from the tales the author heard from Harry Amos: "... he mentioned that the bridge at Tretire was supposed to be haunted by some hedgers who were killed there. I forget how. Harry declared that he and another man had crossed it one night and heard every sound of men at work. They heard the stakes being cut, and driven in, he said. He gave every detail" (Margiad Evans MS 494).

p. 65. *beetle.* A kind of mallet used to hammer in stakes when laying hedges. Living branches are woven around the stakes as the basis for dense growth in the spring.

p. 66. *browst.* Undergrowth – local word. [Note by the author.]

p. 67. *lamp-chimney.* The glass tube placed over the wick of an oil-lamp to protect the flame.

p. 69. *a very simple story about her dead brother.* This is an adaptation of another of Mr Amos's stories: "... he saw Frank Scudamore's brother who was killed in the last war. He saw his figure wheeling a bicycle past the quarry and spoke to it. 'Why,' I said, 'you've got some time off then?' It didn't answer but disappeared. 'I knew he was dead', said Harry. Two days later comes Frank to tell them they'd had the telegram. 'I could've told you, Frank. I saw him'" (Margiad Evans MS 494).

p. 69. *Mesopotamia.* An ancient kingdom in the Middle East, lying between the Tigris and Euphrates rivers. It was occupied by the British in the First World War. Most of it is now part of Iraq.

p. 70. *a clubbed tree.* Probably a tree which has been pollarded. Where the branches have been repeatedly cut back in the same place, encouraging them to produce plenty of fresh shoots, a club shape tends to form.

p. 71. *... when Dad said "Be quiet" ... it sounded like "quack-quack" to me.* In February 1945 Margiad Evans had gone to visit her husband at his naval base at Dartmouth. While staying in a hotel there she witnessed the incident which inspired this detail in the story: "When the man said 'be quiet' it sounded like 'quack-quack' said the little boy to his mother at breakfast. He's a nice little child with his huge flat picture book, sitting by the fire. His father is a naval man .... The mother is an easy young lady – she curls up in the lounge" (Margiad Evans MS 36, 12 February 1945).

p. 71. *left her wan and short.* Here "short" means short of breath.

The Lost Fisherman

This is the longest story in *The Old and the Young* and Margiad Evans had originally intended that it should give its title to the collection. "I'm thinking about my book of short stories, *The Lost Fisherman*", she wrote in her journal on 5 October 1944. This story is based on events in May 1940 when Margiad was living in Ross-on-Wye with her mother and their friend Miss Smith at 17 Brookend, next door to the Friends' Meeting House. Margiad's brother, Roger Whistler, had been taken prisoner-of-war, and their sister Betty Pratt had just come back to Ross with her three children. Betty's husband, William, was a doctor and he stayed on in London. *The Old and the Young* was dedicated to Betty and William because of this story. Originally Margiad Evans had intended to dedicate it to her friend Mrs Joey Hodgkinson, who had lived at Llangarron but moved to London (Margiad Evans MS 36, 5 October 1944).

Margiad Evans seems to have started writing 'The Lost Fisherman' by late 1943, for she noted in her journal on 13 December: "I must get poor Emily down to the river" (Margiad Evans MS 35). In June the following year she was still only "meditating" the story, but in April 1945 she picked it up again and in September offered it to *The Argosy*, a magazine specializing in short stories (Margiad Evans MSS 36, 21 June 1944; MSS 601, 608, 712). When it was refused, she rewrote the ending, which she now saw was "simply awful" (Margiad Evans MS 725, 23 September 1945). The new version was offered to Gwyn Jones, who published it in *The Welsh Review*, 5 (March 1946), 9-28 (see also Margiad Evans MS 746, Gwyn Jones Papers 74/137-8).

p. 73. *the market hall.* Ross market hall, which still stands, is a roofed-over platform with stone steps leading up to it on the lower side where the ground falls away.

p. 74. *submit to noble advertisements ... Be poster-educated.* During the Second World War the government regularly issued series of posters with suitable messages for the civilian population. As the slightly sarcastic wording here suggests, Margiad Evans did not always think very highly of the way the government was running the country during the war, or indeed afterwards.

p. 75. *mumbled.* As if chewed by a toothless person: rough, clumsy, confused.

p. 76. *the ordnance factory at Chepsford.* Chepsford usually represents Hereford in Margiad Evans's writings. She worked at the ordnance factory for a short time at the beginning of the summer of 1940.

p. 76. *The house that Emily and her mother lived in ....* This passage describes exactly 17 Brookend, Ross, where Margiad Evans had lived with her mother and which is also evoked in *Autobiography* (1943). The mill, which stood close by, dominates Margiad Evans's fourth novel, *Creed* (1936).

p. 77. *they would have to move the oilstove.* This detail is taken from Margiad Evans's journal, 12 March 1938, when war was expected. She was staying with her mother and Miss Smith at 17 Brookend: "We were washing up. 'Listening to all that about the war (said Miss Smith) I was thinking we shall have to move that oil stove. Yes, if there's a war that oil stove will have to be moved. You see those shutters fasten over the window with an iron bar: but you can't get them closed when the oil stove's in the way. During the last war you know they came and told my aunt there was a light showing – that shows how nosy they were'."

pp. 77-78. *here in the faded part of town* ... This description of the poorer districts of Ross recalls the more extended account in *Creed*.

p. 78. *when she was a child at Aunt Fran's*. Here, as so often in her writings, Margiad Evans evokes Benhall, the farm on the west bank of the river Wye where her Aunt Annie and Uncle Douglas Lane lived and where Margiad and her younger sister, Nancy, lived for a year from March 1920. In an unpublished memoir of her childhood, 'The Immortal Hospital', written in 1957 (now Margiad Evans MS 23 and NLW MS 22369C), Margiad Evans again calls them Aunt Fran and Uncle Donovan. Since 'The Immortal Hospital' was written a decade later than these stories and has many details in common with them, it is possible that having crystallized the memories in writing the stories she was then influenced by them when she came to set down a more overtly factual account of this crucial period of her childhood.

p. 81. *when she had lived at Ell Hall for a year*. See note above. Ell Hall here and in 'The Old and the Young' represents Benhall. In 'The Immortal Hospital', where it appears as Hill Hall, she explains that Hall was "a common name for a farm in Herefordshire".

p. 83. *the Wellingtonian*. More correctly, Wellingtonia, also called the California Big Tree, *Sequoiadendron giganteum*. This evergreen tree is a native of the Sierra Nevada in California, but is cultivated as an ornamental tree in Western Europe. The foliage smells like aniseed when crushed.

p. 83. *The mother woke up ... Her husband was alive*. Emily's mother is modelled on the author's mother, Katherine Isabel Whistler (née Wood). Her husband, Godfrey James Whistler, died on Christmas Day 1935 and the following summer the family home, Lavender Cottage, was sold. It was then that Mrs Whistler went to live at Brookend.

p. 84. *I hope they don't bomb the bridge*. The railway line crossed the street only a few yards above 17 Brookend and trains passed over carrying ammunition from the ordnance factory at Hereford. The line was closed after the war and the bridge removed.

p. 85. *Hangbury Hill*. This place-name seems to be imaginary. It appears in 'The Widower's Tale', the unfinished novel which Margiad Evans began in the late 1930s and finally abandoned in 1955. In *Autobiography* she evokes one of the characters, who had come into her mind one day: "I sit here by the window of my bedroom, smoking, mending stockings ... I am thinking of Fanny on Hangbury Hill watching the moon float clear of the stiffening grass" (p. 83).

p. 86. *call Emily to ... have her hair curled before going to bed.* In 'The Immortal Hospital' Margiad Evans describes how her aunt at Benhall curled her hair, "During the curling I used to read aloud to her from my favourite books about animals." *The Story of a Red Deer* by J.W. Fortescue (1897) which is mentioned here, was one of the books Margiad found at Benhall and came to love. Others she mentions in 'The Immortal Hospital' are R.M. Ballantyne's *The Dog Crusoe*, Harriet Beecher Stowe's *Uncle Tom's Cabin* and *The Wide, Wide World* by Elizabeth Wetherell.

p. 86. *when you're in bed sing me a song.* Compare 'The Immortal Hospital': "After [the curling] I used to sing to her, for I had a pretty ringing voice and she was proud of it". There too she mentions 'The Keel Row' and 'John Peel'.

p. 87. *P.Q.* Fair, according to the rules.

p. 92. *a pair of sculls.* Small oars, a pair is worked with two hands.

p. 94. *My mother was a musician.* Like Emily's mother, Katherine Whistler was herself a fine singer and pianist and had taught music to her daughters. She was brought up in Chalfont St Peter and before her marriage she used to play for the inmates of the nearby colony for epileptics. Again like Emily's mother, Mrs Whistler had four children, three daughters and a son.

Solomon

Writing to her husband on 15 October 1945 Margiad Evans describes how she was "thinking of a story I mean to start tonight about a house and some children, and it's called 'Solomon'" (Margiad Evans MS 743). Three months later she again mentions "the story 'Solomon' which is Langstone", referring to the house at Llangarron which she took as the setting (Margiad Evans MS 809, 19 January 1946). The story was first published in *Life and Letters*, 48 (1946), 171-81.

p. 97. *Barrabas.* The Four Gospels agree that Barrabas was in prison at the same time as Jesus, and that Pontius Pilate offered to release either one or the other. John alone describes him as a thief (John 18.39-40, compare Matthew 27.15-26, Mark 15.6-11, Luke 23.18-19).

p. 98. *Solomon's lilies.* See note below.

p. 98. *a Bible story about lilies and Solomon in all his glory.* The reference is to Matthew 6.28-9: "Consider the lilies of the field, how they grow: they toil not, neither do they spin. And yet I say unto you, that even Solomon in all his glory was not arrayed like one of these."

p. 100. *Indian red.* A red pigment, originally an earth rich in iron oxide, imported from the East Indies.

p. 100. *glazy.* Glassy.

p. 103. *Rosa, the bitch spaniel.* Margiad Evans loved spaniels and kept a succession of them. At the time of writing this story she had a young bitch called Rosette or Rosie.

p. 105. *a yellow smirch.* A stain.

Miss Potts and Music

Entries in Margiad Evans's journal for 1944 (Margiad Evans MS 36) show that the original title for this story was 'Miss Jelly and the Musical Prizes'; the girl's name seems to have been suggested by Jelly d'Aranyi (1893-1966), a famous Hungarian-born violinist who performed regularly in British concert halls between the two world wars. On 26 June that year Margiad Evans refers to "two stories after 'The People [of his Pasture]' – 'Miss Jelly and the Musical Prizes' then 'The Lost Fisherman'". By 5 October the shape of both her proposed book and this story were becoming clearer in her mind. "First there are those I've written. And then 'Miss Jelly'. Well, we know all about her – her hair, her violin case, her court interest and her aunt who looked like a combination of Sherlock Holmes and – who? We don't know that yet." The title was later modified to 'Miss Jelly and Music' when she was revising it a year later. At this point she told her husband: "unless it improves in the second version it ain't much cop" (Margiad Evans MS 712, 8-9 September 1945). Miss Jelly became Miss Potts a week later and the story was finished by the end of the month (Margiad Evans MSS 718, 722- 3), despite endless interruptions from neighbours which eventually drove her to put a notice on the door: "DANGER. WORKING".

p. 107. *My fellow climber rises dim* .... The final stanza of Thomas Hardy's poem 'Logs on the Hearth. A Memory of a Sister', where a log burning on the hearth reminds the poet of how his sister used to climb the tree, now felled, from which it came.

p. 108. *Lindenfield*. In *Creed* (pp. 60-1) Margiad Evans describes Lindenfield as a wealthy residential district of the town, some distance away from the poorer, industrial area dominated by mill and gas-works. The name may have been suggested by the Ashfield or Archenfield districts to the south of Ross town centre.

p. 108. *combining Rossetti's Beata Beatrix and my own idea of Sherlock Holmes*. 'Beata Beatrix' is one of the best-known paintings by the Pre-Raphaelite artist Dante Gabriel Rossetti (1828-82). He painted it in 1863 as a memorial portrait of his dead wife, Elizabeth Siddal. It is now in the Tate Gallery, London. See also introductory note above.

p. 109. *aerial*. Ethereal, insubstantial-looking.

p. 110. *Jew's-ear fungus. Auricularia auricula,* a brown or liver-coloured fungus which grows on dead tree branches, especially on elder, but also on elm and willow.

p. 110. *One day* I'm *going to play the violin*. It was one of Margiad Evans's greatest ambitions to play the violin well. While living at Llangarron she owned a violin of Dutch or German workmanship, on which she practised regularly. Towards the end of the Second World War she got to know Jan Rosé, a paralysed émigré violinist who gave her her most inspiring lessons. In his memory she wrote an essay on violin makers and violinists, 'The Man with the Hammer', published in *Life and Letters*, 59 (October, 1948), 11-27.

p. 112. *Puss-in-the-corner*. A children's game where one stands in the centre and the others keep changing places from one "den" or "base" to another. The player in the centre tries to capture one of the dens, sending the one left without a position to take his or her place in the centre.

p. 112. *the Light of the World.* Another reference to a Pre-Raphaelite painting, this time by Holman Hunt. It represents Christ carrying a lantern, knocking at the closed door of a house. The first version was painted between 1851 and 1853, and is in Keble College, Oxford.

p. 114. *snowball bushes.* The sterile form of the guelder rose, *Viburnum opulus.* See also "Whitsun bosses" below, p. 148.

A Modest Adornment

The seed of this story can be traced to an anecdote Margiad Evans heard from a friend at Llangarron and recounted in a letter to her husband: "Margaret told me a lovely story about two old women living together in one of Vincent's cottages. One said the other was a 'sooner'. Vincent asked Ernie what a 'sooner' was. 'Oh, don't you know? Sooner do nothing' was the answer. I think those old women will make a story" (Margiad Evans MS 726, 26 September 1945). She began writing 'A Modest Adornment' on 21 January 1946 (Margiad Evans MS 810) but it was March that year before she made much progress with it. On 14 March she told her husband: "I'm writing the story about the woman who was buried in green gloves." It was a Thursday and as usual she had taken the bus from Llangarron to Ross to do some shopping and visit her mother. "All the way to Ross I was thinking deeply of [the story] and it was coming *fine*", but it was dispelled by "anecdotes and interruptions" when she visited her mother at Brookend. 'A Modest Adornment' was probably completed towards the end of the month, for on March 24 she wrote to her husband: "My story about the oboe playing Miss Allensmore [*sic*] is nearly finished in the rough. I must finish it tonight" (Margiad Evans MS 871).

p. 117. *picking some washing off the thorns.* People without washing lines would spread their clothes to dry on hawthorn or blackthorn bushes.

p. 118. *People called Miss Allensmoore "Sooner".* See introductory note above.

p. 120. *vernal.* Spring-like, the colour of fresh grass in the spring.

p. 122. *Mrs Little-So-Big with a burst washer and a roaring tap.* On 14 March 1946, when Margiad Evans was about to catch the bus to Ross and was thinking of this story, she found that her one tap in the kitchen at Potacre had burst its washer (Margiad Evans MS 864).

p. 123. *a-playing on them bagpipes.* On 17 March 1946 Margiad Evans wrote to her husband: "I'll write some more about Miss Allensmore and her oboe – them bagpipes as the villagers call it" (Margiad Evans MS 866).

p. 123. *yowe.* Ewe.

p. 124. *the copper.* See note to p. 25 above.

p. 124. *that daft walk to London she done once.* Margiad Evans's next-door neighbour, Mrs Saunders, seems to have been the source of this strand in the narrative: "Ellen has been in .... She's promised to get the story of the woman who walked to London for me" (letter to Michael Williams, 8 October 1945, Margiad Evans MS 738).

p. 127. *char-à-banc.* A long, open car with many seats, all set looking forward, often used for transporting trippers or holiday-makers.

p. 130. *the Litany.* A series of petitions in the Book of Common Prayer. The petitions are recited by the priest and the con-gregation responds.

The Ruin

This story is concerned with the difficulties of a couple readjusting to married life after the husband's demobilisation from the forces and therefore reflected a common experience when it was first pub-lished in *Life and Letters* 52 (1947), 49-60. Many men were not released from the forces until well after the end of the Second World War, and Margiad Evans's husband, Michael Williams was not demobbed until April 1946. The exact date of composition of 'The Ruin' has not been established, as there are no relevant refer-ences in her surviving journals. However, the date of publication suggests that she had finished it by the end of the autumn of 1946.

In the author's journals in the 1940s there are a number of ref-erences to visits to ruined cottages. The following typical example is taken from an account she sent to her husband of a trip to the Brecon Beacons with her brother Roger Whistler and his wife Doreen on 24 March 1946: "There was one empty rusty cottage on a hillside which could have been made lovely for it was a good shape. I wish we had the means. The very place to paint and fiddle. It had a ruined water butt, a bit of red piping and no garden. Looked as if generations of poor people had lived there like gypsies" (Margiad Evans MS 871). In this story, however, the setting seems to be Cumberland, where Margiad Evans spent a holiday with her husband soon after he was demobbed.

In both theme and treatment, 'The Ruin' is strikingly similar to 'Y Golled' (The Loss), a story by the Welsh-language writer Kate Roberts (1891-1985). 'Y Golled' has a very different setting but is similarly concerned with a wife's sudden awareness of the lack of communication and understanding between herself and her husband. It was included in *A Summer's Day*, a collection of Kate Roberts's short stories in English translation which was published in the summer of 1946. Margiad Evans, who had long been an admirer of the work of Kate Roberts, was asked by the editor Robert Herring to review *A Summer's Day* for *Life and Letters*, so we know that she had read the book (see *Life and Letters,* 51 (1946), 54-8). She was working on the review in July 1946. In both 'Y Golled' and 'The Ruin' the story is seen through the eyes of the wife, and in both an outing starts with happy agreement but ends with a gulf between them. In both cases too it is the wife who is conscious of the increasing distance between them, and feels that while she understands what is in her husband's mind, he has no idea what she thinks. It seems very likely that Margiad Evans was influenced by Kate Roberts in this instance, although perhaps unconsciously.

Margiad Evans felt that 'The Ruin' was one of her most successful short stories. Rereading it after it was published, she noted in her diary; "My most beautiful. A piece of chamber music" (2 March 1947).

p.138. *a bullfinch.* This detail can again be traced to a note in her journal, where she describes how she and her husband had gone for a walk together when he was home on a few days' leave: "Mike sees a beautiful greenfinch but it's a blue tit" (Margiad Evans MS 36, 19 January 1945).

The Old and the Young
This story, which gives its title to the collection, was several months in the making. A journal entry for 19 July 1946 shows that she had

already started it: "Did nothing to 'The Old and the Young' as I wanted to live in the AIR, in the body ..." (Margiad Evans MS 37). She worked at it solidly in September and may have finished it then. The poem which introduces 'The Old and the Young' was published in Margiad Evans's first volume of poetry, *Poems from Obscurity*, where it is entitled 'Children' (p. 12). She was working on this poem in July 1946 after starting the story, showing that during these weeks she was writing both poetry and prose.

p. 148. *Whitsun bosses*. The guelder rose, so called because its clusters of white flowers appear in early summer, around Whitsun. See also "snowball bushes" (p. 114).

p. 148. *cornfactor*. Dealer in corn, corn-merchant.

p. 149. *Mrs Payne from Ell Hall*. Like Aunt Fran in 'The Lost Fisherman' this character is clearly inspired by the author's aunt Annie Lane. Mrs Payne is referred to as 'Aunt Fran' later in the story (p. 163), and here her farm, Benhall, once again becomes Ell Hall. The three young nieces recall the three Whistler sisters, although Betty, the eldest, was away at boarding school during the year the two younger girls lived at the farm. Arabella and Esther correspond to Peggy/Margiad and Nancy, just as they do in the autobiographical novel *The Wooden Doctor* (1933). Betty is referred to as Augusta in 'The Immortal Hospital' as she is here.

p. 150. *New England*. Margiad Evans dreamed of visiting Connecticut some day, for she was deeply interested in writers from that area, especially the nature writer Henry David Thoreau. When in 1949 she received from the Society of Authors an award of £125 for travel abroad, she thought she might go to New England. Unfortunately, the grant was not big enough to pay for both her and her husband to go, and they had very little money of their own, so they went to Ireland instead.

p. 151. *her grandmother ... would always wake up in Welsh*. Margiad Evans's paternal grandmother, Ann Evans, is thought to have been Welsh although she lived in Lancashire, and when the young Peggy Whistler was choosing a pen-name it was only natural that she should borrow her grandmother's surname. A Welsh grandmother features elsewhere in Margiad Evans's work, most notably in the novel *Turf or Stone* (1934).

p. 152. *Maureen*. This character was originally called Fiona: see note below.

p. 152. *the lightning tree*. This first appears, as a strongly visual image, in Margiad Evans's journal during the summer when she was writing 'The Old and the Young': "In the night I thought of the Lightning tree, which is the same as the banana tree. I might use it in 'The Old and the Young'. It's a willow round which the children play – the play place. Like the great willow by the stepping stones it has split itself into four and the quartered trunk loops in great boughs to the ground, like a peeled banana. Esther, Arabella, Pudge and Fiona play there.

But the lightning tree is all mixed up with my unhappy mind, my restlessness, my surly doubts. With many other pictures which are partly mine, partly true" (Margiad Evans MS 37, 13 August 1946).

p. 154. *hubbled*. This word is obscure, but it may be related to "hobbled".

p. 155. *The two sisters loved each other profoundly*. The relationship of Arabella and Esther mirrors that of Margiad and her younger sister Nancy. A close, twin-like bond was forged between them during the year they spent together at Benhall and persisted throughout their lives. This relationship is reflected in much of Margiad Evans's work, culminating in her poem 'To My Sister Sian', composed when the author knew she was dying and published in her last book, *A Candle Ahead* (1956), 25-6.

p. 156. *wishing ... that she could play the violin*. See note to p. 110.

p. 157. *"Katy Hopkins"*. This was the name of one of the fields at Benhall, which Margiad Evans mentions in 'The Immortal Hospital': "Every field had a name ... A few, like the big arable field Katy Hopkins ... were easy to understand. An old lady called Katy Hopkins had lived on the edge of her field in a cottage which was still inhabited" (NLW MS 22369C, f. 39).

p. 159. *she dishes*. A horse that dishes has the habit, while trotting, of moving the forefeet in a circular or scooping motion rather than straight forward.

p. 161. *sproggers*. Sparrows. Margiad Evans picked up this word from her next door neighbour at Llangarron, Mrs Ellen Saunders (Margiad Evans MS 37, 17 July 1946).

All Through the Night

It was Margiad Evans's mother-in-law, Mrs Williams, who provided the core of this story. She told Margiad how, when the family lived at Mitcheldean, her daughter Hilda and elder son Bernard had spent the evening in Gloucester, missed the bus and walked the twelve miles home. The first draft of the story appears in her journal, dated 26 October 1943, where she introduces it as "a story I should like to write" (Margiad Evans MS 35). She sent the completed text to Gwyn Jones, editor of *The Welsh Review*, probably on 5 February 1944, for in a letter of that date she told him she was sending two stories, "not very well copied out but I can't get paper or much time". Paper was in short supply during the Second World War. In a further letter, dated 30 March 1944, she told him to "print H. and A. for that's what they called each other" (Professor Gwyn Jones Papers 74/128, 130). It is not clear from this comment whether the story was entitled 'All Through the Night' when she sent it, but she usually chose the titles for her stories early in the process of composition. She was undoubtedly familiar with the Welsh song, 'Ar hyd y nos/All through the night'.

Gwyn Jones accepted the story for publication and it appeared in *The Welsh Review*, 3 (1944), 159-67.

p. 164. *scutted*. The exact meaning is not clear. To "scutter" is to make a hasty, excited movement.

p. 171. *pigscots*. Pigsties.

Mrs Pike's Eldorado

The germ of this story may have been suggested by Mrs Ellen Saunders who lived next door to the author. In a letter to her husband dated 12 October 1945 Margiad Evans reported that "Mrs Saunders's sister Kate is going to be married. She's a widow and a charming person aged 68. I often see her in Ross" (Margiad Evans MS 740). It was a year later that she began to work in earnest on the story and according to her journal she finished the rough draft of this story on 13 October 1946 (Margiad Evans MS 37). Four days later she was revising it and feeling that it had not come right: "Have yet another try at 'Mrs Pike's Eldorado'. Can't get the end". By the end of the day it was done: "I finished 'Mrs Pike'. I know the end is crowded".

p. 174. *a blowsy nose.* A coarse, reddened nose.

p. 175. *toffs.* Stylish, smart person, especially one who wishes to be taken for such.

p. 181. *hedge-cropping.* Trimming and laying hedges.

The Sea

It was during the summer of 1946 that Margiad Evans started working on this story, returning to it in early November that same year. By 20 November she was able to note in her journal, "'The Sea' is coming clearer – And then the end!"

The port town could have been inspired by one of those, such as Portland and Dartmouth, which Margiad Evans visited after her husband joined the Navy. For the first few years of his service he was stationed at various British ports, and she was sometimes able to join him for a few days.

Although she lived inland for most of her life, the sea and sailors had been part of Margiad Evans's life since childhood. One of her uncles had been in the Merchant Navy, and in her late teens Margiad had spent some time in Pouldu, a fishing village in Brittany. In 1936, when she was twenty-seven, she visited Iceland with a friend, and her essay 'Three Seas' (*Life and Letters*, no. 96 (1945) 90-7), brings together elements from that trip with her visits to her husband at two naval bases, and a few recollections of Breton fishermen.

p. 188. *Melville.* Margiad Evans was a great admirer of the American writer Herman Melville (1819-91), especially his novel *Moby Dick*.

p. 189. *pawky.* Cunning, bold, cheeky.

p. 189. *Spaniels are the most faithful of all.* See note to p. 103.

p. 189. *a barque.* A sailing ship with fore and main masts square-rigged and the mizzen (lowest) fore and aft rigged. The narrator is unsure of the technical details.

p. 189. *They never came back.* This part of the story came to Margiad Evans early on in its gestation. On 26 August 1946 she was making greengage jam in her cottage when she remembered that "I was thinking of my story 'The Sea' as I came down the south bank – how it was just a sound of trickling down a harbour wall and then suddenly its deathly immensity in the old woman's account of her father's death" (Margiad Evans MS 37).

Further Reading

Moira Dearnley, *Margiad Evans* (Writers of Wales series, Cardiff, 1982)

Ceridwen Lloyd-Morgan, *Margiad Evans* (Border Lines series, Bridgend, 1998)

Three further short stories by Margiad Evans were published:

'The Little Red Umbrella', *New Statesman and Nation*, vol. 7, no.168 (12 May 1934), 717-18.

'The Black House', *The Welsh Review*, 1 (June 1939), 242-6.

'A Party for the Nightingale', *The Welsh Review*, 7 (winter 1948), 285-93.

The main archive of Margiad Evans's personal and literary papers is held at the National Library of Wales, Aberystwyth (Margiad Evans Manuscripts and NLW MSS 23357-74, 23577C). These include the letters and journals discussed above. Other important archives at the National Library include the Margiad Evans Papers, compiled in the early 1960s by W. Arnold Thorpe, in preparation for his proposed biography of the writer, and letters from Margiad Evans to Gwyn Jones, editor of *The Welsh Review*, which are now Professor Gwyn Jones Papers 74/115-73. Her letters to Bryher are in the Beinecke Rare Books Library, Yale, USA.

always seen in rel'p to ladscapt